SWIMMING WITH SHARKS

SWIMMING WITH SHARKS

A DI Gillian Marsh Mystery

ANNA LEGAT

Published by Accent Press Ltd. 2016

ISBN 9781783759651

To Steve. Where would I be without you?

Day One

The boat skids across the tide. Every time a wave hits the floor, Nicola's stomach lurches. She cannot see into the night. The ocean is a black oil spill, its vastness disorientating. The stars are bigger here than back home. The reek of petrol is nauseating. Despite the speed, time stands still. It feels like she is going in circles – on a rollercoaster: wind in her hair, her stomach in her throat, gravity defied. Even as a child Nicola disliked rollercoasters – they made her feel sick. She is feeling sick now. Yellow smudges of light from small islands along the way take Nicola out of the spin. She focuses her eyes on them for as long as they last, but they vanish quickly, left behind in the wake of the speedboat.

The skipper – lean and hairless, like a pubescent boy – turns and flashes his teeth and the whites of his eyes at her. She wishes he would keep those eyes on the steering wheel and on the road ahead. But then there is no road, she realises, only the blackness of the night seeping through the blackness of water.

He has switched off the headlights. He is not navigating by what he can see – he is going by instinct. She shudders despite the heat, and tries to distract herself with the bottle of water he gave her at the start of the journey. She takes a small sip just to moisten her tongue. Since landing in Colombo, she has drunk gallons of water. Where did it go? She sweated it out the moment it touched her lips. The air is swollen with moisture. Clammy. The air here weighs twice as much as the air in England. It sits on your skin.

Boy-skipper turns away and speaks to his companion. A gesture of his hand imitates a slap on the cheek. Their laughter drowns in the drone of the engine. Should Nicola be afraid? She is the only passenger on this boat. A female passenger. Boy-skipper and the other man, both black-eyed, black as the oily equatorial night, are ogling her in the rear view mirror. She can see the whites of their eyes flashing. Is her dress too revealing? In Colombo, she had changed from her grey winter layers into a flowing summer dress, one so light that she didn't feel it become airborne as the speedboat took off. She pushes the fabric down and traps it between her knees, but it flaps around her thighs, desperate to break free. The eyes in the rear view mirror stay focused on her, willing her knees apart. They surely threaten an assault, even rape. She could be kicked in the stomach and thrown overboard, then left behind to be torn to shreds by sharks. Her two ferrymen have guessed correctly that no one would miss her: a lone woman in the honeymooners' paradise. Boy-skipper has caught her eye in the mirror. He is smiling with a knowing glint in his eye. His earlier reverence is gone. He could give it to her here and now if that's what she is after. Cheap thrills, that's what she wants. He nods and Nicola shifts her gaze towards the black water.

It offers her no comfort. She can still feel his eyes on her, penetrating her flimsy summer dress. The boat staggers on the waves and her breasts shift inside her bra. They ache. *She asked for it*, Boy-skipper will say if they ask why he did it … And he will be believed. A furtive glance up and there he is – the mirror brings his lecherous eyes closer to her, so close that they can almost touch her.

Horrified, she places the flat of her palm on her chest. Her heart thumps against her hand. The dress is drenched with her sweat; a cold trickle slides from under her finger. She tries to stop it before it goes any deeper, but the nervous rubbing of her chest makes it worse. She gasps for air, looks nervously into the night, begs for it to lift so that their intentions are revealed. It's the unknown that makes her panic. Where are they going? Why is she the only passenger? Who are they? What are they planning to do with her?

Which way is home?

They are staring at her, openly now. The smiles are gone. Without caring what she may overhear, they talk loudly over the drumming of the engine. Boy-skipper leaves his friend in charge of the steering wheel and heads down the two steep steps into the passenger cabin. Nicola holds her breath. Her suddenly lifeless hand peels off her chest, leaving it exposed. *She was gagging for it*, Boy-skipper will say and they will believe him. He leans over her.

A sharp change of direction throws the boat to one side, tossing him at her, his hand landing in her lap –

Nicola screams, pushes the bulk of his body away from her, but in that second, reinforced by the velocity of the lurching boat, he is way too heavy.

Quickly, he pulls himself up, and inquires with the most reverential, customer-centred concern, 'Is madam feeling sick? It is not very much longer. Itsouru is that light, over that way.'

The first lights of Itsouru shimmer weak and tentative, but soon many more of them break up the night.

At first, travelling alone didn't seem like such a bad idea. She bravely joined the queue to check in to her flight to Colombo. Heathrow was buzzing with anonymity – an extension of London where everybody minds their own business and no one establishes either body or eye contact. Nicola was in her element. She had stood in an orderly queue of likeminded travellers. Behind her three women were bubbling with conversation. Three women and no man, and they were perfectly happy. Well, two of them were – the younger ones. The older one – a mother figure after a fashion – sounded rather neurotic. Nicola hazarded a gaze behind her, observing the back view of a titch of a woman with fluffy, fair hair, the compact body of a marathon runner and a high-voltage disposition. She was at a loss to tell why the woman was so paranoid – she wasn't the one going anywhere; the other two were.

'Tara, concentrate please!' She was pulling the tall, blonde girl by the sleeve. 'You must call me the moment you arrive, so I know all is well. Do you hear me?'

'Mum, you can't come with us beyond this point. See? Only passengers with boarding passes.' The tormented young lady was beginning to sound relieved. 'I'll call you. One last hug?' She took her mother into her arms, where the woman briefly disappeared without trace. And then she was gone.

Soon after the two girls vanished as well. Nicola saw them through a crowd of people, chatting with two young men from the back of the queue. They all looked in full holiday swing, laughing, taking selfies on their mobile phones and exchanging text messages even though they stood right next to each other. It was then that Nicola had had her first doubt. She was no longer part of the gang, not even in her own head. They didn't know her from Adam. She was on her own.

'Madam Eagles travel alone?'

At Arrivals in Malè, Boy-skipper could not help himself. He gawped at her modest suitcase, willing *Mister Eagles* to jump out of there and put everything right.

She nodded and pointed to her suitcase. 'That's my luggage.'

'One bag?'

'So it is.' She tried not to look guilty.

As they walked towards the jetty, Nicola's bag rattling behind Boy-skipper, he tried again: 'Mister Eagles, will he be joining later?'

'No, he isn't coming.' She felt the sticky heat creep up to her cheeks, a burning blush. There was no Mr Eagles; had never been.

Nicola had never married. Mr Right had eluded her all her life and she was not the type to go and look for him. She lacked initiative. She was a human koala bear: a recluse content with her own company and easily pleased with a celery stick chewed thoughtfully in front of the TV. She had passions, but they were purely *academic*. Buried in books and furiously typing articles about the angst in Pushkin's verse, Nicola had hardly noticed that her youth had sailed past and disappeared over the horizon. While she had been perfecting her Russian pronunciation, her peers had experimented with Sambuca shots and the morning-

4

after pill. She had instead spent the prime of her life (and most of her parents' money) building an impressive portfolio of honours in obscure subjects.

Nicola could have merrily languished in this relative obscurity for the rest of her days had it not been for her great-aunt Eunice dying. In a blink of an eye, she had found herself a wealthy woman and the proud owner of a charming, period cottage in Sexton's Canning.

The cottage came with a cat called Fritz. She had no heart to send Fritz to a cat orphanage, but neither could she re-home him in her matchbox flat in Hammersmith. Fritz was a country cat – he did not climb stairs and didn't use litter boxes. The sensible option was to sell the flat and move in with Fritz. After that radical move came another brainstorm: a holiday. Somewhere nice and warm – somewhere exotic.

Boy-skipper turns off the engine and the boat drifts towards the shore. The sound of water lapping against the jetty is comforting. Snippets of light punctuate the night. She has arrived.

The solid land is made of sand. It is a far cry from the assuring solidity of London's concrete pavements. It ebbs underfoot. She is unsteady and ungainly as she treads across it. Her feet sweat inside her trainers. Nicola wishes she could take her shoes off and walk barefoot, but she wouldn't dream of delaying her escort. The boy has heaved her suitcase on top of his head. The strain on his face shows how heavy the damn thing is. She has not told him that it is full of books; he does not need to be told. He can guess.

She lags behind him, repentant. Paper is heavier than it looks.

Outlines of palm trees are black sugar paper cut-outs. Spotlights hidden in the roots illuminate some of them, leaving others to stand obscure and sullen. The brightness of the Reception hut approaches fast. Nicola braces herself – there is no going back. She wouldn't risk the oily blackness of the night-time ocean again. She can still taste burning petrol on her tongue and feel the bumpiness of the ride in her stomach. Travel sickness. She swallows it, and steps in.

Boy-skipper deposits her suitcase on the floor. It is a sandy floor, with hundreds of footprints on it. He grins at her, wishes her a happy stay and walks away taking with him the memory of their water crossing and his insolent ogling in the rear view mirror. Nicola discovers she has been holding her breath. She exhales.

Two love-struck newlyweds, seated on wicker chairs shaped like cracked-open coconuts, are holding hands. They have two suitcases – two suitcases for two, Nicola observes pointlessly. A waiter, clad in a sarong, brings them bright red drinks in cocktail glasses decorated with dimpled cherries and floating umbrellas. They clink the glasses in mid-air; she laughs, he feeds her a cherry.

Another couple are dealing with the receptionist. Nicola has to queue behind them. That is something she can do. She is good at queuing. It is in her blood. Waiting her turn takes her mind off her misgivings. She raises her chin and thrusts her chest forward.

The newlyweds kiss. It is a passing kiss – a distraction from what goes on lower down on the level of the coconut-shaped seats. The woman's hand slips from the man's chest and finds something to grip down in his groin. The man's face softens with pleasure. He takes off his hat and places it in his lap over the woman's hand and the bulge in his shorts. Nicola stiffens. She should not be here – not on her own, not with only one suitcase, not a woman alone.

She focuses her eyes on a model of a large fish with what looks like a horn on its nose. It is suspended from the ceiling between two huge fans. Their blades turn relentlessly, threatening to slice the fish into sushi pieces. Nicola knows how the fish must be feeling: the same as her.

Like a fish out of water.

At last the people in front of her have checked in and are on the move. She is next. She is going to tell the nice man at Reception

6

that she has changed her mind. She wants to go home. She wants to be on the next boat out.

Except that, perhaps, it would be better if it was a day-time boat. Equatorial nights do not agree with Nicola. This may mean that, after all, she will have to spend at least one night here, on the island. In that case she will have to check in. Just for the night. She steps forward bravely and that is where she collides with the other couple who are busy crossing her path, unware of her as they are battling with their wheeled suitcases stuck in the sandy floor.

Nicola bounces off the man as he whips his stubborn piece of luggage onto his back. She makes a few unsteady backward steps, while her arms are performing disjointed cartwheels. She is tripped up by her own suitcase. Squawking, she grasps at the air and fails miserably to regain control.

She lands softly in somebody's lap. A pair of strong male hands grab hold of her midriff. A glass in one of the hands tips over – alcoholic liquid soaks Nicola's dress. The wet fabric sticks to her stomach like cling-film. She clutches the arms that caught her: they are covered in a soft fluff of reddish hairs. The hands on her waist feel highly opportunistic. Nicola tries to free herself and pushes the hands away – rises – and falls again. The man groans. She has hit his privates.

'I am, I am … so sorry!' she mumbles.

'No problem,' the man manages to say. He sounds foreign. How else should he sound? This isn't the London Underground! What did she get herself into? How clumsy! She would never lose her balance like that on the tube! The man will think she has done it on purpose!

He helps her up. It feels like he pushes her up, freeing himself from her unwelcome weight. 'So sorry … So sorry …'

She doesn't dare look at him. Her eyes shift between his crotch and his sandals. Desperately she is searching for a hole to bury herself in. Sand. Sand. Sand. Footprints in the sand. She is unable to raise her eyes – they are glued to the floor. Her cheeks are burning in ultimate humiliation.

'It's no problem. Are you all right?' the deep baritone of the man's voice booms over the shrill of her internal demons.

He is holding her arm to steady her up. She frees herself, pulls away. 'Sorry! I didn't mean to –'

'Of course you didn't. No problem.'

From the corner of her eye she watches him pick up the glass. His shorts are also wet, like her dress.

'I'm sorry about your shorts ... I mean, about your drink,' she stammers. 'I spilled it. Can I buy you another one?' She blushes. This sounds awful. This sounds like she is trying to chat him up. He must be thinking she has done it all on purpose!

'No, no need. I've had too many.'

She doesn't know if he is smiling, but he sounds like he is. Is he laughing at her? She dares not look up. 'Well, if you say so.' Is that the right thing to say? Isn't it like saying he is drunk? Accusing him of drunken behaviour while it is she, Nicola Eagles, who –

God! Where is God when you need Him! She is still gaping at the floor – she won't find Him there, but she simply cannot lift her gaze to look the poor man in the eye.

'Good evening, madam! Welcome to Itsouru Island!' The receptionist is grinning at her in a similar way to Boy-skipper, as if he and she share a shameful secret. Nicola feels betrayed. Her lower lip quivers. Everyone is laughing at her. She senses their merriment. At her expense. They must stop! 'Can you –' she starts and doesn't quite know how to finish.

'What can I do for you, madam?' The receptionist looks eager to please.

Can you send me back home, please? she wants to say but that would be childish and would confuse the poor chap. He is only doing his job. His keen eyes are smiling, not laughing.

'I'm Nicola Eagles, um ...' She is fumbling inside her handbag (it is a suitably exotic handbag with large loops of bamboo handles and a clean white canvas sack). It is hard to find anything in it, especially if your hands are shaking. Her fingers brush against the plastic wallet carrying her return ticket home. She clutches it. At least it is still in her bag, ready to be used in due course. Due course being one whole week: seven days; God knows how many hours. She finds her passport and booking form. She hands it to the receptionist. He looks over her shoulder, searchingly. Has she become paranoid or is he, just like Boy-skipper, looking for *Mister* Eagles?

'Something wrong with the papers?' she asks.

He is all smiles again. Oh no, nothing wrong; everything in perfect order. Would madam like to take a seat? Choose a cocktail from our Cocktails Menu?

No, Nicola is not planning to put herself through the torture of being seen drinking alone in a public place. She cranes her neck and peers back from under her eyelashes at the seat behind her. The man with the strong hands and spilled drink is gone. The seat is empty. She gazes at the receptionist pleadingly. Does she have to take a seat? Can she not go straight to her room?

'Of course! I will get someone to escort you to your chalet. Chalet 42.'

Do they allocate room numbers based on the occupant's age? Nicola feels it is a bit insensitive, but she takes the key from his hand. He gives her a map of the island and tells her where her nearest restaurant is. If she hurries, she will still make it for dinner. The kitchen closes at 11 p.m. That gives her half an hour. Of course she can have sandwiches made and delivered to her chalet, if she prefers. Fresh fruit …

'No, it's all right.' Nicola does not wish to cause anyone any inconvenience. The poor cook wants to go home to his family. She will go to the restaurant and grab something quick and simple.

Another Boy-skipper – perhaps the former's twin brother? – hauls her book-laden suitcase onto a cart and drives her to her room. She thought she would walk, but it is late, the island is big and her chalet is at the far end of it. She squats uncomfortably next to her driver. Her knee wedged into the side of her suitcase – her only taste of home in this impossibly exotic world – offers her a modicum of comfort. She would cuddle and kiss it if that wouldn't look ridiculous.

Her room is a large cabin wearing a conical party hat of thatched roof. Her driver drags her suitcase to the front door and lets her open it. A wave of freezing cold air hits her in the face and wipes the blush from it. The suitcase makes it across the threshold.

'I take madam restaurant?' the driver nods with keen conviction. He is not going to go away. He has his instructions.

'I would need to change, refresh … It's late … Maybe not?' she asks feebly.

'I will wait. No hurry.'

She sits on the bed, biting her nails. The spillage has evaporated from her dress. She is not going to change. She doesn't know what to wear. Hopefully, the driver will go away.

Twenty minutes later, as she peeps out of the door, he waves to her, a big, wide grin on his face.

The restaurant is an enormous, open-plan sacrificial temple. The buffet is brimming with hot and cold dishes; aromas mingle; chefs in tall white hats chop pieces of fish and toss them up in the air, using frying pans like tennis rackets. Sarong-wearing waiters look focused and competent. They are friendly. Smile a lot.

Nicola's waiter puts her at a discreet corner table. The lights here are dimmer and the foot traffic less exuberant than in other parts of the diner. Out of character she orders wine. She needs Dutch courage more than a clear head.

There aren't many diners in the restaurant. She feels singled out as a latecomer and a lone female in a place where having a partner is part of the dress code. If there were crowds, she could try to blend in, but all she has is a few cosy couples dotted over tables, drawn into each other to the exclusion of everyone else. She spies a quartet: two women, two men, middle-aged, loud and red-faced from the sun or the alcohol. Germans. They are having a whale of a time even though they are clearly not newlywed or under the age of thirty. Loud outbursts of laughter and slaps on the thighs keep them amused. They are happy on this love island. If there can be four of them here, then sure as hell there can be one of her, Nicola bites her lip. She will be strong. And she will have a good time, if it kills her!

After a couple of false starts, she scuttles to pick something to eat from the buffet. It feels like everyone's eyes are on her. She looks deeply engaged with her potential dinner: examines dishes carefully, lifts big silver domes, sniffs, tilts her head, thinks, contemplates options, goes back to where she has already been and compares. She has to make up her mind sooner or later, and return to her table for one. And then she will have to eat in solitude.

She returns with a slice of bread and a pork medallion. She has forgotten vegetables. Her plate looks empty and inadequate in this extravaganza of culinary excesses. She will not be able to go for pudding. The chefs are already clearing the stalls. She was hoping for a trifle, and those smiley faces of watermelons looked irresistible.

She chews slowly and at the same time peeps from under her eyelashes. Honeymooning couples are radiant. Men look hungry even with their stomachs full – they are hungry for their women. It is in their eyes: the hunger, the lust. The women are more than deserving of that lust: they are young, fresh-faced and beautiful. Suntans glisten on their skin like nail polish. Their hair is long and moist. Did Nicola already acknowledge that they are all so young? On average they are about twenty years younger than their hungry men. That explains things: someone has to be able to afford the price tag that goes with paradise.

Nicola has to slap herself on the wrist: she should not be cynical. Or envious. She is not like that. She is not a bitter old spinster.

Not yet.

One couple is different: she is older than him, though well-preserved. She must be the one with money. Her hair is thick and healthy, and though it is greying, there is lustre and shine to it. It falls in coiled layers onto her back and shoulders. The skin on her upper arms and neckline is withered, one of the signs of age you can't belie, but she wears her years with effortless elegance. She is tiny and he is tall, overwhelmingly tall, acutely so in comparison with her. It is hard to say if his hair is grey or reddish-blond, the colour of straw in the height of summer. There is some length to it – he pushes it behind his ear. His frame is square and strong. He is no boy gigolo. He must be over fifty. How old is she, then? She shakes her head in protest when he orders a drink from the waiter. When the drink arrives – a bottle of wine – the woman puts her hand flat over her glass. The man laughs and fills his own glass. The woman's face crinkles with anxiety. The man kisses her hand and then her forehead. The woman seems appeased, though she still refuses to smile. They are eating in silence. The man's eye catches Nicola's and he freezes for a fraction of a second, a butter knife paused over a bread roll in his hand. Imperceptibly, he nods his head. Nicola looks away.

No, he doesn't. She has imagined it.

She must stop staring, for God's sake!

Nicola gulps down the rest of the wine and squints. She is not used to the bitter taste. The wine wells up in her eyes. Is the man still looking at her? Despite her efforts, she turns red, as red as the wine. She had better leave before she makes a fool of herself.

The footpath is lit by an occasional spotlight; the undergrowth beyond it is thick and dark. It is a jungle, Nicola observes, a tropical jungle, with a twinkle of excitement. Mysterious, wild creatures live in the jungle. Some of them live on the path. They have hairy legs and carry curvy shells on their backs. When danger approaches they freeze and play dead. Nicola knows where they are coming from – not geographically, mentally. She has been known to freeze when events in her life have taken sharp turns, when strangers intruded on her space, when conversations strayed into the explicit.

A few years ago she tried to break away from her isolation. She signed up with a dating website. It was her last chance before turning forty. She had read about the website on

Facebook. It came highly recommended. Her friends had found love there. She uploaded her passport photo and truthfully filled out all the sections about herself, her education, background, interests and dreams. She waited. Nothing happened. She searched through hundreds of profiles of eligible, heterosexual, male candidates of her own age, but she would not contact any of them. It would be too predatory and Nicola, despite her desperation, was firmly committed to the idea of being chased, not doing the chasing herself.

She was dismayed: so many men looking for their true love and not a single one of them showing any interest in Nicola. Why? What was wrong with her? She was not fat. She was not cross-eyed. She wasn't *that* old. She was comfortably well off – she would not be a burden on anyone. She wasn't stupid; in fact, she was well-educated, an intellectual of sorts ... She wished she could ask someone, someone more experienced in the area of dating, but that was out of the question. If she were to ask for help, everybody would know she was desperate – a cat on a hot tin roof. They would know she was looking. She would never get over the embarrassment.

In the end, Nicola put her research and cross-referencing skills to a good use. She began studying the profiles of other females – learning from the experts. She categorised them by age, image and style. The discoveries she made were eye-opening. Online dating wasn't about real people – it was about striking the right pose, sending out a vibe of desire and desirability.

Rescue me and I will take you to Paradise...
Not a day should go by without me by your side...
Looking for love – in all the wrong places? You found me...
Hold me tight, never let me go...

Nicola had always been a fast learner. She made instant adjustments: the passport photo had to go. It was replaced by a full-body shot of Nicola on the beach (taken some ten years earlier). Her interests transformed magically from reading and medieval history to outdoor adventure and extreme sports. Her headline became an invitation: *Take me on a bumpy ride*. With that she hit the nail on the head.

She did not realise what effect her unintentionally indecent proposal would have on the red-blooded male population of the dating site. She did not comprehend the meaning of it. She was a dating simpleton. *Take me on a bumpy ride* sounded rather romantic to Nicola: windswept hills and galloping horses. The sexual innuendo behind the *ride* and the *bumps* along the way was lost on her. But not, of course, on the sex-starved dating site veterans. Offers started pouring in.

Unfortunately for Nicola, the transition from fiction to reality turned out to be quite a challenge. She was not prepared for the extent of filth that evaded her laptop's filters and made it to her inbox. Emails inviting her to tame senders' *dicks*, *cocks* and other bodily protrusions, suggestions of *flayed whips* and *unbridled sodomy* and the slightly less colourful intimations of a good old *fuck under the star-studded sky* made Nicola's hair stand on end.

After the initial shock, she managed to sieve through the plankton of vulgarity and continued corresponding with two potential candidates: Peter and Paul. That their names were also those of the two most holy disciples had nothing to do with her choice. Peter seemed genuine about his passion for water-based sports and Paul was even more genuinely grieving the loss of his family home and half his pension to his demonic second wife and her brat whose paternity Paul was seriously suspicious about.

Nicola enjoyed talking to both men over the internet. She had built an advanced knowledge and professional vocabulary relating to surfing, tides, boating and everything water-related. She excelled at commiserating with Paul and hating his ex-wife. She felt needed and appreciated. But she had to go one step further – she had to meet them in person and she had to choose between them. The state of virtual bigamy could not go on for ever.

She took the plunge with Peter – literally. He gave her a surprise on their first date, and everything went down the drain from that moment on. Kayaking! In her trainers and ankle-length Laura Ashley skirt she was hardly dressed for the occasion. To make matters worse, the puffy, dirty-yellow life jacket she was obliged to wear made her look like a neckless hen with steroid-packed chicken's breasts. And to finish on a high note she dropped her oar in the water, leaned over to fetch it, and capsized her kayak. Unable to bring herself back to the surface, as she hung upside down among weeds and duck poo, Nicola had lost the will to live. She was such a fraud! Peter was bound to know it. She would rather die than have to face him again, but face him she did as he pulled her out of the river's depths and dragged her to the bank.

As soon as the water was out of her lungs, she spat out a couple of snails together with an *I hate bloody water!* It wasn't even true – she had nothing against water in principle, but in that moment of defeat water was her enemy number one. Peter's face creased in disappointment. He drove her home in her dripping, dirty-yellow life jacket, and dropped her at her doorstep. She did not hear from him again.

Paul went as far as inviting himself in. The dinner had gone well – they'd talked about his ex-wife's antics in the divorce court, and Nicola had felt safe and useful being there for him. He didn't look anything like his profile photograph, but then neither did she, so after the initial shock, they reconciled with each other's actual ages, weights and hairstyles.

He wasn't impressed with her flat (she was still living in her Hammersmith matchbox), but the sofa appealed to him. It was a sizeable leather sofa – a deep four-seater capable of housing a pair of consenting adults. Consenting copulating adults. Or so Paul thought. And he also thought that Nicola shared his appetites. Why else would she have invited him to her flat? Surely the '*bumpy ride*' was on the cards.

As his hand rolled up her skirt and reached for her knickers, with his finger poking fervently inside them, Nicola froze. She sat up with her eyes and mouth wide opened and her body as stiff as Paul's organ. Her body went into a spasm, but by no stretch of imagination could that be mistaken for an orgasm. There she was again, back on form: a koala bear who has just had her once-in-a-lifetime chance to reproduce, and lost it. A disappointment. A species on the brink of extinction.

Paul paused and peered into her eyes. 'Are you all right?' She did not answer. She was frozen, playing dead.

Very much like those shelled creatures caught underfoot on the sandy path she now walks in the Maldives.

Nicola feels their fear.

Something screeches up in the trees. She clutches her chest. *Breathe*, she reminds herself. She dares not look up. A rat scampers from under her feet and dives into a clump of undergrowth. Nicola screams. Jumps back. Her heart is racing inside her chest. She runs.

Her trainers are useful, at last. Her feet may be sweaty in them and her white socks may look ludicrous beneath the hem of her floral dress, but she can run! Keep to the path, another reminder crosses her feverish mind. She keeps running, she must not stop.

A couple emerges from the shadows. The woman is draped over the man. Nicola slows down, tries to resume an ordinary, leisurely pace as if she knows where she is and what she is doing. She doesn't want to look stupid and lost. She doesn't want them to ask her if she is all right. Breathing steadily is a challenge. She swallows a gasp and goes red in the face. They pass by without noticing her. She turns to look back at them. The man's hand is on the woman's buttock.

Nicola must go in the direction they have come from. They must have come from somewhere! Some civilised place, somewhere other than just rubber plants. She is staggering. The wine is taking its toll. On the other hand, it could be the tree roots. They encroach on the path and trip her over. She carries on regardless.

At first, she hears the murmur of human voices cutting across the hiss of the ocean. Then she sees lights. Beyond the next curve of the path stands a bar. It is thatched like every other house on the island. Soft, jazzy music soaks in voices and the sounds of nature. There are tables inside and out, separated with screens and plants. People look relaxed. They are sprawled in comfy chairs, their feet on the tables, colourful cocktails in hand. Mainly couples, engrossed in each other. One of the trees is wrapped in Christmas lights: large blue and red bulbs reflect in the pool.

Never in a million years will Nicola gatecrash this party! Not even to ask for directions, because, truth be told, she does not know where she is on the island. She is lost. Nevertheless, she will not go in. She will not introduce into this peaceful equation the discord of a single woman barging in on lovers' privacy. Instead, she crouches behind a leafy branch, and watches.

A twig snaps close behind her. Two half-naked kids are running away. They are laughing – no doubt at her. An adult woman spying on other adults, being spied on by kids! How do the kids fit into it? Where the hell did they come from?

'*Davay, Petya!*' shouts one to the other. Was it Russian? Is she looking at two Russian boys under the age of ten, loitering mother-less on a tropical honeymoon island? Surely, she has had too much to drink!

The boys dive-bomb into the pool. There is one splash after another and they swim with their heads underwater like two slippery otters.

Could it be sunstroke?

Nicola is feeling faint. She is tired. She has travelled non-stop for the past twenty-four hours. She needs rest. She needs to go to her room, and sleep!

Beyond the pool, she recognises the Reception hut. She staggers towards it like a doomed desert traveller towards a mirage. With a wild look in her eye she summons a boy in a flowery sarong. He may be the lecherous Boy-skipper for all she cares. She needs to be driven to her room. Chalet 42.

Out of sight! She dims the lights and shuts the curtains. She eagle-flies onto her indecently huge king-size bed, and lies sprawled across it, watching the relentless fan as it wrestles with the ceiling, wanting to break free. Think of all the

17

homeless people living in cardboard boxes, she admonishes herself, but the guilt does not come. She is beyond caring.

The icy-cold interior has invigorated her. She is not that sleepy after all. The trainers have to come off. They squelch off her feet. Her socks are wet. She peels them off like blisters. Her feet look swollen. Her breasts still ache inside her bra. She unclips it and pulls it out through an armhole in her dress. Her breasts burst out; nipples spring up and harden on contact with the cold air. Even the light dress feels oppressive. She slides it over her head, takes off the knickers. Her pubic mound itches – it's a jungle there! The sweat and the heat make the itching unbearable. Her pubic hair has never seen the sharp end of a razor. She should shave it all off, not just the bikini line – all of it. That should bring some relief from the heat. She will do it now; then shower, moisturise and go to bed.

Armed with a razor, Nicola heads for the bathroom. As the door swings open, she is assaulted by the heat and the bubbling sounds of the tropics. Quickly, she covers her modesty and retreats into her room. Bloody hell! Hopefully no one has seen her! Where is the bathroom? There aren't any other doors: the front door, the sliding door and this one – the one she thought led to the bathroom. She has to discount the wardrobe doors, surely?

She tries the same door again, peers in – indeed, it is a bathroom. But there is no roof over it – it is out in the open air. The walls are high, but are they high enough? She tunes into the sounds. Nature's squawking and screeching, but no human voices. Is she going to crouch here, peeping through the keyhole into an empty bathroom, or is she going to go in?

She ventures in.

It feels awkward to sit on the toilet without solid walls to protect her. She can only hope that flushing won't wake up the neighbours. The water from the cold tap is colder than the air. She will be having cold showers – after dark, only after dark. Now is a good time. First, the razor.

The hairs fall off, twirl around the plug and travel down, out of sight, carried by the lukewarm water from the shower's cold tap. She has to sit down and spread her legs wide to reach deep between the folds and crevices of her most intimate areas, places she does not visit often. It is a painstaking exercise, but at last all is smooth and much, much cooler. It may be a bit decadent, but she moisturises the whole area with her face cream. That is all she has. It is a strange feeling – but not unpleasant – to touch that very soft skin, hairless and softer than her fingertips. It responds to the touch. It tingles. Nicola shudders.

She looks into the full body-length mirror on the bathroom wall. Her nakedness seems even more indecent for the lack of hair. She washes her hands again, splashes water on her face and goes back into her room, back into the sobering coolness.

In her pyjamas, she feels more in control. It is business as usual. Nicola takes out her laptop and installs it on the table, next to the TV. She keys in the wireless code the receptionist scribbled down on the map he gave her. Facebook remembers her password even in this distant corner of the world. She skims through her friends' pages, but has no energy to message anyone individually. She goes to her own page and writes: *Arrived on Itsouru. It is hot – hot as hell!*

She shuts down the computer and rolls under the thin sheets. She is out within seconds.

Day Two

The ebb and flow of sleep comes to a standstill: she is awake. The air conditioning is blowing full blast, but she is perspiring sticky sweat. She rolls from the bed, looks at the time. It is 10.08 a.m. She has overslept. Missed breakfast.

A residue of dreams weighs on her eyelids. Nicola has not dreamt in years. She is too disciplined to allow dreams to infiltrate her conscience. Dreams could easily corrupt her mind. She cannot let that happen so she always gets up at 6 a.m.; she doesn't need an alarm clock. She ups and goes. Not today. It is the first time since she was a teenager that she has missed her waking hour. It must be due to the different time zone and her journey halfway around the globe. Her body is confused; her mind, more so. Dreams have sneaked in. They creep back into her head: an image of an enormous shell with smooth curvy tunnels polished by the constant flow of whispering water. Nicola slips and slides down a twisting canal: round and down she whizzes – a downward spiral. Echoes bounce from the walls. There is an exit at the narrow far end. She sees a bright light, but she is afraid to come out. She tries to cling onto the smooth walls, but her fingers find nothing to hold on to; she gathers speed – down, down. The humming of flowing water perforates her ears. It transforms into the whizz of a rotating fan. It is right above her head and it is the first thing she sees when she opens her eyes. The fan is unstoppable. The swishing noise gets to her. It's a form of Chinese torture – she turns it off. It quietens down, its pulse slowing until the blade halts and remains still. Heat pours into the room. It is suffocating. She pours a glass of water, and gulps it down in one go. She is hungry; raids the mini-bar. A bag of nuts will have to do. She cannot bring herself to start the day on a chocolate bar. She could go out, find a bar and buy a sandwich – except she can't. She simply cannot open the front door and step out; she cannot leave the safety of this room. She might get lost again if she does.

Nicola unpacks her suitcase. Books find their way to the table. She lines them up in a straight row, propping one against the other. Ambitiously, she brought *Anna Karenina,* in Russian. She will start with that. She stretches on a settee, piles up cushions under her back, feet on a glass coffee-table, nuts in the cup of her hand. She does not have to go out at all. She can spend the entire seven days in her room, reading, sleeping and eating nuts and chocolates.

She wakes up an hour later, a dribble of saliva tickling her neck. Her arm is folded awkwardly under her ribs, her body folded in half like a penknife, her cheek resting on a remote control. She must have pressed the power button, for the TV is on. Exchange rates flash at the bottom of the screen; a weather presenter is talking about the scorching temperature of 38°C as if it were something ordinary. Perhaps it is.

She drinks more water – what's left in the bottle. She is thirsty. She will have to get out from time to time, if only to get more water and food. Her neck aches. She must have slept awkwardly. Swaying her head from side to side makes it worse. She gets up, looks in a mirror. She has the pattern of the keypad from the remote control etched on her left cheek. Her eyes are puffy. She needs air.

When she opens the curtains she is instantly compelled to open the door, too. The world behind the glass cannot possibly be malignant: it is calm and blue, its tranquillity complimented by the warmth of yellow sand. She steps outside.

The heat surprises her once again. It sits on her shoulders, her face and her back. It is omnipresent. Her muscles go flaccid. The sun – which does not occupy a clear spot but is spread thinly across the sky as if someone has tried to bleach it out – dazzles her. Its rays bounce off the sand crystals and fly into

Nicola's eyes. She puts her hand to her brow and scans the horizon.

The sublime blueness is broken in a few places: a stilted hut with a rowing boat moored to it; a long pier with a succession of thatched chalets reaching into the ocean; a palm tree leaning towards the water like a teenage girl's long neck. A couple of white yachts are motionless in the far distance. Everything is true to form – picture perfect. She saw many photographs in glossy brochures which resembled this scene, but this is better. This is real. She stands on the deck of her chalet and takes it all in. This will be the best holiday ever.

The ocean licks the land, and retreats; and comes back for more. It is like a children's story book: full of goodness and sunshine. Nicola steps down onto the burning hot sand and jogs towards the water. Her feet sink in. She feels the warm and moist tongue of the sea on her soles. She sees a fish pass by, just a few steps away. You could reach out and pull that fish out with your bare hands, but who would do such a thing?

Nicola has taken hundreds of photographs: panoramic landscapes but also small things – the broken glass of vacated shells strewn under the pier; a root that has abandoned the ground and climbed up the invisible ladder of air to freeze into a coil, like a snake; a clay pot with a ladle, dry and cracked, wood turning to white bone.

She intended to circumnavigate the entire island, but only managed to get to the other end, the end where the Reception hut is, and the bar with a palm tree impersonating Christmas. The place looks less intimidating in broad daylight. Guests camp on deckchairs, surrounded by beach towels, water bottles, sun creams, iPads, sandals, baseball caps and the rich tapestry of summer dresses rippling out of straw totes. An air of lazy indifference hangs low and heavy.

Nicola finds a table where she unpacks the contents of her canvas bag: her phone, towel and *Anna Karenina*, in Russian. A waiter (Boy-skipper's first cousin, no doubt) has materialised in front of her with a tray propped lightly on the fingertips of his right hand, held above shoulder height. He is standing between Nicola and the sun, his silhouette a black hole in the daylight.

'Good morning. Would madam wish for a drink?'

Nicola, indeed, wishes for a drink – a whole two-litre bottleful of water, please. With ice – a glass full of ice. She drinks greedily when the water arrives; crushes ice cubes between her teeth and presses the misted glass against her chest. She rolls it from shoulder to shoulder, over the bumps of her breasts; droplets of water mix with her sweat.

She tries to read, but her brain is cooked. She leaves *Anna Karenina* on the table and ventures into the pool. She does twenty lengths; her body unfolds from the compact ball of tension it has been rolled into during her journey to the island. She wades into the spa corner of the pool for a rest. She won't leave the pool – not yet. It is cool and refreshing.

A child dives in; water splashes. It is an instinct for Nicola to raise her arm protectively over her head. She doesn't mind the water. It is the noise that she objects to, and the taunting laughter. 'Petya, Petya, smatriy!' *Look, Petya!* The diver rolls forward and soon his feet wriggle upside down. Petya grabs hold of the feet; he is preventing his friend from coming back to the surface. There is a scuffle; water boils. At last, the diver emerges, his mouth gasping for air. 'Nu, pagadi!' *Just you wait!* He leaps at Petya. They wrestle like a pair of eels. Petya escapes and swims to the other side of the pool. There they make up without words: just a pat on the back, a nudge in the ribs, more laughs. They are leaning on the wall of the pool, panting – staring at Nicola. They are both tanned to a crisp: deep brown. They must have been on the island for weeks. They act as if they own it.

She is sure they are staring at her. If she recognised those two, then they remembered her too. From last night. Are they whispering? Laughter: rah-tah-tah, rah-tah-tah … They laugh like circus seals, never taking their eyes off Nicola. Her stomach sinks. What if they tell on her? They will tell their parents that she has been spying on them. Which she wasn't, but no one will believe her. You have to be a freak to go on a honeymoon alone. She is a freak!

'They're such a nuisance.' A young woman is sitting on the underwater spa shelf opposite her. Nicola has not noticed her come. Her lean tanned arms are resting on the side of the pool, over her head. She is wearing sunglasses – in the water. Judging by her toned arms and tight skin she cannot be more than thirty. Her hair is blonde and cropped short. She resembles a matchstick.

'Do you mean those boys?'

'Yes. This island's not a place for kids. It's a retreat. They disturb the peace.'

'You think?'

'I do – and so do you, going by your expression,' the woman chuckles.

'My expression?'

'You're scowling.'

'Good God, is it that obvious?'

The woman nods. 'Afraid so.'

And this is where Nicola has been so many times before – she doesn't know what to say next. This is where most of her conversations end, when she hurries to say that she must be going somewhere extremely important, she'll see you later (or, preferably, never), cheerio, she is gone. When did it start, her being afraid of company? When did she become socially awkward? Earlier than she can remember. As a little girl she used to crawl under the kitchen table at night, the white tablecloth hiding her from view, and listen to adults' conversations without them knowing she was there. She didn't understand any of it, she just liked the droning of their suppressed voices, the comforting sensation of their closeness. If discovered, she would cry and be sent to her room, and would slump with her ear to the door to listen some more, until, so comforted, she would close her eyes and slide into sleep. They would find her in the morning, the weight of her small body blocking the door, the corner of her blanket in her mouth, chewed like a pig's ear.

She's been caught again. She looks away from the chatty woman. 'They're just kids,' she says. She has to chill. She is on holiday, basking in the sun, soaking in a pool; free of worries.

The Russian boys are climbing out of the pool. They have forgotten about her. They run back to their parents, their feet wet flippers, water dripping from their chins and noses. They are screaming for ice cream. Their father is a larger version of them: compact like a body builder, with arms and legs puffed up and shiny. He has the round, chubby face of a boy, but he must be in his mid-forties. There is something Asiatic about him. His wife, on the other hand, is blonde and petite, her stomach flat and sunken between her hips. She doesn't look much older than the boys. Perhaps she is not their mother, or perhaps she is just good for her age.

'They're gone.'

Nicola says it just to break the silence, just to say something. The chatty woman smiles at her and raises her glass in mock salute. She is not afraid of them – they are only kids. But they bother Nicola. They've got under her skin. If she could make a second entry onto this island, she would do it differently: she would not be caught with her knickers down by a pair of freckled brats.

'Do you want a drink?' The woman is asking her while at the same time waving to the smiling waiter. Boy-skipper has a large family – to Nicola, the waiter is yet another clone of him. She has to start paying more attention to people's faces. 'Can we have two cocktails, Greyhound for me with plenty of ice, and you?'

Nicola cannot pretend she knows the names, never mind contents, of any of those tropical beverages. 'Just water, thanks.'

The woman pulls a sympathetic face. 'You've just arrived.'

'Easy to tell?'

'Yes. You're white as a lily.'

'Always,' Nicola relaxes. 'You, on the other hand, you've got a beautiful tan.'

'Thanks. I like it here, would come here every year if I

26

could. This is my second time – my second honeymoon.'

'Second? Wow! Congratulations?' Nicola does not know if that is the right thing to say to a serial honeymooner.

'You're alone, couldn't help noticing. Is your ... someone joining you?' This is a sharp and unwelcome turn in the conversation. The woman has strayed into the joys of spinsterhood and loneliness, and the stupidity of people who suddenly come into money and choose to spend it unwisely by coming to places where they have no business being. Nicola feels ashamed: of herself, of being alone and of her persistent blushing. She hopes that the sun in her face will somehow belie the burning cheeks and give her a better excuse for blushing than a teenage girl's embarrassment. 'No. I just felt like coming here. Alone. My great-aunt died and left me ...' She has to wonder how that's relevant.

'Ah ... I see ... You must join us. If you feel like company, that is.'

'I wouldn't want to intrude.'

'Don't worry, you wouldn't. We've been together for years, only got married last week – again!' the woman chuckles. 'We're bored to our back teeth with just each other. It'd be nice to make friends with new, interesting people, like you.'

Nicola smiles. Actually, why not? It is a woman – not a man – who is making the offer. It's innocent. She cannot be accused of stealing someone's husband. She is just making a friend – a girl friend. 'Well, thanks. That's really nice of you. I might take you up on the offer.'

'Please do.' The woman stands up. She is perfectly formed, if slight. 'Shall we go for a swim? We'd better take our chances before the Russians are back. They virtually take over this pool, like it's theirs.'

'It's odd. I never expected to see so many Russians in one place ...'

'In *this sort of* place, you mean? Oh yeah, they're the ones with money, aren't they? Look there.' She points towards the horizon where a couple of luxury yachts are bobbing on the tide. 'They come by sea. Come and go as they please.'

'Nice!' Nicola tries to sound dismissive. It should make her appear worldly, she hopes, even though she is just an awe-inspired little mouse with her mouth gaping and her knickers in a twist.

'So, about that swim?' The woman pulls the elastic of her bikini bottom and re-arranges it on her narrow hips.

'Yeah, sure!'

'I'm Amy!' She plunges into the pool. Nicola laughs when water droplets splatter on her head and face. She dives in and swims after her, trying to catch up. Things are looking up – she's made a friend. She wonders if they live far away from each other in England. Maybe they could meet up from time to time for a coffee. Maybe they could visit each other. It'd be nice to keep in touch.

Another woman is standing on the edge of the pool, her hands on her hips. She is wearing a funny straw hat with frayed rim that looks too small for her, and no sunglasses. She looks like a mother of five: round, earthy. 'Amy, come on, let's go!' She is looking hard at Nicola though she is speaking to Amy.

Amy pops out of water like a buoy. 'You're not coming in?'

Mother-of-Five shakes her head and points to her wrist. 'Lunchtime!'

Amy climbs out. 'This is Nicola,' she tells her companion.

'Hi, Nicola,' the other's tone is dry. 'Nice to meet you. I'm Sarah.'

Nicola squints and hopes the squint can pass for a smile.

'We got chatting.' Amy says.

'Great. Let's go.'

Amy springs out of the pool and lets Sarah throw a protective towel over her shoulders. They walk away; Amy waves back to Nicola, the towel sliding off her back. 'See you later!'

Nicola waves back and sinks into the pool. She has obviously come between two gay women. She would have to laugh if it weren't so embarrassing. It was too good to be true: just a friendly chat with a fellow holidaymaker. They were really getting on. Or was Amy chatting her up? Did she actually

28

find Nicola attractive? That would be the day!

Nicola is back at her table now, wrapped in her beach towel like a chrysalis, pondering her potential as a lesbian. Perhaps that is what she is. This would explain why she has never succeeded at normal heterosexual relationships. Maybe it is genetic – maybe Great-aunt Eunice was gay; that's why she never married. In her time, one didn't reveal such leanings to the world, not if one happened to be a school headmistress. But Nicola ... What's to stop her?

She waves at the waiter with the same frivolous wriggling of fingers as Amy did a few moments ago. He notices her, grins and instantly wonders what he can get for her.

'Greyhound, please. Lots of ice.'

There is a glint in Nicola's eye. Thank God no one here knows her.

The restaurant is buzzing. Nicola feels comfortable in chaos. It reminds her of the hectic streets of London at peak hour: hearts beating, brows sweating, laptops clutched under arms, copies of the *Evening Standard* shared on the tube. Enclaves of privacy cut out from the sea of souls. Indifference. She thrives on being a small fish in the big, blue ocean. She is invisible and she can observe others, or read, or get on with her life. The familiar faces of the four Germans from last night are comforting. Familiarity without intimacy has its advantages. They are laughing: big teeth, big faces, shiny cheeks, bright eyes. It looks like they have been lunching for a while – they are on their puddings – but they aren't in a hurry to leave. For them the restaurant is a temple. They worship here. They worship their food and their own company. Nicola would not dream of joining them (way too loud, way too smug), but she is grateful for their proximity. They make her feel at home. If only she could crawl and hide under their table ...

She is having a hefty meal: a three-course carnivore's feast. With that a glass of wine will go down well, so she has ordered one. Chilled rosé. It makes her head swivel in a nice, mild way. Today she will not scuttle away like a mouse – she will relish

29

her food, enjoy the ambience. She will take her time. She is a lady of leisure.

She can hear people behind her talking: London accents, chummy but slightly critical in the way in which it is clear they are bothered but not enough to do something about it – the good old English way. It does feel like home! She cannot see them but she can picture the ladies' dyed blonde coiffures, sparkling eyeshadow like goldfish scales, full bosoms held up by strapless bras, and the men wearing Hawaiian shirts and sailors' tattoos.

'By comparison, Egypt is a Mecca,' one of the women sings.

'Mecca ain't in Egypt, pet,' a patient, long-suffering male replies.

'I know where Mecca *isn't*. I'm just saying –'

'Tourist-Mecca,' another woman comes to the rescue.

'Exactly! Have you been to Egypt?'

'Course!'

'More civilised.'

'If you don't set foot outside the resort. We were swarmed when we went out. Only once. Once was enough.'

'Oooh, I know what you mean.'

'More wine, pet?'

'Just a touch … A bit more than that!'

'Paula?'

'Oh, go on then!'

'The pyramids are well overrated – don't you think?'

'We went on camel backs. My backside!' Chuckles follow, and a cough – the wine must have gone down the wrong hole.

'I'll be calling Reception if the sheets ain't properly done.'

'Right you are! I can feel every crease. It's torture.'

'Too much sun if you ask me, pet.'

'But no one's asking you, George.'

Nicola tends to agree with George. She feels this place is luxury enough for her, and then, lest she forgets, there are people in London sleeping in cardboard boxes. You don't hear them complain about the sheets.

She is on her raspberry-and-bramble trifle laced with Drambuie. A man waddles by her table. A cloud of body heat envelopes him. The man is seriously obese. He puffs and wheezes, clutching a main course plate which seems a miniature in his hand. He bulldozes his way to a table where the rest of his family sits. There is no doubt they are related because they are all huge people. He drops his weight on a chair and digs in. One of the women speaks to him, her mouth swelling with food. He nods but does not stop eating to respond. Nicola scowls at her pudding. She is sure they are lovely people, probably very jovial and kind (somehow big people are invariably jovial and kind, she finds), but it isn't their character that disturbs her. It is their weight. How did they get to this point?

It isn't any of her business, though. It is so incorrect to ask such questions. But she does. She drinks her wine, followed by a glass of water, and, so detoxified, she leaves the rest of her pudding untouched.

Nicola has never liked Anna Karenina as a person and she sometimes wonders if Tolstoy himself cared that much for her. She was out of control. He let her rave through the story like a woman possessed, and then didn't know what to do with her so he just let her take the easy way out. Got rid of her because – frankly – he couldn't restrain her. But it wasn't really fair of him to inflict that woman on Count Karenin. Now, that's a man after Nicola's own heart! He is the sort of man she could fall in love with, if love was ever meant for her. She would fall in love with a man who does not waver, a man of integrity and a man of his word. Honourable. Staunch. Nicola feels for him and feels with him. She would not betray him, like Anna.

She refuses to see any of the *Anna Karenina* films, convinced Count Karenin would be portrayed as a hapless old fool. Nicola sees him differently. A man of steel. A strong man who can overcome self-pity and rise above base instincts. He is impeccable in his controlled poise. He is larger than Alosha Vronsky – in body and in mind. Nicola imagines that in films he is shown as shrivelled and dry. He is not like that. He has a deep Russian soul. You need a large frame for a soul of that size.

31

Nicola's cheeks are burning as she tears her eyes away from the page. She is back at the bar with the Christmas tree. Amy and her partner Sarah have not returned. Why is she not surprised? She downs another glass of ice water, and calls for more. She might go for a swim. The ritual around here is simple: drinking and dipping in the pool, on a loop. Everyone does it. At some point you stop seeing individual people – just a mass of quivering bodies hydrating themselves in a relentless struggle against the heat.

She watches the heads bobbing in the pool to check if the two Russian brats are there. They are not. But there is a couple that draws her attention. She is not sure what to make of them. They are at the far end of the pool where earlier the two kids were playing. Unlike the two kids, this couple is not aware of her existence. The man's back is to the wall of the pool. The woman's head is just above his, her arms hooked over his shoulders. She seems taller than him. Though their bodies are tightly pressed together, she is going up and down. It is a rhythmic motion that creates small ripples around them. Up and down.

Nicola realises: no, the woman isn't taller – she is sitting astride the man's hips. His arms are submerged. He is holding her. She is sitting – nesting – in his hands. And he pushes her up and lets her fall down, into the water, onto his … Well, it is clear: they are having sex.

Nicola is frazzled. She is worried for them. It is an irrational concern. It is as if she was in on it: an accomplice. What if someone sees them? Will they be in trouble? What if someone sees her watching them without protest? She knows from her travel agent that the Maldivians are repressed that way. The mores are strict: no bared arms or midriffs in restaurants, no public displays of physical intimacy. It is a Muslim country.

The woman starts bobbing faster and faster. It isn't going to last much longer, surely? He isn't going to last – the man. They freeze for a split second. Smile at each other: wickedly, Nicola thinks, like a pair of rascals up to serious mischief. The woman laughs, flips back, detaches herself from her man and swims away on her back. It is over. Nicola breathes relief. She half expects to see a trail of sperm floating on the surface in the woman's wake, but there is nothing to affect the pure blueness of the water. All is well.

She enters the pool and swims to the far end where not long ago the randy pair were doing their best to offend common decency. She fancies that the water here is warmer. Nicola cannot tell whether she is disgusted or fascinated. She is definitely stirred – intrigued. Perhaps she has imagined it. It has been a hot day. She has had too much sun.

It seems like a blessing that the sun is sinking fast on the far horizon. Dusk happens unexpectedly. The pool empties. Nicola climbs out, dries herself with a towel. She slumps in a deckchair, takes out *Anna Karenina*. A wriggle of her fingers brings a Skipper-boy with a tray and a friendly grin. She orders a Greyhound. She needs something stronger to steady her nerves. Before the waiter returns with the drink, the two Russian boys dive into the pool. Nicola sighs, picks up her things and leaves. She cannot take those two little weasels. She tells the waiter she must dash; he can have the drink on her. He stops smiling. His face hardens.

They don't drink alcohol here, do they? Their religion doesn't allow it, you idiot! Nicola scolds herself.

No one has commented on her Facebook page, which does not come as a surprise. Nicola is used to it. Facebook is there mainly for her to keep track of her old friends, so old and distant that, if pressed, they wouldn't be able to recall her face. She knows that but she doesn't mind. She is more of a follower than a newsmaker. She enjoys peeking into people's busy lives. She studies their faces and changing body shapes. Sometimes she will zoom in on their eyes to explore their laughing wrinkles or their hooded eyelids which say more about them than their laconic Facebook entries. Nicola is an exemplary Facebook friend: she is there for others, but she doesn't expect anything in return. She is low maintenance. She can be God-sent when someone needs tender loving care without strings

33

attached. Too much attention would probably send her reeling. So no comments is perfectly OK. In any event, her last entry wasn't much of a ground-breaking revelation. People go on holidays every day. Only for Nicola it is one of those once-in-a-lifetime events, like getting married, or dying …

Today she has all these fantastic pictures to post. The memory card in her camera phone is brimming with them. It is quite a job to select just a few. No, it won't do. She will upload all of them. It is her adventure, her memories. She copies one photo after another. It takes a while. She works tirelessly through the evening; pictures are spilling onto her webpage, impossibly blue, impossibly bright.

That done, she surfs through her friends' pages. She has a bit to catch up on. Fiona – the long-suffering, endlessly jilted, darling Fiona – has broken up with her partner of two years, David. That is her fifth boyfriend in so many years, since she divorced Ben (or he divorced her; exactly which has never been quite clear from her entries). Nicola had high hopes for David. He had the staying power, she thought. Fiona was proud of him and at last at peace with her lot, but even he has let her down. She must be devastated! Not very lucky with men, poor sausage! Ben habitually fails to keep up with maintenance payments; the others care at first but then find Fiona's twins impossible to live with. They walk over her – she lets them go. What else can she do? Some of them get angry: with the kids bumbling under their feet, with the school runs, with Fiona. They flee and Fiona is left behind to pick up the pieces. Nicola sends Fiona hugs. If there is anything she can do … Deep down, she is glad of her own inner peace and her *single* status that points to no men – no pain – in her life.

Good news on Barbara's front: she's got a new job! It's not what she's used to, not as high-powered, and the money is half what she was getting, but it is a change after fourteen months of job-hunting. In today's market it is a success story. But Barbara sounds cautious and a little flat. There aren't as many exclamation marks as Nicola would expect to see. She remembers Barbara's joie de vivre back in their university days.

It has been missing from her posts and it hasn't quite come back with her new job. Nevertheless, Nicola joins seventy-six others in congratulating Barbara.

Her brother, Robert ... She always checks his page. His Facebook is her peephole into his new life. He signed up with Facebook after moving to Australia and since then Nicola has learned more about her brother than she had ever known before. He has a decent job selling IT technologies, though it involves lots of travelling abroad, especially in Asia where the new markets are. Hannah, his wife, stays at home with the girls. She tried to find a job and held on to one for a few months, but lost it and Robert decided she didn't need the stress of looking for a new one. The money is tight, but the children are happy to have their mum around and are doing well at school. There are photos of their escapades into the Outback and to the East Coast. They all look happy and healthy: ruddy faces and white-toothed smiles, bless them! Nicola doesn't leave comments on Robert's wall – she wouldn't dream of imposing. Robert is just like her. He never comments on her wall. She wonders what he makes of her Maldivian holiday. He is probably scratching his head in bemusement. Nicola smirks. She is going to send him a postcard.

On her way to lunch Nicola stops at the Reception hut. There is a small souvenir shop next to it, where they sell everything you don't need but which may capture your fancy if you're in the mood. They also sell postcards and stamps. She buys a beautiful card with an orange-red sunset. She sends her love to all: Robert, Hannah, Tammy and Grace. She wishes they were here.

Meals are proving tortuous: sitting alone at a table, avoiding eye contact, focusing your thoughts on the copious number of dishes on offer until you begin to feel sick, keeping your back straight and a faint smile quivering on your lips as if you are having a whale of a good time and can hardly contain yourself. At mealtimes the spotlight is on Nicola, a lone woman amongst pairings, a sore thumb – a social disaster in the making.

She has claimed the little table in the corner as her own. It is secluded and very much out of sight. Most diners sit with their backs to her, which suits her fine. She can watch them without being seen. She can listen to their conversations and take part in them, by proxy. Slowly, she is becoming one of them. Slowly, she hopes, they will stop noticing her. She is growing on them: the bawdy Germans, the bunch of cantankerous Londoners, the Big Table (as she decides to call the obese family) and the handsome man with an older wife. *Count Karenin.*

He and his wife are sitting at the same table as last night. They are creatures of habit, just like Nicola. It is comforting to discover that she has something in common with others, especially with *him.* She can't help watching him even though he sits at the one table which faces hers; there is a chance of their eyes meeting. Nicola cherishes the thrill. Is this what one calls 'living dangerously'?

Count Karenin tells his wife something that he finds funny but she does not. His laughter is full-bodied and open. He throws his head back. His wife glares at him in condemnation. She tries to keep her face straight, but it doesn't work. His laughter catches up with her. In the end, she has to smile. Is the joke on her? He calls to a waiter and passes him his wine glass – orders another drink. The woman sticks resolutely to sparkling water in a tall glass with melted ice. When his drink arrives, he clinks his glass against his wife's. She scowls at him as he downs his drink in one go. It is an extravagant way of drinking wine, the man can't possibly appreciate it, Nicola observes. And the man observes her ... He smiles and winks at her! He does! Nicola scuttles away, heading for the buffet despite her full plate. What a fool!

She is piling up more food on her plate, pretending to be totally absorbed in the process. The effect is astonishing: a raw fish swimming in beef stroganoff, an odd lamb cutlet on the raw fish's back, a couple of chips stabbing at a mound of couscous like unexploded missiles.

'Here you are!' Amy confronts her by the salad counter. Nicola jumps.

'Oh ... hi! Hello again! Hi! What ... what are you doing here?'

'Having dinner, I should think ...' Amy's tone and the glint in her eye tell Nicola she has been found out – a proper idiot! 'How about you?'

'Same as you. Dinner, it makes sense ... with all that food –' They both glance at Nicola's plate, and laugh.

'What were you thinking?'

'Couldn't make up my mind: fish or red meat...' Nicola thinks back to Count Karenin and blushes. She must not betray herself – she must look the other way.

'You are one greedy carnivore.'

'Actually ... I'm a vegetarian.'

'Course you are. And the red meat was just a ... decoy?'

'I don't know how it got to my plate.'

'Old habits die hard. I still have an occasional fag, after fifteen years of abstinence.'

'I still savage an occasional lamb.' Nicola doesn't even like lamb.

'You brute!' Playfully, Amy punches her on the arm. Nicola's plate tips precariously to one side and the raw fish swims out of the beef stroganoff and into the salad bowl full of celery and raisins. 'Ouch!' Amy finds the fish in a salad bowl hilarious. Nicola has no choice but to agree. Their heads come together and Amy's hand is on Nicola's arm, squeezing it in a spasm of giggles. They're still chuckling when Sarah swoops on them like a frantic mother goose ready to fend off the wicked Mr Fox. 'I thought I'd lost you,' she tells Amy, and gapes at the runaway fish. 'Did you drop it there?'

'Fish ... in a ... bowl,' Amy points, grins and staggers back. Only now does Nicola realise that Amy is drunk. Tipsy at least.

'I did. I dropped the fish,' Nicola confesses.

'It was my fault,' Amy protests Nicola's innocence.

'Let's get back to the table,' Sarah takes Amy by the arm like a naughty girl.

'Join us, won't you?' Amy asks.

Nicola doesn't want to. She can tell Sarah is not too pleased;

she hasn't as much as looked at her. And there are all those people watching them. Amy is being loud and unsteady on her feet, making a spectacle of herself. 'No, thank you, I'd better go back to my table –' Nicola hesitates. Count Karenin is watching them too. She cannot walk past him. The anonymity of her table has been compromised. 'Oh, on second thoughts – why not?'

Sarah smiles woodenly. The waiter brings another chair to their table, and that alone causes enough commotion to make Nicola blush. Amy gets another bottle of wine. There is an empty one on the table. 'You will celebrate with us, won't you?' Amy insists and fills their glasses. Some of the wine spills on the table. Sarah throws her white napkin onto the spill; the napkin absorbs the wine; a red patch forms on it. Amy rests her head on Sarah's shoulder. 'We got married last week.'

'Congratulations,' Nicola mutters.

Sarah is sipping her wine slowly while Amy goes on, and on. She tells Nicola about their first wedding. 'That was a wedding to remember, wasn't it? We had forty guests, including my parents. Sarah's family didn't come. Well, your daughter did – kind of ...'

'She did. She came to the ceremony, but not the wedding reception. Didn't want to upset her dad.'

'Supercilious prick! *And* he kept Matthew at home!'

'That was five years ago. Things have changed since then. Matthew can make his own mind up now.'

'I thought you got married last week.'

'Yes, correct. *Married* being the key word,' Sarah looks hard at Nicola. She either doesn't like her or thinks her stupid. Nicola frowns, trying to take in the importance of the *key word*. She wishes she could leave now. She has had enough of food, of wine, of attention and of Sarah's disapproval.

Amy is pouring more wine. 'Five years ago we did the civil partnership thing. It wasn't the same, Sarah says. Me? I don't mind. I don't need formalities to know how I feel.'

'It's not that.'

'Blah, blah ...' Amy laughs loudly. 'Sarah can be such a prude!'

38

Sarah turns to Nicola. 'You're not married?' There is admonition in her tone, perhaps a touch of insecurity.

'No.'

'So what brings you here, if you don't mind me asking?'

Stupidity, Nicola thinks.

'You must tell us about yourself, will you? I like your type. I like the *veil of mystery*. There is mystery about her, isn't there, Sarah? Do you think?' Amy squeezes Nicola's hand. Sarah glares. Nicola feels like apologising. There is no mystery. There is no story. There is nothing but stupidity.

'Stop pestering her, Amy.'

'I'm not pestering her. Am I pestering you, Nicky?' Her hand is still on Nicola's hand. 'Tell me I'm not pestering you! I'm just curious.'

'You are pestering her.'

'I'd … I'd better be going,' Nicola gets up. Her legs feel like they belong to someone else. 'I've never drunk so much wine in my life. I think I need to go to bed.'

'You'll sleep like a baby.' Amy gets to her feet. She stretches her neck and kisses Nicola on the cheek. She loses her balance for a split second and leans on Nicola for support. Her breath is hot, her lips brush against Nicola's ear. It was just meant to be a friendly and meaningless peck on the cheek, but Nicola dreads to think what Sarah will make of it. Amy whispers in her ear, 'Don't mind Sarah. She takes time to warm up to people. I'll see you tomorrow.'

'See you,' Sarah says louder than it is necessary. 'Sorry about Amy.'

'It's OK.'

'No, it isn't.'

The warm, humid night does very little to sober her up. She feels tingly all over her body. Her brain seems numbed; it swivels in her skull. Tensing her muscles to keep a steady pace has the opposite effect: she staggers. Shelled creatures scurry away from under her feet, but to Nicola it feels as if the sand shifts underfoot. Steady, girl, she tells herself. It can't be too far to her chalet. Only a few more steps and she will shut the door behind her and hide under the table. Was Amy holding her hand? Did she kiss her? When was the last time someone kissed her? Amy's lips were soft and moist. Nicola rubs her cheek. For God's sake, it was only a peck on a cheek! *It didn't look like that to Sarah.* And all those people watching them. They *were* watching ... Nicola felt their eyes drill into the back of her head. Why does she care so much! They don't know her. She'll never see them again in her life.

She is hurrying to the safety of her chalet, hopeful she is heading in the right direction. It has only been two days and she has already made a fool of herself twice. Once a day – what a score! Yesterday it was her manoeuvres in the bushes where she was found out by a couple of kids; tonight it was a liaison with a newlywed lesbian. Her foot catches in a stray root and she trips. A few quick, mangled steps and, just in time, just before falling down on her face, she manages to regain her balance. She looks nervously around. Did anyone witness her drunken antics? Before she can answer the question, a high-pitch squeal fills the air and a pair of flying objects emerges from the bushes. Nicola's thin balance is lost. She tumbles to the dusty ground, clutching her chest. It's an automatic response to her heart's attempt at breaking out through her ribcage.

It takes a few seconds to establish that the two flying objects are her old and well-hated tormentors: the two Russian boys, playing fighter planes with their arms spread out like wings and their throats expelling squeals of menace. Even they are momentarily taken aback by their own success at bringing Nicola down to her knees. They stare at her for a while, furtive at first, then bursting into peals of laughter. From the corner of her eye she can see the stocky figure of their father behind the trees dimly lit by the soft light from his chalet. He is standing on the deck, doing nothing to help. The blinking scoundrels are having a field day with Nicola. They are like the biblical locusts – they won't go away until she is torn to shreds. They're laughing their little hearts out, slapping themselves on the thighs, the rah-tah-tah of their laughter like a machine gun.

Nicola hides her face in her hands and bursts into tears. She doesn't care how old she is and how young they are. She is humiliated. She wants to go home. She can't move. She is stuck on the ground, her legs are useless and her eyes shut tight. She doesn't want to see her own disgrace.

The boys stop laughing. Someone has stopped them. A male voice is shouting at them in Russian. She can tell it is in Russian, but her mind is too frayed to decipher a single word of what the man is saying to them. All that matters is that they have stopped laughing and are running away. She thinks it is the boys' father. She looks up towards him, but he is silent. Angrily, he takes a few steps towards the path, towards where the voice is coming from, but halts in his tracks. The fury in his face fades away. He cocks his head – he is intrigued. Stealthily he steps behind a tree. With a deep and still focus, he is watching the man who scolded his kids but he does nothing to confront him. Meanwhile, that man approaches Nicola. He leans over her, takes her by the elbows, helps her up.

'Are you all right? Can you walk?'

It is Count Karenin.

He takes her to her chalet. He knows exactly where she is staying. 'We are neighbours,' he tells her. 'I am next door, on that side,' he points to the left. 'We came two days ago, you arrived last night. We will be neighbours for a few days, I hope.'

'Oh dear! I tried to be as quiet as a mouse, but with the bathroom outside … Did I wake you up?'

'No, you didn't wake me,' he flashes his teeth at her in a wide grin. 'You don't remember, do you?'

Nicola fears she has experienced some kind of blackout. What is she supposed to remember?

'You sort of dropped in my lap the day you arrived.' He is laughing.

Nicola's eyes round in horror. 'It wasn't you, was it?'

'I'm afraid it was.'

'I'm so sorry …'

41

'Why? It was the highlight of my day!' He stretches his hand out to her. 'You've got the key?'

She hands over the key without hesitation. Inside, he sits on her bed while she is standing hapless and alien in the middle of the room. 'Those shoes, they are uncomfortable? Hot? Are they?' he points to her trainers. Nicola gawps at her feet and views them with disbelief. Do they really belong to her? She is an ugly duckling, which wouldn't be that bad except that she has little hope of turning into a beautiful swan. A bit too late.

'I'm sorry,' she is speaking to her feet, though she means it for Count Karenin. She is sorry he had to witness her humiliation – twice! She is sorry he had to come to her rescue, sorry she is wearing inappropriate footwear. 'I'm so sorry!'

'What for?'

'I mean … thank you.'

'Those boys deserve a smack on the ear. I've been keeping an eye on them – and on you since the first night we met … I saw them follow you from the restaurant. I knew they were up to no good.' His broad, singing accent aside, his English is perfect. 'They must have scared you witless. Sit down, they're gone.' He pats the side of the bed to his right. It is an innocent gesture though to Nicola the thought of the man's close proximity is both unsettling and exhilarating. She can't make up her mind whether to run or to take those dreadful trainers off and join the man on the bed. This is the man she named Karenin! Close up and personal he looks even stronger and more assertive than from a distance. His weight has made a dent in the bed; the white sheets have crumbled like broken icing. She does need to sit down. She needs to sit down desperately, before her legs go to jelly.

'Drink?' He is up heading for the fridge as soon as she lowers herself next to him. Clearly he doesn't have any untoward intentions. Nicola is disappointed and, at the same time, relieved. She nods. Yes, please, she wants to say, Greyhound with ice. But she says nothing and the nod gets her a glass of plain water.

He watches her as she drinks greedily. Smiles. 'Well, I

would take off those shoes if I were you.'

Nicola kicks off one of her trainers. Wriggles her toes.

'I had better go,' he says. 'Shout if you need anything. I am just over the wall.'

'Thank you again.' She passes an empty glass back to him. He takes it, puts it on the table. 'May I have another glass, before you go?' She doesn't want to be left alone. Not by him. His presence reassures her. She needs plenty of reassurance. She needs a man's hands to hold her together.

She is drinking the second glass as slowly as she possibly can. He sits next to her. He smells of aftershave. She could never tell the brand. The scent is exotic and manly.

'How about the other shoe?' He is smiling again. It's a boyish smile, like there is a prank somewhere behind it. She would've never suspected a Russian man to be so childlike. Carefree. She has always thought them somewhat severe.

'I don't know why I'm telling you this, but I don't want you to go. It's a very wrong thing of me to say, but –' She starts crying. The tears haven't really gone away. They have been welling up ever since she arrived here.

He puts his arms around her. 'Don't cry. I can stay for a bit if that makes you feel better. Don't worry about those boys – they won't come near you. They know I'm watching over you and I'm just that much bigger than them!' His smile is wide and open, laughter lines shoot out like fireworks. Nicola sniffles and presses herself hard against his chest. She clings on to him, her fingers digging into his back. She is too strung up to remember who kisses whom first, but they are kissing, more hunger on her part than his. She isn't even surprised that she knows how to kiss a man. Everything flows naturally; everything that happens seems preordained. His hand slides under her dress and parts her thighs. His fingers are cold and moist from the glass of iced water he took out of her hand and put on the floor by the bed. She wants to be closer to him, skin on skin. She eases herself out of her dress. No shame. No propriety. No hesitation. She is drunk. She does not know what she is doing.

Day Three

The morning finds Nicola's nakedness wrapped up in the sheets. Her heart is thumping in her temples. It's the hangover. She crawls out of bed in search of water. On her way to the fridge, she knocks over a glass – *the* glass. Karenin put it there last night after he had taken it out of her hand and before they made love. She picks the glass up and examines it. It is real. It is here. It must have happened.

She uses the same glass to quench her raging thirst. As she is drinking, she catches herself in the mirror. It is the upper part of her body, from the point where her hips narrow into her waist and open up towards her breasts underlined with sinuous curves that travel to her upper arms. She looks herself in the eye. There is something settled and satisfied in her face, something she hasn't seen before. She smiles at herself, raises her glass and says, 'Good morning, Miss Eagles. And how are we today?'

'Couldn't be better,' she replies. 'Haven't been better. Last night I had sex with a stranger. Well … I had sex, full stop.' She drinks to it.

She feels her inner thighs. They are sticky; it could be sweat, it could be something else. There is also dried blood. There are blood stains on the bed sheets, too – she has only just noticed. It is her blood. She is no longer a forty-year-old virgin. She is a woman.

She pulls the sheet off the bed, rolls it up and hides it in the wardrobe. Nobody needs to see it, nobody needs to know. It is her sweet secret. Nicola doesn't see that there is blood on the other sheets too, a couple of small patches that soaked through in the night.

In her newly acquired boldness, she pulls up the curtains

while still stark naked. Why should she care? She is a worldly woman, experienced in the arcane arts of sex, drugs and rock 'n' roll.

The ocean is tranquil, the sky bears no clouds. A figure is wading out of the water: tall, muscular, familiar. It's him: Karenin! Nicola's heart misses a beat. To her surprise she discovers that it is not just a manner of speech; her heart truly stumbles over itself, *misses a beat*.

Her camera-phone must be somewhere. She fumbles through her bottomless beach bag. There! She is holding it in her hand in triumph. Before it all becomes a myth, a figment of an old spinster's imagination, she will capture him on camera. She will have proof that it has all really happened.

By the time she gets back to the window, he is already crossing the strip of sandy beach, heading for his chalet next door. Didn't he say he was her neighbour? Nicola zooms on him and presses the button. She has him! He stops, looks to one side – she takes another picture. After that it is too late; he is too close not to notice her naked in the door. She scampers to her laptop. Her hands are shaking as she thrusts the memory card into her laptop and uploads her two most precious photographs onto her Facebook wall. With her trembling fingers she can only manage a two-word caption: *Count Karenin.*

Sitting in front of her laptop, she is gazing at the photos. *This is the man I made love to last night*, she wants to add. *I don't even know his real name, but I am head over heels in love with him.*

She does not type any such thing, but she is thinking it. Her hands are trembling. *Oh my God, my God! What have I done! A married man ... How incredibly bad! How amazing! Oh my God! I seduced him. I begged him to stay. What will he think of me? What will his wife think of it? He won't tell her ... Surely ... Oh my God!* Her thoughts are as shaky as her hands. Though she should worry – ought to be ashamed of herself – she is walking on air. And her hands shake because of the high. The thrill of her crime.

She cannot go to breakfast with blood caked on her thighs

and the smell of sex on her skin, though if she could she would carry it around like a badge of honour. Regrettably, she has to wash. She ventures into her outdoor bathroom. It feels like the heat hasn't ebbed in the night. It assaults her with vengeance. Before she turns on the shower, she hears voices: a man and a woman.

'Mishka, gatovyi?' Nicola translates in her head: *Are you ready, Mishka?*

'Niet, niey gatovyi, Matushka. Ya budu bystrah. Uhadee.' *No, Mum. I'll be quick. Go without me.*

Could this be Karenin? Nicola is almost sure she recognises his voice, but maybe she just wishes it was his voice. Did he call the woman *matushka*? *Mother*? Not a wife after all? A wave of relief washes over Nicola. And it washes away her guilt. Not that she has been feeling particularly guilty; not that she gave a second thought to the man's wife when they made love last night ... But it would be nice if he wasn't married to that woman, or to any other woman on this planet.

Nicola has to make sure. She can hear him whistling a plaintive little tune, just there over the high wall that separates their bathrooms. A towel drier is attached to the wall on her side. It looks robust. Nicola must see for herself if her Russian neighbour is indeed the man she gave herself to last night – at the drop of a hat – for a glass of water. She starts climbing the frame, reaches out to the top of the wall to pull herself just that little bit higher, so she will be able to peek over to the other side. Something gives, her foot or the frame. Nicola screams as she plummets to the ground.

His face hovers over hers, only inches away. He smiles his mischievous boyish smile when she frowns at him, trying to focus her vision. The wrinkles around his eyes are deep, but benevolent. The smile deepens them. He has short stubble, only a day old, greying. His eyes are pale. His hair falls over his face, still wet from his morning swim.

'What happened? You fainted?'

Nicola nods. What is she supposed to say? That she fell from her makeshift ladder while spying on him?

'You hit your head. Nasty bruise. Here, put it over your head.' He gives her a wet towel. It's pleasantly cold.

'Thank you. You saved me again.'

'I carried you to bed, I hope you don't mind. You didn't have any clothes on.'

'I don't mind anything.' Nicola has never been this bold. That's what love does to you, she ponders: it emboldens you.

'Good. I think that's good,' he looks relieved. 'Is there anything else I can do for you? Now that I am in the habit –' His eyes rest on the red blotches of blood on the sheets. 'Are you bleeding? Have you cut yourself?'

'No. That's from last night.'

'I haven't hurt you, have I?'

'Oh no! Not at all. It's a ...:' What does she call it? What does she say now? She has no name for it.

'Is it your period?'

'No. Yes! I mean, yes!'

His eyes sweep over her body and stop on her thighs where the blood has dried. 'You're not bleeding now ...' He knows. Something changes in his face. He touches her thigh gently, tenderly. 'It is not your period.'

Nicola is a rubbish liar so she doesn't try. She nods, puts her hand on his and pushes it into her thigh, manoeuvres it higher and presses it in to stop the throbbing. 'No, it isn't.' She should be feeling exposed and powerless, here with a man ogling her nakedness and demanding most intimate confessions, but she feels liberated. Her only anxiety is about him leaving her. Once again she wants him to stay. 'Is someone waiting for you ... in your room? Next door?'

'No, she's gone to breakfast.'

'Your wife?'

He laughs. 'No, not my wife – my mother.'

Nicola exhales. She wants to get up but her head hurts. She winces and groans.

'Stay here. Stay in bed. I'll bring you something to eat from the restaurant.' He lifts her hand to his lips and kisses it like a gentleman. Like a true count.

Nicola limps to the shower. Her ankle hurts. It looks swollen. She puts pressure on her toes and balances awkwardly like a three-legged dog. A cold shower is what she needs, she tells herself, for the swelling in her ankle and for the fever in her head. It is burning with excitement. She washes her hair, lathers her shoulders, breasts, stomach and legs; watches the water carry away in rivulets the scents and stains of last night. As she steps out of the shower the sun dries her skin almost instantly. She moisturises it with her face cream. At first it feels like paper, then it softens and gives in to the touch of her fingers. She brushes her hair, slips on a long beach dress. She is pampered, dressed, fresh and radiant, like a bride. She has almost forgotten about the ankle. Anyway, the pain feels good; it's a reminder that this is not a dream.

They come along the beach. Karenin is carrying a plate. He waves to Nicola as soon as he notices that she is watching from her veranda. His mother puts her hand to her forehead and strains her neck to take a look. She is tiny compared to her son. She is walking in quick, small steps, her long, striped dress restricting her movement. She is also carrying a plate. They are both heading in the direction of Nicola's chalet. She bites her lip: she will have to meet Karenin's mother. Nicola is not good with people, the woman won't like her. Is he bringing his mother with him to prevent any more intimacy? A safeguard – a chaperone …

Not too far behind them another man follows. He is alone. It strikes Nicola that he appears to be hiding, staying close to the line of bushes, ready to dive in should one of them turn to look back. Nicola recognises the man: he is the Russian, the father of the two boys. She knows him by his thickset frame, deep tan, roundness of the head. She is also sure that he isn't just taking a stroll on the beach. He is following them, stops and looks away when the mother pauses to take off her sandals and pour sand out of them. She decides to carry on barefoot, flinging the sandals over her shoulder. The Russian moves too, maintaining the same distance. He is obviously annoyed with Karenin for shouting at his boys, but he is also, for some reason, reluctant to approach him directly. Perhaps he is afraid of him.

'We bring gifts!' Karenin lifts the plate over his head and produces his trademark naughty-boy's smile.

'Is it for me?' She makes an attempt to get off the deckchair, but stands on her sore foot and winces in pain.

'Don't get up! I've got you!' He is holding her around the waist and ushers her back to the chair. He puts the plate in her lap. 'I hope you like bacon and egg for breakfast? It isn't called *English breakfast* for no reason ... You *are* English, I am guessing, looking at your rosy cheeks.'

'I've got cereal and fruit,' says the tiny woman by his side. 'In case you don't like English breakfast.'

'Ah! And that's my mother. She knows better, of course!'

'I am Agaata. Call me Agaata.' She is a no-nonsense, straight-talking woman, who looks Nicola in the eye with calm interest. She doesn't have her son's fiendish smile, but she has his directness and her English is less accented than his. 'Now let me look at that ankle,' she touches the swelling gently. 'Move your toes. Good ... It's a sprain. Mishka,' she turns to her son, 'Yey nadah prinimat' aspirine.' She instructs him to bring the aspirin from her bag and the two women are left alone. The Russian man has also disappeared. Maybe he was on his way somewhere, minding his own business, and Nicola has imagined everything.

'I'm Nicola,' she says. 'Thank you very much for –'

'That's no problem – you have to help when people are in trouble.'

'Your son has been very kind ...'

'Has he? What has he done?'

'I was being taunted by a couple of boys, nothing really, but I guess I was tired and a bit confused where I was, and he, well – he chased them away for me, brought me home.'

'It must have been a long chase. He only came back at dawn,' she nods knowingly, but without sarcasm. Nicola blushes. 'I didn't miss him, don't worry. We'll have to elevate

50

that foot,' she fetches a pillow from the bed. Nicola wonders if she noticed the faint blot of blood on the sheet. 'Do you have any ice in your fridge? It'll bring down the swelling.' She is rummaging in the fridge. 'Oh, I found it! It will do wonders.'

'Thank you! You're very kind.'

'Stop thanking me please. You'll make me blush.'

'Your English is very good.'

'It should be. I taught English Literature at St Petersburg State University.'

'I guessed you were Russian. I heard you speak. I understand Russian a bit ... very little.'

'That's unusual ... We speak Russian with each other, yes, but we're from Karelia.'

'I see.' Nicola hasn't got a clue what that means.

'And we now live in Finland.'

'Finnish?'

Agaata nods. 'I am. Mishka ... Mishka is Russian. He lived his whole life in Russia, born and bred. St Petersburg and the Karelian country – that was the only home he knew until we left Russia.'

Nicola is not making much sense of it. The woman looks pensive, regretful in some way. 'We moved to Finland fifteen years ago. After Mishka's wife Daria died.' She looks sharply at Nicola, then pats her hand. It's an affable gesture. 'I shouldn't be talking about his wife. He wouldn't want me to. Not with you! I think he likes you.'

Nicola feels something grip her stomach. It is a mixture of delight and guilt. Delight because he likes her and because his wife has died and won't stand between them; guilt because it is wrong to be happy about it. What do they call it? Schadenfreude?

'I'm sorry to hear about it ... I mean, about Mishka's wife ...' It is the first time she has uttered his name – his real name. This makes him more real. He is no longer a character from a book. He is a man, a real flesh and blood man – a man in Nicola's life.

'It was fifteen years ago, but it feels like only yesterday.

51

Everything changed that day. It all fell apart. Mishka gave up everything ... he had a good job, a comfortable life ... What do you call it? He was a *high-flyer* ... Is that right?'

'Yes, a high-flyer – someone who does well for himself.'

'She died in a car accident. Just an accident. It happens! Nobody's fault ... Nothing could be done to prevent it. Mishka took it hard. Left his work, left St Petersburg, came to me and said, "Mama, we must go. You and I." "Where do you want to go, son?" I asked him. "As far away as possible," he said. "Finland." He had never been to Finland. I had only memories of it, distant memories from my childhood. He never as much as asked before and suddenly there he was: "Finland"! So we left as we stood. I just packed a few things. He insisted we went the same day. It was the most bizarre day of my life ... Grief does strange things to people. It was hard at first, but we are settled now –'

'What stories are you telling her, Matushka?' Mishka returns with the aspirin in hand and his big smile. 'Don't believe a word she is saying! It is all lies!'

'He doesn't like to speak about it,' Agaata whispers, and then adds out loud, 'I was telling your friend about my birthday treat.'

'I did it for me. You just came along – there was a spare seat on the plane.'

Agaata wags a reproachful finger at him. 'As if that were true! My seventy-fifth birthday ... Mishka came and said, "Mama, it is time you saw a coconut tree." And I said, why would I want to see a coconut tree at my age. He said, "Because you may never get another chance." And so here we are. Mishka has always been like that: spur of the moment, hot headed! As I told you ...'

He is laughing. 'Matushka, Matushka, you're giving me a very bad reputation!'

'Not at all,' Nicola says. 'It all sounds very romantic.'

'How about that aspirin?' He swiftly changes the subject. Is he embarrassed by his talkative mother who has dragged into the daylight all of his life's secrets?

'Oh yes, aspirin! Two tablets. It'll bring down the swelling. Get a glass of water, Mishka, don't make the girl suffer!'

Agaata left them an hour ago, claiming a headache, yet she did not ask for her aspirin back. Mishka told her he would follow her soon. 'Don't even think about it,' she said. 'I need peace. Give me space!' So he has stayed with Nicola. They talk, sitting on the veranda, gazing over the quiet rolling ocean, laughing at his jokes. Strangely Nicola does not feel like they could ever run out of subjects. There is no koala-bear awkwardness she would so often experience with strangers. She doesn't feel the need to escape, excuse herself and run away. She wants this moment to stretch into infinity. 'Your mother is a lovely lady. I don't know how to say how grateful I am.'

'No need for that. She enjoys being indispensable. And she knows everything about sprains and broken arms. She had me, you see, and I was so damn accident prone!'

'Were you? You're such a ... strong man – stable.' She blushes.

'In Karelia, when I was a kid, I did what kids do: climbed trees, swam in the river, tamed horses and teased guard dogs. Everyone else would get away with it, but I wouldn't. I would get caught or injured. She would have to ... what do you say? Bail me out. My father was a lieutenant in the Red Army – I didn't see him much, didn't know him that well. My mother was my guardian angel even though I didn't believe in such things as angels. She believed. She still does. The Finns are very superstitious. My father used to laugh at her, I remember, but she stuck to her way of life.'

'How did your parents meet?'

'Impossible, wouldn't you say? Finnish and Russian, mortal enemies. Well, miracles happen – according to my mother. When Karelia passed to the Soviet Union after the war, Mother's family stayed put – they wouldn't let go of their land. Mother was only twelve. There were few Finnish left in the area – most of them ran back to Finland. My father was from St Petersburg, Leningrad we called it them. He was older, sixteen years Matushka's senior. They met in 1956. When he was stationed in Karelia in the fifties, he saw her – *milk and honey*, he used to say about her. That was it: head over heels he was in love. They were married, had me and ... all the troubles started,' he chuckles. 'I was a handful! When I was out of primary school, we moved to St Petersburg. Mother took up teaching. And so it goes ...'

'Your mother said you moved to Finland? You live there now, permanently?'

'We do now. I always suspected she wanted to go back there. It was only a matter of time so when she retired fifteen years ago –'

'She said it was your decision, after your wife died –' Nicola bites her tongue. Too late. She notices how his face darkens.

'Enough about me. Tell me about you.' He controls the emotion, and covers it with a wide grin. 'Do you realise I don't know your name?'

'Oh dear! Nicola. Eagles. Nicola Eagles.'

He picks up her hand, kisses it like an old-fashioned gentleman. 'Mikhail. Lakso. Mikhail Lakso. Misha for short. It is my honour to meet you.' He charms her with another kiss planted on her hand, and with his round, faintly blue eyes and with his mischievous smirk. 'Now you will have to tell me everything about you. Everything there is to know!'

Nicola fears there is little to tell. Her whole life story may take no more than a couple of minutes to relay. She starts with Maidenhead and with the wave of memories come little things: her and Robert's tree house, the day when she fell from the swing and broke her leg, the night she spent home alone when Robert's appendix burst and they rushed him to hospital, forgetting her at home, frightened of those liquid shadows gliding on the ceiling from the headlights of passing cars. She tells him she doesn't see Robert that much these days. In fact, she doesn't see him at all. He left England soon after their parents died, one after the other, like in one of the Brothers Grimm's tales. She was left on her own, though of course she'd still had Great-aunt Eunice, until she died too ...

Nicola worries she has strayed into the doom and gloom of her life. 'I studied Russian,' she says merely to change the subject, but instantly a thought occurs to her that perhaps it was meant to be: it was her destiny to read Russian so that she would meet Mikhail – Misha – Mishka …

'I had better watch what I say to Matushka behind your back,' he laughs.

'I wouldn't understand much of what you say to each other. My Russian isn't half as good as your English.'

'Ah! I think it is much better than you care to admit. I saw some Russian books in your room. *Anna Karenina* is not an easy read.'

Nicola smiles with all due modesty, but she is pleasantly tickled. 'Well, I worked as an interpreter for Amnesty International for a short while, then for *The Ritz Hotel*. Funny thing is they didn't need me. Their Russian guests were perfectly fluent in English.'

'So what do you do now for a living? If you don't mind me asking.'

Nicola doesn't mind anything he asks. Without shame or embellishment, she tells him how five years ago she found the perfect job for an overqualified spinster – the position of librarian at the Manuscripts Department of the British Library. Her work with the dusty manuscripts on the second floor is as undemanding as it is uninspiring, but she is content with her lot. She travels to work by train and does not own a car, which is just as well since she cannot drive. She is paid peanuts but that doesn't bother her either because of Great-aunt Eunice leaving her lots of money. And a cottage in the country. The cottage in the country, she tells him, comes with a cat called Fritz and strawberry fields smelling good just over the hedge. It is not such a bad life, Nicola ponders, it is lonely, but not bad.

'I wish I had your life,' Mishka says, 'very little could go wrong with it. Given a chance, I would like it better than mine.'

'Surely yours is much more exciting!'

'Oh, exciting! Exciting it has been: parties, drink, gambling; the high life!' He smiles at his memories, and out of the blue, mentions his wife: 'Daria was a ballerina. With the Kirov Ballet. We knew all sorts of people. We lived our lives to the fullest. Top of the world – that's how it felt! Like your lungs were bursting with air and the world lay humble at your feet. She used to wear those soft, soft furs and the jewellery – it sparkled. She sparkled … Why am I telling you that?'

'I don't know. I guess I asked.' Nicola feels small and insignificant. A little grey moth. He must have realised that as well. The illusion is gone. This tropical island, the heat of the sun, the remoteness and the glamour has made her into someone she is not, and now the veneer has fallen off. He knows. She is such a fraud!

'I need a swim!' He jumps to his feet and takes her in his arms. 'Come on! Let's go! Into the ocean!'

'My foot! I can't!'

'I'll carry you! No such thing as *can't*!' He is holding her folded and curled, clutching onto his neck, and he is running across the hot sand towards the edge of the ocean. His laughter is loud and open and in that instant she knows he is no Karenin – he is Vronsky, a daredevil, a show-off, a man who doesn't take 'no' for an answer, a man who is used to having it his way. Nicola laughs with him. She sheds her inhibitions. What the hell! She screams. She tells him she is wearing nothing under her dress. Even better, he replies, and his eyes light up with lust. He is strong. He presses against the wall of water, trudging deeper into the ocean, crossing the shallow lagoon with her in his arms until the water levels with her back. He lays her on the surface. 'Tilt your head back,' he tells her, 'relax your muscles. Just float.' Which she does. She trusts him infinitely. He withdraws his hands from under her back. The wave rolls her gently. She closes her eyes so that the sun doesn't bore into them, and she drifts, lost but not alone in the deep blue sea. When she opens her eyes, he is gone. Panic sets in, her stomach muscles tense and she starts dropping, waving her arms, splashing, choking on water. The shore seems miles away: tiny huts in the distance. Where is he!

The water bubbles and he shoots up a couple of metres

away. She spots him just before she is dragged under and before she catches her last breath. Has he abandoned her? Her eyes are wide open under the water. A colourful fish glides by, ignoring Nicola and her efforts to stay afloat. She can feel the sharp sea bottom with her foot, the healthy one that doesn't shrink from touching down. And there he is. His face materialises in the murky depths and his hand reaches to her and grabs her and lifts her and pushes her out of the water. He is standing firmly, holding her up with one hand and showing her something with the other. 'Look! It's a starfish! It's beautiful!'

Nicola coughs as she chokes on air, which she has tried to gulp down too greedily. She spits water. He hasn't even noticed she nearly drowned. He is grinning proudly. 'It's for you,' he says.

She takes the starfish out of his hand. It feels rough. She throws it back into the sea, wraps her arms around his neck and presses her forehead to his. 'You gave me a bloody fright,' she whispers. Her dress has opened up like a parachute on the waves. She feels his body as she clings to him. Urgently, with the agility of a monkey, she folds her legs around his back and sits astride him. There comes a memory of those two lovers rocking against the wall of the pool. He must be reading her mind for he pulls her down and into him, and she is bound to him and safe.

Day Four

He has stayed the night with her. When Nicola wakes the next morning she finds him fast asleep on his stomach, his knee bent, his arm stretched across her chest, his face buried in the pillow. She examines his naked body – it is toned and still youthful. Not like hers, but it doesn't matter that she is a bit flabby and pale, because he likes her the way she is. He likes her, full stop. And he has stayed the night with her. Agaata doesn't mind, Nicola is sure of that. Agaata is used to being alone. Her husband, Mishka told Nicola, died suddenly of a heart attack three years after they moved to St Petersburg. Agaata had never remarried, never cared for another man. She must have been worried that Mishka took after her: a one-woman man, and that he would not find – or search for – anyone else after his wife's death. But Agaata must worry no more because he has found Nicola. A touch of miracle, Nicola marvels, and miracles are what both she and Agaata believe in. Maybe Mishka, against his better atheist's judgment, believes in them too.

The previous evening is a blur. They drank a lot of champagne. He had brought it from the bar in an ice bucket with silver handles. They drank it from the bottle; poured it into each other's mouths. Made love and fell asleep letting the champagne dry on their skins. Nicola was wasted. This morning her head is throbbing and her tongue is swollen inside her mouth. She can believe now that thirst kills. She slips from under his arm and staggers to the fridge. A large, icy bottle looks like salvation. She swallows in loud gulps.

'Where do you think you're going?' His voice is gritty. 'You're not trying to escape from me already?'

'No!' The thought scares her. 'God, no! Just having a drink.

I'm so thirsty.'

'It is called a hangover.'

She sits on his side of the bed (*his side of the bed*, she rejoices) and passes him the bottle. He sits up, pulls himself up to the headboard. His stomach is flat and muscular even when he is sitting, folded in half. He drinks – his Adam's apple bobs like a buoy.

'I wouldn't dream of escaping,' Nicola says. 'I can't imagine when it is all over and you go back to Finland and I go back to the UK ... I just can't bear the thought of being separated from you. I know it's silly. I know I've only known you for two days. But I can't bear the thought –'

'It doesn't have to come to it. I won't let it.' The bottle is empty. He puts it aside and pulls her towards him. 'Don't even say it. Let's not worry about it. It won't happen.' He kisses her on the forehead, a strange paternal gesture after a night of passionate lovemaking, but Nicola finds it reassuring. *He won't let me go* ... she reminds herself to keep that reassurance afloat. Deep down, a nasty little voice whispers in her head that she is one of many conquests, she is a little grey moth attracted to a bright light. He must've told many women the same thing and then walked away to his high life and the sparkling memories of his ballerina wife. Nicola banishes those thoughts from her mind. She is too afraid to doubt him. She wants to believe him. Somehow he won't let it happen because he says so, but she won't ask him how exactly. If she did, she would hear the truth: *how can he not let it happen, how is it at all within his power to not let it happen* ...

'Chin up!' he tells her. 'Let's go for a swim!'

Her foot is better; the swelling has gone down a lot, but he insists on carrying her like he did yesterday. Except that today she has managed to put her costume on. He doesn't object. His hunger for her nakedness has gone down just like the swelling of her ankle. He is spent, Nicola fears, but tries to combat her insecurities: he is spent but not bored. How many times have they made love in the span of two days? She has lost count. He is spent, not bored.

He dives in and pulls her with him. 'I love water!' he shouts, 'Ever since I used to go to pioneer camps in the Crimea. The Black Sea is just like this!' And he is gone. Nicola bobs on the surface, waiting for him to emerge. She scans the hazy horizon. Someone is waving to her from a pier, a lonely, small figure sitting with her legs up, knees drawn to the chin. Nicola recognises the matchstick body. It is Amy. She waves back. Mishka pops out of the water, shakes droplets out of his hair, grasps her arms and pulls her in before she is able to draw air into her lungs. Underwater, he gives her a kiss of life.

Agaata has checked Nicola's ankle and declared it 'on the mend'. She has been staying away for most of the day and refused to join them for dinner. Mishka has come up with the idea of a French restaurant, not part and parcel of the holiday package but something more luxurious and secluded. A bit of the high life. 'I want you to myself,' he tells Nicola. 'I don't want all those people around us. Just you and I.'

'What about your mother? She'll have to dine by herself, she won't like it.'

'She'll love it! She knows what she's doing. Do you call it *giving us space*? That's what she is doing. She's done some matchmaking in the past. I know her: she's rubbing her hands with glee.'

A tiny niggle at the back of Nicola's mind: all that matchmaking … Did anything ever come out of it? She has the urge to ask but bites her tongue. She doesn't really want to know. She would be stupid to want to know.

The restaurant is on top of the island, on a secluded peninsula that stretches into the ocean. Mishka has hired a rowing boat: the quickest way to get there with an invalid in tow, he laughs. Nicola's foot isn't that bad, she protests, though she loves the idea of being ferried on a rowing boat, far away from all those preying eyes. How her life has changed in the span of a couple of days, she marvels as she leans back in the boat and dips her fingers in warm water. Her work in the Manuscripts Department seems like a pointless exercise in reversing the flow of time – something that has been eating away her life, nibbling on precious moments like this one here and now. Her home is an empty shell that belonged to a different snail: an old aunt who has squandered her own life on pointless exercises. Nicola will not make that mistake. If Mishka – her dashing, mad Alosha Vronsky – asks her to go with him to Finland, to Russia, to the ends of the world, she will.

If he asks …

The sun is setting in deep hues of crimson. In the distance a couple of white yachts break into the crimson. The two Russian boys are building a sandcastle on the beach. One of them runs with a bucket to get water, the other is patting a conical shape that looks like a turret. They are two innocent kids, Nicola reflects, playing in sand. Only two days ago she saw them as the devil's own, now they make her smile with warm affection. They have brought her and Mishka together. Everything changes when your own perspective shifts and you see the world from a new angle, and it surprises you how different it is. The boy's father rises from a beach chair and pulls a towel from his face. He is watching the ocean or the bobbing yachts; perhaps he is watching the two people in the rowing boat. The young, gorgeous mum also gets up and starts dusting the sand off her legs. She is wearing a wide-brimmed straw hat. She stands next to her husband, shades her eyes from the sun, and watches. In a surge of affability, Nicola waves to them. She feels like she knows them. The woman responds but the man puts his hands on his hips, shouts something to the boys, and they all begin to collect their belongings. An idyllic family snapshot. Only yesterday she feared them and suspected the man of sinister intentions. She has to smile.

'Why are you smiling?' Mishka asks.

'I think I am happy.'

'I am smiling too. Have you noticed?'

In the restaurant he tells her about all the things he wants to show her in St Petersburg. His face is animated and flushed with colour. She can't keep up with his drinking. Shot after shot

62

of neat spirits. 'We take drinking seriously in Russia, you know?' His accent becomes more pronounced; he stretches and softens vowels and starts throwing Russian words into the mix. Nicola loves his accent. And that's not all, but she is too afraid to admit that even to herself.

'What the devil,' he says, 'I'll take you there! I don't care! *Ya byl durak*! *Trus! Payedziom!* I will take you to that restaurant near Ermitazh. They serve proper Russian borscht. Then I will take you for walk. I know places ... I was stupid to leave! *Durak!* You come with me? Say you will!'

'I will.'

'That's my girl!' He seizes her hand and lifts it to his lips. 'You will see life in *Rossiya*! Ahh, it will dazzle you, I bet you all I have! You will be dazzled ... When we partied, in those days – I was younger then, but I can still do it! You watch me! When we started going, the morning would never come. We could go on day and night. Champagne was flowing in rivers. A never-ending ball ... Whoever said Rossiya was sad and dull was a fool. *On nye znayet!*'

His eyes are sparking with a feverish light. They are a bit bloodshot from the amount of alcohol he has had, but they are alive and almost insane with excitement. Nicola tries to imagine the wonders he is talking about. How she wants to be part of it! She downs a whole glass of champagne in one go, like he does. She can do it! What the hell!

You only live once!

Day Five

How quickly things change. Unexpectedly and without a warning. Thinking calmly about it – if she ever does – she will realise she has had it coming. Her mother used to say it often: if it looks too good to be true, then it probably is. It has been too good, way too good to be true. And it is so easy to get used to the good thing, so easy that you find it impossible to let it go.

They wake up together, once again at an ungodly hour well past breakfast. Nicola recognises the symptoms of a hangover and drowns them in a pint of water. She joins Mishka on the deck. He is gazing over the waters of the peaceful ocean which rustles and whispers, and sighs and murmurs as the waves throb only skin deep while the depths remain unmoved. The invisible heat is beginning to rise, but it is still relatively cool. Nicola wonders if she has enough money to be able to live here permanently. Probably not. A few months and she would have to pack up and return to London to earn a living. She shudders thinking about it. She wraps her arms around Mishka's body; it is a reassurance. For now, for here, nothing is impossible. Almost too good to be true.

The sun isn't yet high or powerful enough to dazzle. In the distance the two regular white yachts are joined by a third one. It is bigger than the others – a cruiser rather than a yacht – and it is blue with white lettering on the side. Nicola recognises them: Russian letters. Like Amy has said, they have all the money in the world to come and go as they please, and even to live here permanently if that takes their fancy. Nicola can only dream.

'My ankle is fine,' she says. 'I'm walking today. In fact, I think we should go for a long walk around the island. I've been planning to do that ever since I arrived. Got lost a couple of times,' she chuckles. Mishka doesn't respond. His body is rigid and he is stubbornly staring into the horizon. He hasn't even looked at her, not once, not since she joined him on the deck. 'What do you think?' she asks, 'about that walk? I'm perfectly capable ... no more carrying me around, mister!' She doesn't think he has heard her. Or he is ignoring her on purpose. His face is inscrutable, the mischief in it has vanished and so has the wide grin. 'Is your head as bad as mine?' she guesses. 'Too much vodka. I think I'm due for another glass of water. You too?'

He turns, pushing her away. Her arms fall off his waist – he doesn't notice. He strides inside. 'Have you got a pen?' he demands and looks at her for the first time this morning. His eyes are cold and focused. She hardly recognises him.

'A pen?'

'Pen and paper.'

She searches through her bag. Pen and paper, not something you have lying around handy. She finds a pen and passes it to him together with the flight itinerary, which is the only scrap of paper she has. He snatches it, almost rudely. 'What is your address in England? And your telephone number.'

'Why?'

'I need to know.'

Her stomach sinks to the bottom of her pelvic floor. She dictates the address to him and he takes it down quickly, making several spelling mistakes, which she does not dare to correct. 'This is ... rather sudden,' she says quietly.

'I want to be able to contact you. I'm leaving today.'

It is the most unexpected revelation she has heard from him even though she has been expecting it, fearing it. It was going to happen. He was going to go home, and so was she, when their time was up on this island. But this strikes her like a hammer on the head. Perhaps it is the way he is telling her: he is cold, matter-of-fact, indifferent. What has happened between last night and this morning? 'I didn't know ... I mean, that you were leaving so soon.'

'I have to be going.' He folds her itinerary with her address on it, and puts it into the pocket of his shorts. In all her dismay she is able to consider whether or not she may need it to travel home. She starts crying. 'Sorry, sorry,' she apologises. 'I didn't know. What am I saying!'

'Sorry,' his face softens for a fleeting moment of regret or sadness, 'if it is sudden. I will be in touch.'

She decides to be brave. 'Can I be in touch? Will you give me your address then?'

There is a hesitation in his eyes, and that tells her that he has never intended to contact her and that he doesn't want to be contacted by her. But he chooses to be polite (probably to avoid a scene). He takes the itinerary from his pocket, unfolds it, scribbles something on it, tears the bottom half off and puts it on the table. 'Here, my address and telephone number.' His tone tells her he doesn't want her to call him, or to write. It is hard. He is just getting rid of her. Probably the address is made up.

'Thank you,' Nicola says weakly.

She can hear a commotion next door. He and his mother are speaking fast, so fast that she can't make out anything. She is listening in so that she can make some sense of it. They must be packing. She wonders if Agaata will come to say goodbye. She was supposed to be their matchmaker. Or does she know not to interfere in her son's affairs? Does she know how quickly he tires of women? Does she enjoy the fact that she is the only woman in his life? Nicola searches in her memory for any early signs of this sudden and brutal parting. She finds nothing. How would she know anyway! How often has she been in a relationship that she would know when it ends?

The door to their chalet is shut closed. Nicola peeps through her own door: Mishka is carrying two suitcases, Agaata trots beside him, muttering and waving her arm in agitation as if she were trying to convince herself of something. The suitcases must be heavy, but Mishka has not called for a cart to take them to the Reception hut. Are they really heading there? Are they really leaving? Is this a trick? Against her better judgment, she follows them down the sandy path. She wants to make sure he has not lied to her. As if that should make any difference! Because if he had lied and this whole circus is just to be rid of her, then it is worse than him just going home at the end of a holiday. Because going home would hurt less than growing tired of her. But she still hopes that as suddenly as this has started, he will as suddenly turn back and run towards her and laugh out loud, and tell her what a silly numpty she has been to believe him. And he will do that with that trademark wide grin of his, full of mischief.

He doesn't turn back. They reach the Reception hut. They enter. Nicola stands outside and watches as they check out, return the key to their chalet, tell the receptionist that they indeed enjoyed their stay. This is final.

The two Russian boys, as is their special talent, pop out of nowhere and glare at Nicola. Once again they have caught her with her knickers down. She doesn't care. It's a Mexican standoff. She glares back at them – the cause of her heartache. Their father hurries from the bar behind the reception hut, instructing them to go home, now: '*Petya, Vanya, davay doma! Bystrah! Ya skazow!*' It is at that very moment that Mishka and Agaata emerge from the reception hut. Mishka bumps into the Russian, they look at each other, taken aback and potentially apologetic; it looks like Mishka is about to say something, but the other man turns on his heel and runs after his boys. Towards Nicola. Mishka's head turns after the man. Nicola steps back behind the bushes. She can't be seen. She couldn't bear the embarrassment of being discovered. Thankfully, he didn't spot her. His gazed is focused on the Russian man. Mishka watches him walk away and only when the man finally turns the corner does he tear his eyes away from him. He points his mother towards the jetty and urges her to head that way. He puts the smaller of their suitcases in her hand. There is a boat moored by the jetty; holidaymakers have poured out of it, loud and excited. A group of about ten people is beginning to board the boat. Mishka pushes Agaata towards that group. He says something to her – it sounds urgent and angry. She tries to grab his hand to pull him with her, but he frees himself from her grasp and is starting to explain something. He gestures towards the path and the bush where Nicola is hiding. She'd better disappear now, before he finds her spying on them. She starts walking back to her chalet, or just walking without any particular aim.

The more she walks, the more strain she puts on her ankle. It now begins to hurt, or it is only now that she realises that the ankle hurts. She begins to limp, but she cannot stop walking. She is walking away from it all: from her stupid old spinster's past, from her job in the Manuscripts, from pointless exercises in living a life, from her table tucked away in the corner of a restaurant where only couples dine. She is walking away from her awkwardness. And her naiveté. Though she will never be able to walk away from her Alosha Vronsky's curse and from how she felt when they made love, when he smiled at her so openly that there was no doubt in her mind. Not only will she not be able to walk away from him – she won't be able to let him walk away from her. At least in her mind, that is, because in reality he just has.

She cannot put the snippets of her grief and shock into any cohesive pattern of thought so she keeps walking – limping – along the beach at the height of the day. The waves that brush by her feet are warmer than chicken broth. The soles of her feet burn, which is a welcome sensation for her inner pain needs to be superseded by something, anything!

She must have circumnavigated the island several times over – she keeps seeing the same trees and hideaways with the same people slumped on the same beach chairs. But she cannot stop. She glances at the apathetic ocean – another speedboat shoots across. The one that carried Mishka away from her must be long gone. It may be in Colombo by now. He may be boarding the plane back to Russia. Or Finland. Or wherever the hell he has come from.

On the pier a matchstick figure cuts a familiar sight. Amy. She is in the same place she was yesterday. Has she been there all night? Daft question. It is only polite to acknowledge her, to wave, even if you don't care and don't want to speak to anyone. Manners will never desert Nicola, even if everything and everyone else does. She waves. Amy responds in a half-hearted way: her hand goes up but not her arm, a tiny quiver of the wrist – that's all. Surprising, coming from the jovial Amy. Her body language is altogether despondent: her shoulders are dropped, her back curved; she is gazing at her feet. Nicola cannot ignore these signals. She breaks from her course and goes to Amy.

'You all right?'

Amy gazes at her and manages a feeble smile. 'Come, sit with me,' she asks and Nicola settles next to her and, like her, dips her feet in the water. Amy makes little waves with her dangling feet; Nicola does the same. They sit like that for a while without speaking. Nicola likes this companionable silence. She has someone to share her misery with though there is no need for words and windy explanations. She couldn't put it into words if she tried. She can't even put her misery into thoughts! Such a mess in her head! Bewilderment. Every thought, every emotion, every understanding shattered into tiny pieces.

Chaos.

In the deceptively shallow water the sandy bottom seems to be ankle deep and it feels like she could touch with her toes the occasional fish that passes by. A strange fish sails beneath: ugly, shapeless, puffed up. More or less how Nicola feels. The fish heads into the deeper ocean. It soon disappears. It is followed by a shark: one of those innocuous small sharks, but magnified by the prism of water and highlighted by the sunlight that penetrates the depths. It is a magnificent creature. Will the shark savage the fish? Will anyone care? It is such an ugly fish.

Amy rests her head on Nicola's shoulder. That makes her slightly uncomfortable. What if Sarah sees it and gets the wrong end of the stick? But she can't bring herself to withdraw her shoulder because she can tell Amy seeks comfort and solace. Why would Nicola want to withdraw that from her? She could

70

do with some solace herself, though she wouldn't dream of asking for it.

'I'm leaving Sarah,' Amy says.

It is beyond Nicola to understand that statement, but she nods and says, 'I see.'

'You probably think I'm a callous cow.'

'I don't think that –'

Amy lifts her head from Nicola's shoulder and turns to face her. Her eyes are puffy, her skin patchy. 'You're thinking: why? This is our honeymoon! Just got married! So many years of waiting for this to happen, so much grief, so many alienated people, tears, dramas! And at last we're here – we're married!' She draws her fist to her lips as if she wants to muffle her words, 'I'm thinking the same. I don't know why I'm leaving Sarah. I don't know how I'm going to tell her.'

Simple: wake up in the morning, look out the window when you're telling her – don't look into her eyes – and say it: 'I'm leaving today.' Nicola won't say it out loud. It'd be cruel. She is bitter, but she won't be cruel.

'Are you sure?' she asks.

'We ran our course. I knew it before we tied the knot but I had to do it for her. She's lived for it the past few years! How could I tell her it was over?'

'How can you tell her now?'

'I don't know! But I must. I must do it now – today, before we go back home. Or I'll go bonkers. The thing is I won't be able to tell her why, and she'll ask. I don't know *why*! I don't know how it came to it, but this is where I am. I don't love her. I don't want to be in it. She suffocates me.'

'I think she knows,' Nicola realises. She can see now how protective Sarah is over Amy. It's not protectiveness – it is insecurity. She doesn't trust her. She *does* suffocate her because she knows she is about to lose her.

'She knows? She can't know.' Amy shakes her head. 'We just got married! How could she possibly suspect what goes on in my sick mind?'

'Because ... well, I don't know ... It's hard to put your

71

finger on it.' Nicola observes another fish – two of them, two of the same kind; orange, and snappy in movement. 'Well ... I think I do know. Because she doesn't strike me like she's happy. She doesn't look happy. She looks – she acts – anxious, gloomy, dark ... Because, I think, she knows. Though maybe I'm wrong. What do I know? I don't know Sarah, I didn't know her when she was happy – that's *if* she isn't happy any more, which –'

'She knows!' Amy grabs Nicola's wrist. 'You're right, she knows! God, she does know! Oh God, poor Sarah ... How long has she known? It must've been torture ...'

'How long have you been feeling like that?'

'Years ...'

'You'll still have to tell her. Because she knows but she doesn't believe.'

'Yes, I'll tell her. Tonight. Take her out of her misery. Thank you.' Amy hugs her. Her arms are tight around Nicola's neck. It feels awkward but there is so much neediness in that hug that Nicola has to reciprocate it. It comforts her too. That human contact, the warmth of another's body, that vulnerability, that closeness – Nicola needs it too.

'I hope I'm not interrupting?'

They draw their arms away from each other as if on cue. How long has Sarah been standing there, listening and watching? She doesn't look hurt, or anxious. She looks angry.

Nicola couldn't bring herself to go to dinner. She doesn't feel hungry, but even if she did she couldn't face the buzz, the affection and the happiness of all those tables-for-two. Her legs wouldn't carry her there. The swelling in her ankle has returned anyway, and the skin is peeling off the soles of her feet. She is picking on it. The TV is playing with more of the same weather forecast and exchange rates are flashing before her eyes, carrying no meaning.

There is a knock on the door. Loud and clear. No one has ever knocked on her door here. She knows. She beams. She always knew: Mishka and his practical jokes! The rascal that he is! He has never left! He just … He will pay for this mischief, she tells herself as she dashes to the door, though she knows that he won't. She has already forgiven him.

Day Nine

It is the ninth day today. Detective Sergeant Gillian Marsh has been living on the edge: getting no sleep, jumping at every telephone ring, and following the *Six O'Clock News* for any sign of cataclysms, abductions or acts of international terrorism. Eight days ago her daughter went globe-trotting: Thailand, Australia, South Africa – in that order. Forty days of living on adrenalin and crackers, then back home –with, Gillian hopes, life lessons learned vicariously through other people's misfortunes. Forty days – like The Flood ...

Tara is not alone, she has a friend with her, but that is of little consolation. Both girls are only eighteen and have not seen much of the world outside the sleepy safety of Sexton's Canning. Although Tara was born in South Africa she does not remember any of its perils. Tara had only been four years old when her parents' marriage fell apart amidst tears, the spittle of angry words and clenched fists. And South Africa was not a place for a single mother with a little girl in tow. Gillian returned home with her tail between her legs. Her parents were delighted. Tara's father Deon, on the other hand, declared the move a personal insult and withdrew into silence. Then, out of nowhere, three years ago, he got in touch: his second marriage in tatters, another ex-wife on the run, and a teenage son in a boarding school somewhere in Somerset.

Deon wants to get to know his daughter. It is his right – who is Gillian to argue? For years, she has been feeling guilty for depriving Tara of a father. Those days are gone.

It was great when Deon came to visit and met Tara. They hit it off straight away, father and daughter, like two peas in a pod. But Gillian knew the day would come when Tara would want to go and see her father on his turf. She had hoped it wouldn't be too soon. Her prayers had not been answered. Tara decided to run to her dad as soon as she turned eighteen. There was no stopping her. She is a foolhardy girl, Gillian knows, and her friend Sasha is bad news. It is their gap year. They are adults, and they do as they please.

Gillian is in for forty long days of sheer dread.

She will keep herself busy. The other option is to go mad with worry. For the past eight days she has been mulling over the mortal dangers her daughter is facing: human traffickers, tsunamis, food poisoning, AIDS-infected syringes buried in sand, sharks and enraged elephants. Gillian will try her best to put such things out of her mind. Next week she is going to London: three weeks of training. She has been putting it off, citing the demands of single parenthood, but with Tara gone she has run out of excuses. Her promotion to the rank of detective inspector has been hanging over her head like the sword of Damocles. She will have to let it fall.

Her desk is the windmill of her mind, with the sawdust of closed but undocumented casework threatening to suffocate her. She will have to deal with it in the next two days. Anything would be better than her single-finger typing. She often thinks of the keyboard as her personal punchbag. It is a battered old thing, but indestructible if you consider the amount of coffee spilled over it and the flurry of invectives thrown at it, all in vain.

Any distraction from her worst fears and even worse desk jobs is a good distraction, so when PC Miller ushers in an elderly couple, who in loud tandem demand to speak to someone in authority, Gillian is at hand to lend a sympathetic ear.

'She told us she'd be back yesterday, lunchtime.'

'Did she say *lunchtime*, dear?'

'She did. She said *by* lunchtime, actually. The plane, she said, was landing at 8.40 at Heathrow, Terminal Four. I have taken it all down. Flight number, the date, the time … I've got it here.' Mrs Devonshire's bird-claw hand submits a notepad bearing the flight details recorded in immaculate cursive handwriting. 'If you could take a copy. I'd like my notebook back, please.

'The problem, you see, is that Miss Eagles knows we're going away tomorrow. We told her straight away when she came to ask if we'd look after Fritz. We said, it's fine, we don't mind taking care of Fritz, but we'll be off on Monday morning. How fortunate, she said, that I'll be back before you leave, otherwise I'd have to take Fritz to a cattery. He wouldn't like that, I said. Eunice would never part with him. Eunice, you understand, was Miss Eagles' aunt. Sadly, she passed away last year. We've always been good friends with Eunice. We've been neighbours for forty years. Miss Eagles moved into Eunice's cottage, what ... would you say five months ago, dear? Maybe four ... I lose count.'

'She told us to call her Nicola,' Mr Devonshire gazes pleadingly at his wife. He has a narrow face with pale, arched brows that give him a look of permanent bewilderment.

'We couldn't, dear, not right away ... We've only known her for five minutes. Well, I couldn't anyway. You can call her what you like, though *I* simply wouldn't go as far as using her first name ... I'm particular that way. Anyway, we don't want to bore the police with details.' At this point Mrs Devonshire's attention returns to Gillian. 'As I was saying, Miss Eagles was very excited about her holiday. She's never been to the Maldives, she said. Neither have we, I told her, small world! We had a giggle, didn't we dear?'

Mr Devonshire nods agreement and pats his wife's hand with affection. Gillian is copying the details from the notebook: a flight from Colombo, UL4016, lands 8.40 a.m., Saturday, 7th February, mob: 0785291022 ...

'Have you tried calling her on her mobile? She left you her number.'

'Well, no!' Mrs Devonshire looks horrified. 'The cost is prohibitive even if she weren't abroad – which she may well be, considering that she isn't here, don't you think? We thought the police should be making the telephone calls, especially the ones abroad ... We *are* pensioners, and like I said, we've only known her for five minutes ...'

'We wouldn't want to intrude on her privacy.'

'No. But we *are* leaving tomorrow. We've had a holiday home booked for months. The same holiday home we book every year. We go every year, you understand, without fail. We couldn't cancel if we wanted. It just wouldn't do! On the other hand, we simply can't walk away from it, can we dear? We owe it to dear old Eunice, don't we, to look after that girl.'

Gillian feels a cold sweat run down her spine. She is thinking of Tara. What a bad idea it was to let her go. God, what a damn stupid idea!

'How old is Miss Eagles?'

'Oh, we don't know, do we dear? We wouldn't dream of asking. She isn't a spring chicken. I don't want to sound rude, you understand, but she's ... what I call *beyond the childbearing age.*'

'A bit frumpy, lots of layers on her, like a sheepdog,' Mr Devonshire adds with surprising competence. 'Late thirties. Tallish. Mid-built. Brown hair, sort of – wiry and bouncy. Pleasant manner ...'

'Dear, you're talking of her as if she were dead! She may still be alive, just ... delayed, or detained somewhere. I dare not speculate ...' Mrs Devonshire covers her mouth, stifling a gasp. 'Though I'd say she's more in her forties, early forties – that's what I mean by *beyond the childbearing age.* It takes a woman to know these things. Does her age have any bearing on her disappearance?'

'No, not that I know of. It's just that you called her a *girl.*'

Mr Devonshire smiles. 'If you were our age ...'

'Let's not detract from the matter at hand, dear. You see, Miss Eagles is missing. We are going away tomorrow, and that leaves us with the small problem of Fritz.'

'Fritz?'

'Fritz, the cat. We've been looking after him, didn't you hear me? He used to belong to Eunice, and when she passed away

78

Miss Eagles took over, very kindly – she could've sent him to an animal shelter.'

'Most people would ...'

'Now, we've been looking after him in her absence. Not much trouble, wet food at night and cat biscuits for breakfast. Quite a pleasure looking after old Fritz, isn't it dear?'

Mr Devonshire smiles at the idea of old Fritz. 'So it is.'

'But now, since we're going away, we can't leave Fritz on his own until Miss Eagles' return, can we? What, if the worst comes to the worst and she doesn't return? I know we shouldn't be thinking on those lines, but we can't take that risk – we can't leave Fritz alone. We couldn't do that to dear old Eunice, could we?'

'No, we couldn't.'

'Now, where is he, dear?'

'I left him with the officer on duty, at the Reception Desk downstairs.'

'So there! Fritz is at the Reception Desk. Please, bear in mind that he is not used to being confined. He's a free-spirited young man.'

'You mean the cat? You left the cat with PC Miller downstairs?'

'We couldn't leave him all on his own in an empty house to fend for himself, could we?' There is unmistakable admonishment in Mrs Devonshire's tone. 'His owner has gone missing. We are reporting her missing, do you understand? You are the person in authority, are you not?'

Gillian agrees and assures the old lady that steps will be taken to track down Fritz's owner. She shows the elderly duo out and waits for them to say their goodbyes to Fritz, who is yowling in his cage, much to PC Miller's dismay. Gillian shakes her head, silently prohibiting the constable from querying the animal's presence at the station.

On the step outside Sexton's Canning Police Station, Mr Devonshire grabs hold of Gillian's hand and presses a large key into it. 'It's to the cottage. We're leaving first thing tomorrow morning, but I will be putting a note in the door for Nicola to contact you for the key and the cat, if you don't mind.'

'No, not at all. We'll look after Fritz.' This probably breaks every rule in the book, Gillian thought, but what do you say to an elderly couple expecting your help? Direct them to the nearest RSPCA?

'That's good.' He shuffles away, his head leaning towards his left shoulder. He catches up with his wife at a red estate car – she is already strapped into the passenger seat, ready to go. They have a brief exchange and, hurriedly, Mr Devonshire waves to Gillian to wait. He shuffles back, this time with a page from Mrs Devonshire's precious notebook. 'Our telephone number in France. As soon as you know what's happened to Nicola, let us know, will you? We promised Eunice we'd look after the girl.'

And then you promised the girl you'd look after the cat. Gillian smiles but says nothing out loud other than to wish the old man a good holiday, and not to worry – she will be in touch.

A call to Nicola Eagles' mobile renders no results; Gillian is taken straight to voicemail. A polite female voice, sweet but expressionless, says: 'Hi, I can't take your call, but please do leave a message. I'll get back to you as soon as I can.'

Gillian introduces herself and asks Miss Eagles to contact Sexton's Canning Police with regards to her cat as well as her whereabouts.

'They're not bad people,' Gillian informs PC Miller.

He shrugs. He is a dog person himself. 'What do you want me to do with the cat?'

'Keep it here for now. Someone will pick it up. Looks like the owner is delayed.'

'Scarface won't like it.'

'I'll make a few inquiries. It's probably the flight. The owner's due back from holiday, or rather *was* due back – yesterday. Missed the flight would be my guess.'

'We aren't an animal shelter.'

'You're beginning to sound like Scarface. Have a heart …

Look at him, isn't he cute! His name's Fritz.'

'Like I care.'

'You should, PC Miller. We have to be seen to be caring.'

Fritz gives out a harrowing mewl.

'You see, you've hurt his feelings.'

It seems like an easy job at first: a phone call to the carrier to check the passenger list. It takes for ever to get through to a live person. Gillian is offered several automated options, none of which apply to her type of inquiry. Finally, she is invited to press zero to speak to an operator. She is put on hold. The music is soothing. The longer she listens, she figures, the more likely she is to forget about her problem, become fully pacified and, ultimately, put the phone down.

She is chewing a pencil. It is an old habit of hers, a habit she developed early in life when the choice was either her nails or school pencils. In the end, both the nails and the pencils got a good seeing-to. Habits stay with Gillian for life. She has the stubs of her nails to testify to that. Plus, every pencil she lays her hands on sooner or later becomes her personal celery stick.

She is through to an operator. 'DS Marsh, Sexton's Canning CID. I wish to make an inquiry about a passenger on yesterday's flight number UL4016 –'

'I'll have to put you through to my manager. Please wait.' The soothing music kicks in again. Gillian's teeth sink into the fibres of the wooden pencil. She has as much patience for automated phone inquiries as she does for Christmas shopping.

'Good morning! Sorry to have kept you waiting,' says a cheery voice of unidentifiable gender. 'How can I help you?'

'I want to check if a passenger by the name of Nicola Eagles boarded flight number –'

'May I just verify your details? Procedure – I *do* apologise.'

Gillian repeats her details, which are dutifully taken down, letter by letter, number by number, rank by rank. 'Right, thank you. I have to keep a record –'

'I understand. Now to Nicola Eagles.'

'Yes ... what flight did you say?'

Gillian quotes the flight number in full this time. There is a brief pause filled by vigorous clicking of the keyboard. 'No, Ms Eagles was not on that flight. She purchased the ticket, but she didn't make it onto the plane.'

'Did she check in on any subsequent flight, can you verify that, please?'

Click-click. No. Not with Sri Lankan Airlines, anyway.

'Was she meant to be on any connecting flights? I understand she was returning from the Maldives.'

Click-click. Yes. She was meant to arrive on a flight from Malè. And no, she wasn't on that either. Nicola Eagles had travelled to Malè on Saturday, January 31st, her journey commencing at Heathrow on January 30th; she had then transferred in Colombo to an outward flight to Malè – the 'manager' can confirm she did that, but nothing since. He – if it is a he – sounds concerned, but it is only a token apprehension. His questions are superficial. Has the lady gone missing? Is there anything else he can do to help? Gillian thanks him for his help and asks him to call her if Miss Eagles attempts to make a booking. The manager is delighted to be able to be of some assistance: Miss Eagles' name is being flagged in the system as they speak.

Detective Chief Inspector Scarfe, affectionately known as Scarface due to both his name and a slight curling of his upper lip – he had been born with it cleft – shows scant interest in the missing woman. 'It's the usual holiday romance. The lady will turn up sooner or later, intact and in love with some Caribbean gigolo.'

'She went to the Maldives.'

'Yes, I know, you told me. Trust me, she'll complain we intruded on her privacy. It wouldn't be the first time! Anyway, it hasn't been forty-eight hours.'

'With respect, sir, it may've been eight days. We don't know if she got to where she was going. We know she landed in Malè eight days ago. After that, it's anyone's guess. I'd like to check which resort she is – was – booked into. Whether she made it there in the first place. I'll take a look around her house, with your permission. It may pay to check with the relatives, there may've been a postcard, a telephone call which would explain …'

'Fair enough.' Scarface is already distracted. He's tapping his fingers on the arm of his swivelling chair. Gillian wonders whether it is a game of golf or early lunch plans she is keeping him away from. 'Have it all done and dusted by Friday. I don't want any loose ends when you're gone the next three weeks.'

'Sir.'

'And be *discreet*, Marsh! I don't want you pulling out heavy artillery just to solve the mystery of a holiday fling, understood?'

'Sir.'

Mr and Mrs Devonshire materialise within seconds of Gillian arriving at Field Cottage. The name of their residence is etched onto a post box. It is a very appropriate name – the cottage is at the end of a narrow lane, which winds around a massive beech and splits into two driveways, one leading to Field Cottage, the twin to the Devonshires' almost identical dwelling. Beyond the two houses there is nothing but fields – strawberry fields, now in winter lull.

'Any news?' Mr Devonshire's brows twitch on top of his forehead.

'I'm afraid not, other than she wasn't on the flight she was booked on.'

Mr and Mrs Devonshire exchange looks of horror.

'Would you happen to know the name of the resort Miss Eagles intended to stay in?'

'Oh dear, she did mention, didn't she? Such a tongue-twister, if you ask me, it went in and straight out again. I didn't take much notice, didn't think it mattered. So many things to remember … Vincent, dear, do you recall? No, I didn't think so,' Mrs Devonshire assures herself without waiting for her husband to collaborate. 'We weren't paying attention when she told us. She showed us some photographs, didn't she? Though, frankly, one of those faraway places looks exactly like the next one. I couldn't tell one from another if it hit me in the face, could you, dear?'

'Never mind, I'll have a look in the house.' Gillian manages to turn the key in the door. It opens with a comforting squeak of the hinges. 'There may be some papers, booking confirmations ...'

The Devonshires follow her resolutely into the house. They are not fully convinced about the weight of her authority. What is a slight female with a pixie hairstyle and plain clothes doing being a policeman, or a police-person as they call themselves these days?

The place is cluttered: a mismatch of furnishings, the old and the new thrown together in a heap. Two of the same kind of everything point to two households being merged into one. In the last five months Nicola Eagles' effects have been added to Eunice's, thus two sofas facing each other in the lounge: one tawny leather, deep and soft, sprawled on the floor like an oversized beanbag, the other framed in polished wood, standing on curved legs, with upholstery threadbare in places – the sort of stiff furniture you wouldn't feel particularly welcome to sit on for too long. There are plenty of books; some are scattered on the floor: a series of *Cadfael* novels in hardback, the National Trust guides to various countryside walks and countless volumes of *Reader's Digest*. On the shelves spanning across the width of an entire wall, there are more books. Gillian can't read some of the titles. 'What language is that? Russian?'

'Oh yes, Miss Eagles is a fluent Russian speaker. Eunice was very proud of her niece, wasn't she, Vincent? Russian, out of all languages! Did you know it is the fifth most difficult language in the world? Or is it the sixth, I forget –'

'Any living relatives?'

'Pardon me?'

'Miss Eagles – does she have any other relatives I could contact? She is unmarried, I take it?'

'An orphan, I'm afraid. And a spinster ... Not that she isn't a good-looking lady, and well-educated, at that. I guess men don't like over-educated women, don't you think? Men don't like being outdone by women.'

'She struck me as rather shy,' Mr Devonshire gets a chance to wedge in a sentence.

'So nobody you know of?'

'A brother. She has a brother.'

Gillian takes out a pen. 'Would you know how to contact him? His name? Where does he live?'

'Robert, I think. Robert or Ronald. Robert, more likely. They don't call them Ronald these days, do they? He didn't visit poor Eunice when she was alive, did he? No, never. Not a family man.'

'He lives in Australia – that could explain it,' says Mr Devonshire.

'He only moved there a few years ago. Did he visit poor Eunice before that? No, he did not.'

Gillian ponders the possibility of Miss Eagles paying a visit to her brother. The Maldives are in the same neck of the woods as Australia, she has a vague idea. Geography has never been her strongest point. Is the distance between the two places a matter of a day trip? Worth checking. An old-fashioned address book lies next to a telephone. Hopefully, it can tell a story. Gillian pages through it. Robert is under E, not R – for Eagles, of course. Not unlike Mrs Devonshire, Miss Eagles isn't one for a first-name basis approach, even when it comes to her own brother. Exactly how formal – and impersonal – can these people get, Gillian wonders. An address in the UK, recorded in a neat young hand, is crossed out. Beneath, a new address is written down, a bit untidy, offhanded, trailing off, as if the writer was reluctant to make the change.

'Yes, that'd be correct. I recall something about him living in Adelaide.' Mr Devonshire is peering over Gillian's shoulder. She shuts the book closed. The old man gives her a hurt look, 'I'm only trying to help.'

'Yes, thank you. I know. I appreciate it. I mean – anything you can tell me –' She puts the book in her pocket. A questioning glare from Mrs Devonshire forces her to explain herself: 'We'll get in touch with her contacts, see if anyone can shed some light on her disappearance. She may be with friends.'

'She doesn't seem to have any friends or ... *contacts*. No one ever visits her.' Mrs Devonshire puts Gillian's line of inquiry into question.

'She's only been here for a few months,' points out Mr Devonshire gallantly.

'That's exactly when people visit you the most, Vincent, to see your new house, how you're getting on in the new place, who your neighbours are. It's human curiosity.' Mrs Devonshire shakes her head, 'Between us, I really don't think she has any friends.'

Gillian proceeds upstairs, followed by the Devonshires. A small room – filled with stacks of files, bills and folders, a dismantled printer next to a box of early nineties-style hardware and a collection of outdated cables – bears the semblance of a study. A quick glance at the papers confirms that they belonged to the previous owner. But Gillian also finds a laptop. It looks discarded and forgotten, but it does not go with the rest of the antiques: it is at least twenty years younger. With any luck it belongs to Nicola.

The bedroom is south-facing and warm. The warmth radiates from under the window and it is only now that it occurs to Gillian that the central heating is on. She opens a wardrobe. A collection of floral skirts of varied shades and patterns, but consistent in their maxi-lengths, points to a woman of conservative taste, the Laura Ashley type. Jumpers are folded neatly on the bottom shelf, casual joggers and tops in the middle; schoolgirl white blouses, each with its own hanger, have been immaculately pressed. She even irons her underwear, Gillian notes. Nothing seems to be missing. Nothing seems to have been taken out.

'You're sure she's gone away?'

Mr and Mrs Devonshire blink at her in unison. 'I can't imagine she's letting us take care of Fritz while she's hiding under the bed,' Mrs Devonshire says.

'She gave us her flight details. She was so excited! What makes you think –'

'The heating is on.'

'Oh, that! She left it on for Fritz. He doesn't like the cold.'

'Of course, Fritz!'

Mrs Devonshire picks up a stack of magazines from a bedside table. 'Here, you see? These are the pictures she's been showing us.' Baby blue skies stabbed with umbrellas of palm trees roll from the covers. On the back of one of the leaflets, the details for Thomas Cook in Shepherd's Bush are circled in pen. Gillian adds the leaflet to her loot.

No one knows anything. Nicola Eagles has vanished without a trace. The Thomas Cook shop closed down over three months ago, and the head office has no record of Nicola Eagles. It is a dead end. And so is the address book. It dates back to its owner's university days. It is sparsely populated with names, and half of the contacts are either dead or married, many with a new name, address and telephone number; many have not heard from Nicola Eagles in years and find it hard to recall her face or how they came to know her in the first place. She seems only a shadow of a real person, not even a memory. How incredibly easy would it be to wipe out her existence? No one would bat an eyelid. No one has. If it wasn't for Fritz …

Scarface has not returned from his extended lunch engagement or golf tournament, or both. Chances are Gillian won't be able to speak to him until tomorrow. He is canvassing for a promotion to Detective Superintendent. He will make a good one. His skills lie in management, not ground work. Getting his hands dirty and desk cluttered is not his idea of professional satisfaction. Gillian wouldn't dream of interrupting his campaign. She is used to making her own decisions and running them by Scarface after the event. On that note, she has left Nicola's laptop with Forensics for a priority analysis. She needs information – anything. Jon Riley at Forensics is a true maverick, commonly known as Jon the Geek. He says it sounds almost as good as John the Baptist. If there is anything to be found on that laptop, he will find it. He has nothing better to do. Despite being only in his twenties, he already has a failed marriage behind him. How he managed to find a wife in the first place is a mystery: he is fat, hairy and speaks in code. However he had found her, the wife did not last. He had lost her quickly after his addiction to late-night computer gaming and poor personal hygiene came to light. Now he can dedicate his entire life to his first love: I.T.

PC Miller is going home. 'What do I do with the cat?' he asks.

'RSPCA.'

'I've got to be going. Picking the kids up – I promised. Missus is having a doctor's appointment.'

'Leave it here.' They push the cage with Fritz in it under Gillian's desk. Fritz hisses at Miller for a goodbye.

'That's the thank you I get!'

'For what?' Gillian raises an eyebrow. Miller never knows whether she is joking or being serious. He shrugs and takes himself out of the cat's peripheral vision. The creature settles down for a nap.

Gillian is hell-bent on closing this missing person's case today. There has to be a simple explanation. It isn't a case of lost luggage – it is a case of a grown-up woman somewhere between one of the most popular holiday destinations on the planet and home. There is only so much that could have happened to her in that part of the world. Anything serious, such as drug trafficking or drowning, would have been reported by now. An impromptu visit to the brother in Australia sounds an increasingly viable possibility. Gillian is not entirely sure what time it is in Australia, but she is promptly informed by Robert Eagles. He sounds like a man with a heavy hangover when he finally picks up the phone.

'Hello?'

'Mr Eagles? Am I speaking to Mr Robert Eagles?'

'Yeah, you are … What is it? Who the hell are you? Do you realise what time it is? It's bloody three in the morning!'

'I am sorry to wake you at this hour. I'm calling from

Sexton's Canning. DS Marsh.'

'DS? As in *the police*? What's it about?'

'Please, don't be alarmed. It's probably nothing serious –'

'Then why the hell –'

'It's about your sister.'

'Nicola ...' his voice trails off. 'Something happened to Nicola?'

'We don't know. She has not returned from her holiday. She missed her plane. I was wondering if maybe you have information about her current whereabouts –'

'Holiday? She's on holiday? Nicola doesn't go on holidays.'

Gillian rubs her forehead. The next of kin is another dead end. 'According to her neighbours, she went to the Maldives. A week ago. You haven't heard from her, I take it?'

'No ...' the man begins to sound softer, almost apologetic. 'We haven't been that close since our parents died. Or before ... I ... I'm a busy man ... We don't really keep in touch. I thought of inviting her over, but you can never find the right time ... It's always something or other ... Anyway, she doesn't go on holidays! The Maldives? It doesn't sound like Nicola. She's more of a B&B in Wales sort of person. Are you sure?'

'We know that she missed a flight back home yesterday. We know she did not book herself on another flight. We know she intended to be back this morning. There may be a perfectly innocent explanation –'

'Nicola doesn't miss planes. She's very ... um ... punctual, organised. I don't know what to say.'

'Can you think of anyone back here in the UK? Anyone she's close to, anyone she would've been likely to contact?'

Long pause. Then: 'No. No one. She keeps herself to herself ... I really don't know anyone my sister is in touch with. Is that bad? It is, I suppose ... I can't believe it – there must be a simple explanation!' He goes silent. 'Now you got me worried ... Can you keep me advised? Please. Any time – day or night. What's your name again?'

Gillian leaves her details with Robert Eagles. He is grateful to her for getting in contact with him. He is the only close relative Nicola has, though he should've kept a closer eye on her … In case of her death, Gillian ponders, would he be the sole beneficiary of her estate? How much is Nicola Eagles worth? Field Cottage alone must be close to half a million pounds.

Jon Riley calls just as Mrs Clunes puts on her vacuum cleaner. Once she has put it on, she will not switch it off until she is done – not for any reason – she is a busy woman, efficient. If she waited for every cop to finish their business, she would be here at midnight.

'Hang on, Jon. I can't hear you! You've got something?'

There is a *yes*, followed by an elaboration that is swallowed by the relentless whine of the vacuum cleaner, the nozzle of which is circling Gillian's chair. The cleaner avoids eye contact. 'Hang on, I'll be with you in a minute.' Gillian puts the phone down and shouts a farewell to Mrs Clunes who, as is her custom, does not respond.

Something smells around Jon's desk. It is hard to say if it is Jon's person or the contents of his drawers. The odour must have been there for a while – Jon doesn't appear to be conscious of it. 'Here,' he says without any preliminaries, 'this laptop hasn't been used since December 25th. The last logon was at 10 p.m. that day. But she didn't drop off the face of the Earth just then. Have a look here!' He waves Gillian to come closer, which she does despite her strong reservation about the smell. He starts in his typical tabloid headline style: 'Hotmail inbox. It didn't take much to hack into – laptop memorised her password. Nothing to hide. Limited contacts, very limited. Historical evidence of liaison with two men. Very historical: dead and buried.'

'How dead?'

'Two and a half years ago – last contact with both men – Peter Bird and Paul Collins. Emails – restrained. No meat on the bone. Polite. Boring. She met them through a dating site, but that's gone too. No life to speak of.'

'Just like you then?'

'Takes one to know one,' Jon snaps back, sharp as the morning frost. If only he smelled better. Gillian steps back to the business at hand: 'Is that all you've got? Anything current?'

'Since December, emails accessed from a different machine, IP address ... let me see ...'

'What sort of emails?'

'Impersonal. Lots of junk, but she opens every one of them ...'

'And?'

'A month ago she makes an online booking, a holiday – Maldives.'

'Booking agent?'

'Primechoice Destinations. Never heard of it. People traffickers for all I know ... So she's lured under false pretences to ... just kidding!' Jon chuckles. His small but perfectly formed teeth and wispy facial hair render him in the likeness of a Chinese mandarin, or a sort of hairy Buddha. He switches to a different window. 'Nicola Eagles' Facebook page. For the past five years since she joined in January 2010, she never misses a day, logs in every bloody day like a Swiss clock, 'likes' every friend's every post, but doesn't post anything herself ... In the first couple of days in February she starts posting manically, tons of snapshots, then – bang! – she goes silent. Her last activity on Facebook was five days ago. She's either dead or lost the use of her arms. People don't stop like that. Not unless there's a good reason. It's a habit. It's stronger than heroin.' If anyone, Jon should know something about computer addictions.

Smell or no smell, Gillian draws a chair next to Jon and starts skimming through Nicola's Facebook entries. *Arrived on Itsouru. It is hot – hot as hell!* Photos follow: typical exotic location snapshots and that's it. That last entry is made on Tuesday, 3rd February. And then nothing. Silence.

Gillian scans Nicola's Facebook friends: only a dozen of them or so. Amongst them she recognises four of the names from Nicola's address book, all of whom have claimed not to have heard from or even really remember who Nicola Eagles was. Robert is also on the list: his photo that of a man in his mid-thirties, his colouring that of a sun-dried tomato, the background an orange Australian sunset. So he did know his sister was taking a holiday in his very backyard … it is all there, on her Facebook profile.

Jon clicks on Nicola's avatar. It is a head-and-shoulders picture of a smiling woman with a heavy brown fringe half-covering her trusting, round eyes. She is smiling; her jaw is square and widened by the smile. So this is who Gillian is looking for.

'Print me a few of her photos, Jon, thanks.'

Hassan, the Day Manager at Itsouru Island Retreat, speaks some English, and what he speaks has all to do with his guests' creature comforts and the restaurant menus. Nevertheless he is able to convey his deepest concern about Miss Eagles: she had not checked out by noon the day before yesterday as she should have; her belongings are still in her chalet, but she is not; it is as if she has stepped out of her room and vanished into thin air. The police have been called in from Malè – their arrival is expected later today. A *discreet* search has been carried out – the idea is not to unduly alarm other guests. The search has rendered no results. Miss Eagles is not on the island – this can be said with a degree of certainty.

'People don't just disappear,' Gillian says. 'She couldn't have walked away …'

'It is an island, madam, so no,' Hassan sounds as if he is about to add *unless she can walk on water*, but thinks better of making flippant comments.

'Drowning?'

'We never had a single drowning, madam. We are an atoll island. We have shallow waters – we are safe indeed!'

'Miss Eagles' belongings – are they still in the room?'

'They are, but we are fully booked. Chalet 42 overlooks the lagoon – it has views … Our next guests arrive tonight. I will put Miss Eagles' items in storage –'

'No! Don't touch anything! Leave it as it is. It may be a

crime scene. It probably *is* a crime scene.'

'We cannot hold the room back! We are fully booked!' Hassan's voice rises by half an octave. 'The police are here soon –'

'*I* will be there tomorrow. Leave it all as it is until tomorrow.' Gillian knows she has no jurisdiction over the man, but she puts on her most authoritative tone. It works. He agrees to wait. He is used to doing his best to please.

It will take some convincing to get Scarface to sign off the trip. The cost will make a big dent in his budget. He will argue against it. He will say the Malè police are perfectly capable of dealing with such cases, but Gillian will hit the PR button: we look after our own, no matter what it takes, no matter how far we have to go, especially when some of us are vying for the position of Detective Superintendent and need to have the public's confidence on their side.

Gillian only realises how tired and hungry she is when she gets home. The house feels cold and empty. Colder and emptier than usual. There is an inexplicable sense of emptiness that niggles at the back of her head. Something is not right; something is missing … She cannot put her finger on it. She forgot something important – that much she knows, but having forgotten it, she can't do anything about it until she remembers what it is. It is bound to relate to the missing woman's case. Gillian is going over it in her head. She must have overlooked some small but vital detail. Perhaps something – some clue – she had missed in the woman's house. Perhaps something the old couple told her, or the brother, or Hassan the resort manager … Somewhere there amongst snippets of conversation, books strewn on the floor of Field Cottage, and Nicola's cryptic Facebook entries, lies a detail Gillian has missed. It is there. It's staring her in the face yet she can't see it. Gillian hates having these senior moments: memory lapses, missed appointments and words that escape her. Deon used to call them *her blonde episodes*. He was so annoyingly superior! Why does he suddenly spring to mind? He is in the distant past, but he was the last man to witness her bumbling incompetence on a day-to-day basis.

The fridge is almost empty: there are eggs, but they require some form of cooking. Rashers of bacon look mummified – they are at least five days out of date. Perhaps they aren't suitable for human consumption but the label says nothing about any expiry date for cats. Fritz yowls in the cage. She had to bring him home with her. By the time she remembered his existence it was too late to take him to an animal shelter. It was almost 8 p.m.

Gingerly, Gillian opens the cage. Her experience with cats is limited. Do they bite strangers? 'Go on then, Fritz, make yourself at home!' He shoots out and makes Gillian jump back. 'Damn animal!' His glare is unforgiving, his miaow a resentful yodel. He pads across the floor panels and towards the front door. Another yodel. Do cats yodel? This one does. It is a desperate sound. 'Hungry?' Gillian cuts a strip of bacon and throws it on the floor. Fritz inspects it and turns his nose up on it. He sits and sulks. 'Suit yourself.' Gillian decides to fry the bacon with a couple of eggs.

To block off the silence, she puts on the radio. The news is on. She tunes in instinctively and listens for revelations of humanitarian disasters. She has been doing it over the last nine days with religious regularity. It hits her: Tara!

This is what has been missing in her day – her daughter! The sense of emptiness, of something not quite complete … She has missed Tara's call! They agreed Tara would call every day between six and seven in the evening. It was the condition of Gillian letting her daughter go. It was Gillian's condition, and she has missed it! With a shaking hand she reaches for the phone. The receiver tumbles to the floor, sending Fritz out of the room. Gillian curses the cat. It's his fault – if it wasn't for him, Gillian would have been home to hear from her child. But she got drawn into the cat and his missing owner's case. Yet another case that has eclipsed her home life. When will she learn to keep her work at arm's length? What will it take? Dread flushes through her stomach, like that day when, deep in thought, she had left Tara on the bus, in her pushchair, turned back after a few steps and seen the bus door close, and chased the bus on foot until it turned a corner and disappeared out of view. Or that night when she was too late and too tired to pick Tara up from her mum and dad or even call them to say she wasn't coming, the very night when Tara drank a whole bottle of her grandmother's anti-histamine and had to have her stomach pumped, and that gut-wrenching morning when Gillian turned up at her parents' house to find it empty but for a note on the kitchen table: *We're at the hospital. It's Tara.*

Thankfully there is a message on the answer phone: *Hi, Mum! As promised. Will call tomorrow. Love you too!* Frantically, Gillian dials Tara's number. It does not ring. Not even once. No signal? She has turned it off? Engaged? She tries again. Leaves a disjointed message. An apology which is cut short halfway through a sentence by Tara's mobile.

She is a crap mother.

Fritz has regrouped and is back before her, yodelling even more desperately than before, being a pain in the arse. 'Fuck off,' she tells him, but he won't take orders from her. The smoke alarm goes off! Bacon and eggs! Gillian heads for the kitchen. Insidious smoke hangs on the walls like cobwebs. Gillian grabs the frying pan – drops it on the floor, convoluted bacon rashers bounce out. The cat is nowhere to be seen, but when Gillian opens the window, she thinks she can see the spooked creature bundle onto the windowsill. Or maybe it's just the thick, swirling smoke?

'Fuck!' She waves a tea towel under the smoke detector under the stairs. At last it stops – cold air soothes it into silence. The cat is gone.

Day Ten

At Colombo airport Gillian tries again. She has been trying to call Tara for the past twenty-four hours. She is now so close to her that she contemplates the possibility of putting the missing person inquiry on hold and jetting over to Phuket. Only there are no guarantees that Tara is there. She has been very vague about her lodgings. In fact, she is what Gillian calls in her professional jargon of *no fixed abode,* moving between youth hostels and B&Bs of dubious repute. It is a daunting prospect for an eighteen-year-old gullible girl in a country where people get hanged for carrying too many boxes of aspirin. Gillian is paralysed with worry. And Tara's telephone does not ring – it goes straight to the answer phone and in the same cheery voice Tara tells her to leave a message. Gillian hangs on to the off-chance that Tara called when she was in transit flying over the Indian Ocean with her phone switched off, but the empty voicemail contradicts that.

The moment Gillian gets off the plane, she checks: no messages. She leaves one of her own: *Tara? Mum here. Please call me on my mobile. I'm on a case – out of the country; won't be at home. Call me as soon as you get this message. Did I say you must call my mobile? I have now. Call me. Love you!* Nothing. Two hours later nothing. What time is it now in Thailand? It is 6 a.m. in Colombo.

Another plane: to Malè. It is small and it rattles. As instructed by the captain, Gillian switches off her mobile and she resents the guy next to her who, in defiance of the rules, continues working on his laptop. 'All electronic devices,' she tells him in a half-whisper. 'That includes laptops.' The man smiles at her, nods politely and carries on with his work.

97

Doesn't speak English. Gillian tips her head back and closes her eyes. She just wants to get there.

In her head she is *inventorising facts*. She has a name for it because she does it all the time. It reflects her thought process accurately as something halfway between inventorying and prioritising – *inventorising*. Gillian's mind works in mysterious ways, and so does her vernacular. Whenever a new case opens, Gillian mounts her spinning wheel of inventorised facts. She goes over the facts of the case over and over again, constantly reviewing the old and regularly adding the new to the spin. Like a hamster. She only stops when the case is solved. She doesn't write it down; all she does is relentless mental revision. And now she has very little to go on: a forty-two-year-old woman, a spinster, fairly well off, in regular employment suddenly breaks the habit of a lifetime and goes on a holiday. Travelling alone, she chooses a traditional honeymoon destination in the Maldives. Her decision appears sudden and unexpected – no one is aware of it apart from the neighbours who are asked to look after her pet cat. They are told the day before she departs. Her brother doesn't know. Her acquaintances do not know … Correction: the woman makes it known on Facebook but it looks like nobody reads it. This will be verified – Jon is checking the viewing statistics on her Facebook page. Other questions to be asked: one, was she meeting someone in the Maldives? Jon is running background checks on Paul Collins and Peter Bird, the only two potential romantic interests in her life who they can verify. Both over two years out of date, however … but that was just emails; they could have evolved to meetings in person, telephoning each other (Jon to check her line and mobile calls history). Question two, who would have interest in getting rid of her? The brother seems like the obvious candidate. He is her only relative, most likely to inherit her considerable wealth. According to Jon's intelligence she is worth close to a million pounds. Unless there is a will (to be checked), the brother would get it all. If, contrary to what he says, he knew she was coming this way, then this was his perfect opportunity. The flight from Adelaide would have taken him just over seven hours – it is doable. Robert Eagles travels around the world for work. Jon is verifying with the Australian authorities if Eagles has travelled anywhere near the Indian subcontinent in the last ten days.

The defiant man with a laptop tugs at Gillian's sleeve and points her to a flight attendant hovering over their heads with what looks like a steaming jug. 'Coffee or tea?' the flight attendant asks with a withering smile. Gillian chooses coffee, which tastes bitter but will do for now to keep her awake. Maybe Scarface is right – maybe all there is to it is a midlife crisis, a woman wanting to get away from it all, losing herself a bit in the world, looking for adventure, all in one: taking time off and wishing to be left alone. If only she had told someone! That would have spared Gillian the seventeen hours sleepless air-ferrying across two continents and missing out on her DI training (though that could be considered an unforeseen bonus!).

'Business or pleasure?' the man next to her asks in perfect English. She had been sure he hadn't understood her admonishment due to a language barrier. Clearly, he'd chosen not to heed it!

'Didn't you hear it?' she asks, astounded.

'Hear what?'

'About switching off all electronic devices!'

He smiles with a nonchalant wave of a hand. 'Oh, that! That really means nothing. I always use my laptop in flight. It's harmless, believe me. And it's business for me. Lots of homework to catch up on!' He salutes her with his coffee. 'So, is it a holiday? Where are you heading?'

'Well, in that case, I've got an important telephone call to make!' Gillian rises to reach for her mobile buried in her back trouser pocket. She turns it on. It takes a moment to light up. Hopefully Tara has called back.

Nothing. No messages.

'You won't get any reception here,' the man tells her.

The flight attendant passes by with her steaming jug, offering more tea or coffee. She directs a warning scowl at

99

Gillian. 'Please switch off your phone, madam. All electronic devices must be switched off.'

As soon as Gillian gets off the plane she puts the phone back on. While queuing through Border Control, she checks her messages. Nothing. She checks if she has reception. Reception, yes; messages, no. She dials Tara's number again, and again gets the same no-rings silent treatment. The answerphone kicks in and invites her to leave a message after the beep. 'Bloody, bloody hell!' she mutters. The beep comes between the first and second bloodies. Gillian rings off. She hands her passport to the officer in a booth.

'Welcome to the Maldives. Enjoy your holiday!'

She only has hand luggage: toiletries, a couple of fresh shirts, sensible pyjamas. This is going to be a short stay. Everything costs and the budget gets smaller by the minute, Scarface informed her sourly after she managed to twist his arm into signing the trip off. The positive outcome is that she doesn't have to queue for the conveyer belt. She pushes by the *Nothing to Declare* gate. If only she could clear her head! She won't have peace until she gets hold of Tara. Her brain cannot multitask: she can't turn it off to solve the missing person inquiry while it is frayed with constant worry. She decides to call Deon. It is not something she does lightly. His number in South Africa is stored on her mobile, but so far she hasn't used it. It rings. At least it rings; she prays for him to pick it up. In the Arrivals Hall a wiry man dressed in white is holding a cardboard sign with her name on it: DS Marsh. It must be her taxi driver. She beckons him while balancing her mobile between her cheek and her shoulder. He looks surprised, and – oddly – ignores her, looking over her shoulder for the real DS Marsh. The telephone keeps ringing. 'Come on, answer the damned phone!'

Answer machine! Gillian curses under her breath, drops the phone, picks it up – Deon's voice says he can't come to the phone but will get back to her as soon as he can. Beep! She starts walking towards her driver, calling out to him: 'Here!

Over here! I'm DS Marsh!' He raises his eyebrows.

'Oh hi, Deon. It's Gillian. Have you heard from Tara? Let me know. I seem to be missing her. Her phone is off. Can you pick up? I'm a bit worried ...'

'DS March?' the driver asks.

'MARSH. Yes, yes!' Gillian fumbles in her pocket for her ID card. She flashes it in the man's face. She passes him her suitcase. 'Are you parked somewhere nearby? Central Police Station, please.' She realises she hasn't rung off. 'Deon? Call me, all right? On my mobile. Thanks.' She presses the end call button.

'Let's go, then,' she tells her driver. He leads her out of the airport and into the steaming Maldivian pressure-cooker. It occurs to Gillian that even in her light bomber jacket and jeans she is seriously overdressed. She begins to sweat. 'Bloody heat!'

'Indeed!' says the driver.

He stops by a police car, opens the boot, and shoves her suitcase in.

'You're a policeman? Sorry, I thought –'

'Detective Nasheed.' He shuts the boot. 'You thought I was a taxi.'

'You thought I was a man,' she counters smugly.

'Not any more,' he beams in acknowledgment and opens the passenger door for her, 'Are you sure you want the police station? I could take you to your hotel – give you a chance to unpack, refresh,' He looks pointedly at her bomber jacket. 'We booked you into Holiday Inn.'

'I'd rather we got straight down to business. I didn't fly here for refreshments.'

In the car Gillian strips down to her white vest. She positively smells; she screws up her nose. 'Sorry,' she says.

'What for?'

She doesn't have the will to explain. He knows anyway but is too polite to admit it. 'Right, so what do we know so far?' she demands.

'Very little. No trace of her. It may be drowning. The body

may not emerge for days, possibly – never. It depends on how far the currents would've carried it into the open waters.'

'The resort manager told me drowning was unlikely.'

'It wouldn't be good for business, true, but it is the only logical explanation. You can drown in a spoon of water, you know?'

'Without a body we can't make any assumptions.'

'No, nothing apart from the fact that she is missing.'

'Did you preserve the crime scene?'

'What crime scene? There aren't any indications of foul play. Like I said, she is missing. This is a missing person inquiry as far as we are concerned.'

'Yes. I mean her room. I asked the resort manager not to touch anything in her room. He was rather reluctant ...'

'We secured everything – all her belongings. We've got them here –'

'You removed all the evidence from her room!' After she specifically asked them not to! She wanted to inspect the room as Nicola Eagles had left it – to see where every single item was placed, on purpose or accidentally. Did Nicola Eagles prepare for her departure? Did she pack? Or did she leave unexpectedly, her belongings scattered on the floor, a glass of water left half-empty, toothbrush still in the bathroom, bed unmade? Perhaps there were signs of a struggle? Was the door locked, or left open? Was the TV playing? Gillian needs to know. She needs to get into the person's house – it is the same as getting into their heads. It helps her build a picture of the last few minutes before death. Or disappearance. Or both. Visiting Nicola Eagles' house in Sexton's Canning gave Gillian several vital clues. The fact that she had left the central heating on for the cat and made arrangement for his care until a specific date told Gillian that Nicola Eagles was not suicidal and had every intention of returning. The way her clothes were tidily folded and organised in the wardrobe told Gillian she was not likely to have done anything on the spur of the moment, anything spontaneous. The fact that, despite the clutter, Nicola Eagles had kept both her own furniture and her aunt's old pieces side by side without being able to dispose of either set said a lot about the woman's character: conservative, indecisive, reverent; not the kind to sail into the sunset on a whim. Everything that Gillian had learned about Nicola Eagles in her house was turned on its head by her disappearance. People like Nicola Eagles do not disappear; they do not leave any loose ends. They are too dutiful and too caring to put anyone out, to cause any trouble. They would feel awfully guilty if anyone had to worry about them, like that lovely Mr and Mrs Devonshire. Gillian has a picture of who Nicola was – is; now she wants a picture of how – and why –anyone would want to get rid of her. Evidence left in her room would point Gillian in the right direction – in *some* direction – if it was there, but the hotel manager got it his way!

'I can't believe you didn't seal the room! I can't believe you didn't wait for me –'

Nasheed gives her a hard look: 'It is *my* jurisdiction, if I can point it out to you. *I* have satisfied myself that there was nothing in that room to indicate crime has been committed there. *I* have had the contents of the room brought to Malè for forensic examination.'

'I just wish you'd waited for me!' Gillian sighed. 'Can I at least have a look at what you have here?'

'I don't see why not. We've looked already, found nothing, but be my guest!' There is resentment in his tone which contradicts the flippancy of his reply. He takes her down the stairs to a cool basement. He requests Nicola Eagles' evidence box from a male officer with a thick mane of greying hair and the gritty voice of a heavy smoker. They are led to an empty room without windows and presented with a cardboard box. When the officer leaves, Nasheed says, 'The only thing that puzzles me is the blood.'

'Blood?'

'On bedsheets. We found a bloodied bedsheet hidden in the wardrobe, and some stains on another sheet on the bed.'

'And you call that a classic case of drowning? What did you say? *No indications of crime being committed?*' Gillian is appalled.

'The blood could mean anything: she could've cut herself. It could be menstrual. We don't even know it is her blood. There was only a small quantity. Definitely not enough to point to a serious wound. She did not bleed to death if that's what you're thinking. You need to get a perspective before you jump to conclusions.'

'We will send samples to the UK for DNA examination. We need to know if it is Nicola Eagles' blood. If it is –'

'Even if it is, it means nothing unless we have a body. Remember that this is still a missing person inquiry.'

He must have said that twice already. She found his defensiveness irritating. Nothing must be allowed to disturb the tranquil image of the Maldivian paradise! Gillian has to hold her tongue. She depends on Nasheed; she needs his co-operation. 'I realise that. What I want to know is this: how do you disappear from an island? How do you leave an island without being seen? Dead or alive.'

'The only way is drowning.'

'There are other ways: killing, abduction, kidnap for ransom … Shall I go on?'

'We've excluded those. You imply we're doing nothing, but you're wrong and I am beginning to take offence.' Nasheed's face muscles tighten and his speech becomes more accented. 'We've explored all possibilities, interviewed potential witnesses, checked all departures from the island, talked to owners of yachts that moored at Itsouru in the last ten days … We searched. We sent boats out. Nothing. She's gone.'

'We need to find her, if only to eliminate foul play,' Gillian insists.

'All we can do now is wait.'

'You didn't search hard enough.'

He snorts, throws his arms in the air. 'We don't have the manpower to comb through the entire Indian Ocean! There are limits to what we can do.' He is irritated as much as she is. Gillian has a feeling that they are going to be stepping on each other's toes a lot …

Gillian's mobile makes her jump. She answers it without looking at the number of the caller. Deon's voice is like a call from beyond. She is momentarily covered in cold sweat. 'Deon? What's happened? Has something happened!'

'Not to my knowledge, it hasn't.' He sounds his typical patronising self: a bit tired of her, a bit bemused.

'Then why are you calling me? You gave me an almighty fright. Thought something happened to Tara. Don't do this to me!'

Nasheed realises it is a personal call, mutters a vague excuse and leaves the room just as Deon hollers in utter exasperation, 'I don't believe this! You asked me to call you, Gill! Get a grip on yourself!'

Of course, she remembers now, she did call him. If only he had answered then and there! She has forgotten – the case, as every other case in the past, has hijacked her, body and mind. 'No need to shout, Deon.'

'How do you think I felt when you called in the middle of the night? I thought something happened to Tara, for God's sake! I should ask you *not to do this to me!*'

'I was worried – I *am* worried! I can't get hold of her. Something may have happened ...'

'Nothing happened.'

'How do you know? Have you spoken to her in the last two days?'

'No! And for a good reason! She's gone elephant riding, somewhere in the jungle. She didn't expect to have signal. Two – three days. Do you ever listen to what your daughter tells you?'

'Of course I do! I wasn't home when she called. She left the most enigmatic message –'

'What's new?'

'Whatever do you mean?'

'You're either not listening or not there at all! Nothing's changed.'

The hurt tone of the old supercilious Deon is unmistakable. Gillian remembers precisely why she had to leave him fifteen years ago. 'Nothing's changed, indeed,' she concedes. Her mind is elsewhere already.

'Thanks for calling back. Must go. Bye.' She takes great pleasure in pressing the end call button. An expedition into the heart of the Thai jungle presents new challenges, but Gillian refuses to face them. Not now. She has an explanation for Tara's silence. That's all she needs for the time being.

Back on the case, Gillian takes out object after object from Nicola Eagles' evidence box. She has little interest in shampoos and toothbrushes or various items of the woman's rather dull clothing, but by being left behind they are the confirmation that whatever happened to her was not planned: you would normally take your basic necessities with you if you were going away. The type of sensible outfits Nicola Eagles brought with her on her holiday adds another piece to the puzzle: she was definitely not meeting up with a lover. Kinky nighties, lace knickers, suspenders and bright red lipstick are conspicuous by their absence.

Gillian finds a few books, some of them in Russian. That reminds her that Nicola Eagles can speak Russian. Good Russian! If she can read *Anna Karenina* in original, she has to be fluent in Russian. Gillian flicks through the book, marvelling at the alien Cyrillic alphabet. Fluency in Russian is something that sets Nicola Eagles apart – one of her most unusual characteristics amongst the dull and the ordinary. But does it mean anything? Does it have any bearing on the case? Gillian doesn't know but she inventorises this fact at the back of her mind.

Her telephone rings again. It's Jon Riley.

'How are the tropics? Hot?'

'What have you got for me?'

'Not much. The woman is a non-entity. No one knows anything about her. They haven't heard from her at work. She was due to return today. Her boss said she was a reliable employee but called her Nicolette instead of Nicola. That tells you something! I got hold of Paul Collins.'

'Paul Collins?' Gillian is not quick enough to keep up with Jon's sharp turns and twists in conversation. There are usually plenty of short cuts in his verbal reasoning, which she is accustomed to (as he puts it, *great minds think alike*) but today she is jet-lagged and on the edge.

'Paul Collins – one of her blokes from that dating site, remember?' Gillian nods to herself. Jon sniggers: 'He pretended not to remember her, said I got the wrong man. Turns out he got married a few months ago and his wife is sitting right next to him when I call! Anyway, preliminaries aside, he claims not to have heard from her in two years. He admitted he met her – once. "And once was more than enough," is what he said. Maybe just for his wife's benefit. Though he did say Miss Eagles – he actually called her Miss Eagles, not Nicola – Anyway, he said she was awkward. He used the word awkward and when I asked him to clarify that, he said: "weird if you must know, son, as weird as they come. Out of touch. Psychotic!" Strong words, if you ask me, but the guy struck me as over the top: agitated, nervy…'

'Wouldn't you be if a cop called you about a missing ex-girlfriend in front of your wife?'

'That wouldn't have happened. I only have an ex-wife. Now, the other bloke – Peter Bird – wasn't home. Spoke to his mother. Blimey, she must be a hundred, couldn't hear a word I said, had to repeat everything twenty times. Like talking to a stone, as in stone deaf?' He sniggers.

'Get on with it, Jon!'

'So Peter wasn't home, travelling on the continent – some river kayaking thing in France. His deaf mother's never heard of Nicola Eagles, but then … she's deaf, isn't she, so she wouldn't't've *heard*!' Jon chuckles. Gillian is not in a mood to acknowledge his quips. 'I want you to check that.'

'I checked it – deaf as a post,' another chuckle.

'I've no energy for this, Jon. Check where Peter Bird is. Check where he's been in the last ten days.'

'Hang on a second!' Jon protests. 'Don't you have DC Webber to do your dirty jobs?'

107

'Webber is on holiday. I only have you,' Gillian tries to instil a purr into her voice.

'Ahhh,' Jon has been tickled under the chin. He loves being indispensable – he doesn't have much else going for him these days. He can deliver a star performance – as long as it does not involve getting out of his chair. Gillian will have to push her luck this time. Now that he is temporarily appeased, she demands, 'Anything else? How about her calls history?'

'Nothing of consequence. Actually no, scrap that! *Nothing* is the word. She hasn't made any phone calls nor received any in the last three months. Do you want me to go further back than that?'

'No. Mobile?'

'Can't help you there. No mobile in sight.'

'Hang on!' Gillian explores the depths of the evidence box. A mobile phone lies at the bottom with a charger still plugged into it. She was charging it when she disappeared – more proof she didn't intend to walk into the ocean and die. It is an old-fashioned cheap job with a conventional keypad. 'Okay, it's a Virgin mobile.' Gillian reads out the number.

'Got it! Will let you know tomorrow if anything of interest. Don't hold your breath. Her Facebook statistics are a record low. There are weeks when no one as much as glances at her page. Weeks! And then once in a blue moon one or two clicks. Poor woman! Never known anyone living in deeper obscurity than that! She could disappear tomorrow and no one'd notice.'

'She *did* disappear and someone *has* noticed.'

'Oh yeah, the cat! You'll like this. Listen good!' There is a faint echo of excitement in Jon's voice – a rare occurrence. Gillian often wonders if she has ever known anyone more detached from the rest of humanity than Jon the Geek. 'Hey, ho! Here it goes: the brother! Robert Eagles flew to Hong Kong five days ago precisely. Business trip. He's a sales rep for a software company, one of those Aussie Silicon Valley mavericks.'

'Except how did he know she would be here?'

'Yeah, well ... you could ask him.'

'Clever, Jon! I did that trick already. He sounded genuinely surprised –'

'Those sales bastards usually sound very bloody genuine. Whatever they tell you, it means fuck all!' Vaguely, Gillian recalls a sour car deal Jon fell victim to a few weeks ago. He is obviously still very sore about it. That gives her a new perspective on the level of Jon's personal bias against Robert Eagles. 'Anyhow, he could be one of those few and far between views on her Facebook page.'

'If only she'd made any prior announcements. If I remember correctly the first entry about the Maldives was the day she got here.'

'Well, whatever you say. Just don't write the guy off.'

'I never do. Few more things, Jon, are you listening?' There is a grunt at the other end of the line. Gillian proceeds: 'Get a DNA sample from Nicola Eagles' house. We'll be sending some blood samples from here, see if they match.'

'Got that. What else?'

'Find out if she has a will and who gets how much when she dies if there's no will.'

'Right … That's it?'

'Find the cat.'

'Say again?'

'The cat took off yesterday from my place. Answers to Fritz. Must be on his way home. Find the cat, get him into a cattery. The neighbours will kill me if I don't find that cat, never mind his owner!'

'How am I supposed to find a cat?'

'He'll be loitering somewhere around the woman's house. That's what cats do.'

'What the hell does it look like?'

Gillian ponders the question for a minute. 'Like a cat,' she says, 'fluffy and fat.'

'That narrows it then.'

'Thanks, Jon!'

'You'll have to thank Miller. I'm passing this one to him. I don't do outdoor commissions.' He rings off.

Gillian gets back to the box. She pulls out a laptop. This must be the one that replaced the old one left at the house. The switch button doesn't work: the screen remains black. How much she needs Jon to be here at hand!

'It's the battery – gone flat,' Nasheed is leaning against the door frame. She is glad she hasn't said anything critical about his handling of this case on the phone to Jon – he must've been outside, eavesdropping.

'Where's the cable?'

'In the box, I guess.'

'You guess?' Gillian is certain he has not inspected any of the box contents. He couldn't be bothered to so much as turn on the laptop. *Drowning; case closed!* She is fumbling in the box for a cable, finds it and plugs it in. The laptop makes a joyful noise and lights up. Luckily there is no password. Once on, the machine takes her to the last place Nicola Eagles visited before her disappearance. It is her Facebook page. With a draft entry awaiting posting. For some reason Nicola failed to press *PUBLISH*. Did she decide against it? Was she interrupted? Did she forget?

Gillian purses her lips and knits her brows as she tries to make sense of that entry: there is a photograph of a well-built, middle-aged man wading through water, heading towards the beach. The photo is of poor quality. It was probably taken through a window as there is a reflection of – probably – Nicola Eagles holding a camera, which is interposed against the image of the man. A short enigmatic caption underlines the photo: *Count Karenin*. Gillian contemplates it. The name sounds strangely familiar. It is a Russian name – sounds it, like Lenin or Stalin. Then it comes to her: *Anna Karenina!* Naturally, it cannot possibly be a real name of a real person. *Count,* at that! Nicola Eagles has been called weird ... What was the term: *out of touch*? The man in the picture is real enough, but it seems to Gillian that Nicola Eagles has taken the picture without his permission: he isn't exactly posing and she is hiding with her camera behind glass. Weird indeed!

'Could we enlarge this photo, do you think?' she asks

110

Nasheed. He comes close and looks over her shoulder. 'It may be nothing, but –'

'We could enhance it, get rid of the overlay, yes,' he says, suddenly intrigued and unexpectedly co-operative. '*Count Karenin*?' he asks. 'A count? It shouldn't be hard to find a count.'

'She was reading *Anna Karenina*. Count Karenin is Anna Karenina's husband.'

'A character from a book came to life?'

'My guess is as good as yours.'

It is not yet lunchtime when Gillian feels numb with fatigue. She hasn't slept a wink in the last twenty-four hours. In England this would be her bedtime – a well overdue bedtime. Her brain is fuzzy; she doesn't even know what she is looking at as she wades through the contents of the box. Mindlessly, she is paging through every book. A scrap of paper is all she finds. It looks like a flight itinerary. She thinks she recognises the flight number from Colombo to Heathrow. The paper is well crumpled, torn in half; something is scribbled on the back: words which mean nothing and some numbers, which may constitute a telephone number, or may not. Probably random notes. Gillian gives up the ghost. She asks Nasheed if he could take her back to her hotel. 'Holiday Inn,' she says, 'sounds like paradise on earth. Can't think of a better place to be right now.'

Nasheed smiles. His teeth are large, whiter than white and so even that they seem unnatural. Gentlemanly, he opens the door for her and lets her through. He is glad to be rid of her for the day. He drops her in the foyer and watches as she staggers to the lift with the key to her room in her hand.

In her nice, air-conditioned room Gillian drops onto the wide double bed with fresh white sheets and instantly falls asleep.

Day Eleven

When Gillian's telephone rings, she thinks it is the alarm. She slams her hand on it in the dark. It stops; then it rings again. A glance at the bedside clock, she realises it is the next day – the early hour of 1.32 am. This time she checks the number displayed on her mobile. 'Tara! Thank God! Where have you been!' Gillian knows the answer but is too worked up not to demand it.

'Mum,' Tara sounds mature and in cold control. She has been here before – she knows how to handle her mother. 'I left my itinerary with you at home. On the fridge. You knew – you *should* have known – that I'd be in the jungle, elephant trekking. You knew – you *should* have known – that I may not have been contactable. Jungles are like that: *impenetrable*.'

'It's no good leaving things on the fridge, for God's sake! You should've told me –'

'Which I did. If only you listened ...'

'You sound just like your father!'

'How are you anyway? And *where* are you?' Even now, when she is asking after Gillian's wellbeing, Tara sounds just like her father: supremely indulgent of Gillian's inadequacies.

'Malè.'

'Where's that?'

'The Maldives. Are you all right?'

'Why shouldn't I be? What are you doing in the Maldives?'

'A case. I've got a case: missing woman. Went on holiday and never came back – holidays for you!'

'I see ... a case. Of course! Could it ever be anything else! What was I thinking?' When did Tara learn all of her father's tricks: the one-word put-downs, the superior tone of someone in

113

the know, the forgiving indulgence for the feeble-minded and straying souls of this world, like Gillian? Tara knows how fallible her mother is. She knows only too well how good Gillian is at bringing her cases home and depositing them on their doorstep like a cat does its kill, or dragging them all the way to her bed and sleeping on them – with them – until they are solved, while the rest of the world has to stand still and wait its turn.

'What do you mean *you see*?'

'Mum, just because some person has gone missing ... I mean, you can't leap to crazy conclusions. *I'm* all right! In fact, we're having a great time! There's a whole bunch of us now –'

'A bunch?'

'We met some people from Kent.'

'And who are those *people*?'

'Muuum ...' there is a warning in Tara's voice.

Gillian knows not to push her luck. She asks, 'Nice people? Your age sort of people?'

'Yes, and yes. And no – I'm not giving you their full names! You'll have to trust me.'

'I do trust you.'

Tara laughs.

'So you're having a good time?'

'Didn't I say? OK,' there is a clear, undisguised yawn, 'I'm knackered. We only just got back to Phuket. It's very late here – I should be in bed – but I called you as soon as I got back because I know how paranoid you get.'

'I only want you to keep in touch.'

'Last time I called you weren't even there.'

'I'm sorry. You know –'

'I do! I do ... Mum, I've really got to be going. Just remember we're flying to Melbourne tomorrow morning. I mean ... this morning. OK? Are you listening?'

'I'm all ears!'

'Good.'

Gillian is now fully awake. She remembers suddenly. 'I thought you were flying to Sydney.'

114

'Change of plans. Josh and Charlie have friends in Melbourne and we can stay with them ... Plus, we were going to get to Melbourne eventually.'

'Josh and Charlie – is that the *whole bunch of people*?'

'Muuum ... Don't.'

Gillian becomes conscious of her breathing: soft puffs, inhaling regularly, just as when she was giving birth to her daughter. She has to take it easy. Tara is a big girl – silly as a turnip, but big enough. 'Yeah, yeah, I'm listening. Get in touch when you get there, OK?'

'As long as you're there to answer the phone,' Tara sneers.

'Watch it, young lady.'

'Goodnight, Mum.'

She doesn't remember the exact moment she fell asleep. Once she had heard Tara's voice – bubbly and full of life – the stress level in her bloodstream had miraculously subsided and Gillian could at last put her weary head to a pillow and sleep. Her mobile – with a charger cable twisted around her neck – is still in her hand when she wakes up in the morning. This time it is the alarm clock on her mobile that demands her attention. She grabs the phone and lifts it to her face, tightening the cable around her throat. It chokes her. She coughs and wheezes, unplugs the charger, loosens the cable and turns off the alarm just as it reaches the crescendo of 'Amazing Grace'.

Detective Nasheed is on standby, ready to escort her to the airport and on her merry way back to the UK. Sitting over a small thimble-cup of espresso, he watches her patiently as she goes for the second round of buffet breakfast. Gillian may be a tiny pixie of a woman, but she can eat for England. It's the nervous energy that metabolises everything she puts in her mouth with the speed of a turbo food blender. She is now on eggs, two golden rashers of bacon and sautéed mushrooms. Her brain is ticking, doing some morning inventorising of facts. She is hardly aware of her Maldivian counterpart's presence at the table.

'The plane leaves in an hour and a half. Theoretically, you

should be checked in by now. Don't rush,' Nasheed raises a calming hand in the air, 'I'll get you on that plane – I've contacts.'

'But I'm not going back,' Gillian gives him an innocent, round-eyed look. 'I haven't got anything yet. I can't go back empty-handed.' She shoves two mushrooms and half a rasher in her mouth.

'You won't find anything! We looked!' Nasheed is visibly agitated. He downs his espresso in one go, nearly swallows the cup.

While still chewing the mushrooms, Gillian realises she forgot sausages. She gets up. 'Excuse me. The sausages look yummy.'

Nasheed follows her to the buffet. He is talking to the back of her neck. 'She has drowned. You've nothing to find here. I told you: if the body turns up, you'll be the first person I'll call.'

'That's nice.' Gillian is back at the table, tucking into the sausages. 'Look, Ali, I need to satisfy myself. I'm going to Itsouru after breakfast. I was hoping you'd make the arrangements, get the clearances for me … I hope we're still working together?' It feels awkward calling him by his first name, but Gillian tends to fly into informalities when she is irritated. Somehow her respect for the rank disappears.

Hassan is not in the least pleased to see her arrive. He is large and meaty, dressed in an airy linen suit with an exotic palm trees pattern. He reminds Gillian of Marlon Brando in *Apocalypse Now*. He shakes her hand which she offers to him in the hope of long and fruitful co-operation. It is a lame offering of truce, she concedes, and the man's face says as much. He has already expressed his dismay in a lively telephone conversation with Detective Nasheed, of which Gillian has – probably luckily for her – understood nothing.

'We spoke on the phone. I told you everything I could tell you about Ms Eagles' stay with us. I do not know what else I can help you with, madam.'

'DS Marsh. Please don't call me *madam*.'

116

'How long do you intend to stay with us, DS Marsh?'

'I don't know – a day or two.'

'What can I do to help you close this … case?' His discomfort is tangible. He has the reputation of his resort to protect, which is rather incompatible with the idea of one of his guests vanishing into thin air. Unless she is found fit and sound, that very reputation he is trying to protect will be in tatters. He glares at Gillian as if she were the author of his predicament. They are sitting in his nice and friendly office with its softly whispering air-conditioning and unintimidating wicker furniture. If it wasn't for his guarded, almost hostile tone, it would seem more like taking afternoon tea than investigating a case.

'I need to speak to your staff, guests –'

'I would prefer if our guests' privacy was respected, DS Marsh.'

'I'll try to be as discreet as I possibly can, but you must accept that this is a police inquiry and that I expect your full co-operation.' Gillian is still a bit jet-lagged and she doesn't quite appreciate Hassan's tone. 'If you continue obstructing my investigation, I may stay longer than I originally intended.'

'There is no need for threats. I believe I have been very forthcoming with all the information you asked for.'

'I asked you not to remove anything from Ms Eagles' room.'

'I didn't – the police did.'

'Fair enough. I still want to look at the room. Is it occupied at present?'

'No. We moved our next guest to another chalet. Luckily we had an early departure. We are fully booked at this time of year.'

'Good, then I'll start with Ms Eagles' room – chalet.'

'If you intend to stay the night with us then that's the only chalet we have available in any event.'

'Excellent! Who could be better to obliterate what's left of any evidence than me! Lead on!'

Hassan winces and rises from his chair. Gillian is not good at niceties. She is walking in step with Hassan, but without a word. He is maintaining a dignified silence, and did not offer to help her with her bag. Not that she would expect him to. She really doesn't give a toss about his principled stand on his guests' privacy, and all that tosh. When Gillian follows a scent, she is like a hound – all sensitivities fly out of the window. He hands the key over to her on the front step and – unable to restrain his inbred hotelier's politeness – tells her that if she requires anything at all, he and his staff are at hand to render assistance at any time of day or night. He says that in one breath, with a smile and without the slightest hint of sarcasm. Gillian thanks him with much less panache.

If she was hoping for any shred of evidence left in the wake of the Maldivian police's cleanout, she has now abandoned that hope. The room is in pristine condition: the bed has been made, furniture dusted and polished, crisp white towels are piled neatly in a roofless bathroom, taps gleam and the toilet paper ends with a triangular fold like a bow tie. There is no trace of Nicola Eagles. Not a footprint. It is as if she has never been here. It is as if she has never existed. If it hadn't been for a stupid cat ...

Gillian sinks into a wickedly comfortable settee: deep and soft. Nicola Eagles sat here a few days ago, she thinks. She was probably loving her holiday in the tropics. According to her brother she had never had one like that in her life. It was an adventure of a lifetime. And now she is wiped out, gone, missing, vanished – perhaps drowned, perhaps murdered, maybe kidnapped and still alive. Gillian was hoping that was the case, but five days has gone by since her disappearance and no ransom demand has been made. Every fibre in Gillian's body tells her Nicola Eagles is dead. This whole case may be the reason why Gillian is obsessing about Tara. Every change of plans, every unexpected development unsettles her. Tara is right; Deon is right – Gillian has grown paranoid. She can't take separation from her child. If it was North Wales or maybe even France ... but Thailand is just that one nautical mile too far for comfort. Gillian will go bonkers by the time this gap-year experiment is over. Who could blame her? She has never been parted from Tara for more than a few nights here, a weekend there, sleeping over at her parents when Gillian was on a case. But that was work. This is torture. She wishes she knew how to cope with it.

The best person to ask is her own mother, Gillian realises. Once upon a time, it was she who had to cope with Gillian's absence. At the tender age of almost twenty-one Gillian had decided that South Africa was the place for her. She upped and went just like those men you sometimes read about in the newspaper: *Gone to the corner shop for a pack of cigarettes and never heard from again.* There could be months before Gillian would call home or send a letter. She was so busy living her enthralling life that it never occurred to her that on the other side of the world her parents waited. They never complained. Never told her off. They just waited. How did they manage to hold it together? She was their only child and she was gallivanting around the globe without a care in the world, without a second thought. While they waited.

It may be because Gillian feels guilty, or maybe because she suddenly understands or maybe because she needs some reassurance that she dials her parents' number.

'Mum? Gillian here.'

'I had a feeling you were going to call us.' Her mother's voice is thin and gentle, a bit shaky, the elderly voice of a nice old lady. 'How are you, darling?'

'OK. Just been thinking about you.'

'Oh, that's nice. Dad and I rang you yesterday.'

'I'm not at home. You can always call me on my mobile. You've got the number.' She makes that suggestion for a hundredth time but she knows they'll never do that. The concept of a *mobile phone* is for some reason incomprehensible to them. A phone has to be attached to a line, otherwise it isn't a phone – it's a trick and anyway, *they can't hear her very well*.

'Oh, that's all right, darling, we'll wait till you get back. We can wait, we aren't going anywhere, are we, Ted?' There is a faint murmur of consent Gillian imagines she can hear. She wonders if patience comes with age or whether it is something you're born with. 'How are you both doing?' she asks.

'Oh, we've got each other for company. And to nag ... So where are you, if it's not a top secret?'

'It's a missing person inquiry, in the Maldives.'

'Oh, the Maldives, did you say? How is the weather there?' That's the beauty of it. Nothing shocks her. Gillian's mother can make everything sound so perfectly ordinary. She puts things into perspective. Gillian should be spending more time with her.

'It's very hot, Mum,' she can't help a smile.

'Oh, I'd imagine it is! That can't be too far from where Tara is. She called this morning – said the same thing: hot, hot, hot! Well, that's the tropics for you!'

'She called you? Tara called you?'

'Oh yes, she calls us every day. If she can. She said she'd keep in touch. Dear girl ... I think she's got herself a chap.'

'A chap?'

'What do you call them these days? A boyfriend?'

'Is that what she said?'

'No, silly, she didn't have to say it in so many words. She just jabbered on and on about that Charlie chap –'

'I see ...' Why does Gillian know nothing about *that Charlie chap*? Why does she have to find out from her mother? Isn't she supposed to be the first port of call for her own child? Obviously not.

In all her innocence, her mother is oblivious to her misgivings. She says, 'So when are you coming back? It's just that when you do, you could pop over for tea. I know there is little point cooking for one –'

Gazing out into the horizon, Gillian notices two people emerge from the chalet next door and head towards the water. 'Must go, Mum! Talk later!'

They are going for a swim. The woman is slim but shapely with a narrow waist and a perky behind; she is wearing a bikini that is made of narrow strings and knots, and very little else. The man is past his prime; his overhanging stomach and thinning hair point to someone over forty. They're holding hands. It is an unpleasant chore, one Gillian is most familiar with, to barge in on their intimate moment, but she has a job to do. She charges towards them and nearly knocks the woman over as she stops unexpectedly to dip her foot in water.

'Oh, sorry! So Sorry! Are you all right?' Gillian is brimming with apologies.

The woman gawps at her and nods. 'Yes, I'm fine. No problem.'

Gillian sighs with relief. 'Great … And hello …'

'Hello,' the man says and eyes her up and down as if she was a nasty barnacle stuck between his toes. Gillian is glad to hear he is English. At least no language barriers to reckon with – only his attitude!

'Sorry I ran into you like that …'

The woman presents a friendly smile. She is not as young as Gillian first thought: at least in her mid-thirties. 'I'm fine, honestly. Don't worry.'

'I couldn't help noticing you're my neighbours. I'm staying in number 42,' she points to her chalet.

'Oh …' The man has little interest in Gillian's revelations.

'Nice to meet you,' says the woman.

Gillian is no good at diplomacy. This is as far as she can take her *respect for guests' privacy*. 'Same here,' she tries to smile. 'I've only just got here. This morning, as a matter of fact. A woman was staying here before me. Nicola Eagles.'

The man is gaping at her. He is puzzled and annoyed in equal measure. 'OK, if you say so. We're going swimming if you don't mind.'

'I do. I mean – I don't mind you swimming. I need to ask you about that woman. Nicola Eagles.'

'We don't know Nicola Eagles.'

'Early forties, shortish brown hair, average build? I have a photo –'

'No,' the woman shakes her head and furrows her brow. Unlike her partner, she looks like she wants to be helpful. The man on the other hand, doesn't.

'Look, lady, we don't know Nicola Eagles. And we want to go for a swim. We'd really appreciate if you –' The end of that sentence would have been *buggered off* or something to that effect, if Gillian hadn't interrupted: 'I am investigating her disappearance. DS Marsh, Sexton's Canning CID.'

The man closely examines her ID card. 'Far away from home,' he comments and returns the card to Gillian. 'We still don't know Nicola Eagles.'

'Here is her photo. Have a look, please.'

'We only got here last night,' the man explains. Gillian realises their arrival date should have been the first thing to ask them about before she embarked on the full-blown interrogation.

The woman is examining the photo. She asks, alarm rising in her eyes. 'How did she disappear? How can you disappear here? I thought it was safe –'

'We don't know yet. Please don't be alarmed. This is just an informal inquiry,' Gillian says sheepishly. 'Enjoy your stay.'

As she is strolling back to her chalet, she can hear the woman ask her husband, 'Do they have those Somali pirates operating in these waters, Mark?'

'How should I know?'

Hassan is openly dismayed to see her. He has only just left her at her front door. She has found him in one of the restaurants, kitchens to be more precise, discussing the menu with the chef. The kitchen is hot as hell, hotter than outside, which says a lot about the unbearable temperature. How can people function in this heat? Gillian pushes across the sandy floor, manoeuvring amongst stainless steel tables and steaming hobs.

'Sorry, I need to ask you for something,' her manner is matter-of-fact but she tries to avoid eye contact with the distraught manager. In vain.

'Can it not wait? I am busy,' Hassan's eyes are large and bulging – accusatory.

'The quicker I get what I need the sooner you'll see the back of me.'

He speaks, fast and furious, to his chef, presses the menu into his hand and leads Gillian out of the kitchen. For which she is hugely grateful. They sit at one of the tables in the restaurant. It is nearly lunchtime and tables are beginning to fill with diners: colourful, relaxed, laughing, radiating heat through their sun-tanned skins. Hassan steals a few nervous looks, but no one seems to take any interest in his tête-à-tête with the dreadful policewoman.

'What can I do for you?' He is patience personified – his hands are clasped together and placed on the table with his chin resting on them.

'It occurred to me that some of my witnesses may no longer be on the island. People who were here a week ago may by now be long gone. Am I right?'

'The standard stay is for a week, sometimes two weeks,' Hassan agrees, still unsure how he can be of any assistance short of herding all the last week's guests back to the resort.

'Yes, precisely. I need to talk to anyone who may have witnessed something when Nicola Eagles was here. That includes all staff members as well as the guests. So that takes me to your guest list. I need a full list of your guests – everyone who stayed here between January 31st and last Friday ... that'd be 6th February – I'll need their contact details, names, etc. ...'

'That is *out of the question!*' Hassan's chubby cheeks and his double neck are shaking with indignation, his eyes bulging even more than before, his fingers clutching the edge of the table. 'I'm not prepared to disclose personal information about any of our guests.'

'This is a police inquiry.'

'This is an *informal* police inquiry. I'd lose my job! We'd lose custom if this got out –'

'If it gets out that a guest has vanished from this resort without a trace, you will *definitely* lose custom. I suggest discreet co-operation –'

'No! I can't do that. You'll have to go through official channels, DS Marsh. The privacy of our guests is paramount.'

'I do suggest you get in touch with your superior.'

'I will. And he'll get in touch with yours. This is an intrusion! I have co-operated fully with the local police – Detective Nasheed. I know how far you can push me. I know I don't have to do this!' He is hitting the table with the flat of his palm. The table vibrates, which makes him stop. 'I have to get back to my duties. If you excuse me!' He is getting up, the conversation over. Nasheed has obviously done some damage control before releasing Gillian on his patch.

'Staff members?' she shouts after Hassan. 'Can I have their names?'

He stops, thinks. 'You can collect that from my office. Tomorrow.'

A svelte, brown-eyed waiter arrives, wearing a sarong, sandals and a friendly grin. Oblivious to his boss's wrath, he greets Gillian with utmost cordiality, inquires after her wellbeing and asks for her chalet number. He wonders if she would like a drink with her lunch. A cool beer would be nice – but she was on duty. She orders orange juice. She is told to help herself to the buffet. That is when she realises how hungry she is.

Jon calls her halfway through sushi with green salad – Gillian's first starter. 'What time is it back there?' she almost chokes. 'Must be close to midnight! Do you ever sleep?'

'Going that extra mile for you, you should be grateful. Do you want to hear it, or not?'

'Fire away!'

'Boring stuff out of the way first: Peter Bird. He checks out. Water sports freak. He was where he said he would be, came back yesterday. Spoke to him. He said something similar to what Paul Collins said, except he phrased it better – called her *strange*. Said she lied about a few things, but then everyone lies on those dating sites – his words, not mine.'

'Yeah, right,' Gillian smirks under her breath.

'Interesting thing he said …'

'I'm all ears.'

'He said she was a crap swimmer. Nearly drowned when he

124

took her kayaking.'

'Ahhh ...'

'I thought you may find it to your liking. Maybe she did drown?'

'That's what the police here think.'

'And what do you think?'

'Would she go swimming if she couldn't swim?'

'Maybe she wanted to drown?'

'That takes us back to suicide and I don't believe she was planning to do that.' Gillian catches a moment to push the last medallion of sushi into her mouth. She speaks with her mouth full, 'The blood? Do we have a match with Nicola Eagles'?'

'They haven't sent any samples from Malè.'

'Bloody-minded Nasheed!'

'Interesting bits now. Ready?' While Gillian mumbles encouragement, Jon gets on with it, 'The will. Spoke to her lawyer. You owe me – had to go out, put on a suit and sweat like a pig. I bloody hate lawyers. My ex's –'

'Is there any profession out there you don't hate, Jon?'

'Never mind that. You owe me, like I said. House calls are not in my job description.'

'Thanks, Jon. Will take you for a drink when I get back.'

'Right you are! So then – spoke to the lawyer. He handled her inheritance and the sale of her flat in London. Doesn't look like she might have another lawyer. So he says no will. He had suggested she made one and she was going to, but it didn't happen. So as things stand, guess who gets it all?'

'The brother?'

'Exactly. Robert Eagles, our friendly salesman! And this is where it gets juicy – the man is broke. Flat broke. He works on commission: high stakes and that, but the software company isn't doing too good. Nine months ago he lost his house: mortgagee sale. He's renting now ... some rent-to-buy scheme. Wife's unemployed. Two kids. The guy would be interested in a nice little windfall ...'

'He most certainly would.'

'And he was in Hong Kong around the time of her death!

Tell me I'm good.'

'Almost, Jon, except that Hong Kong isn't precisely in the heart of the Maldives. And you aren't telling me he's come this way ...'

'He could've hired someone to do the deed for him. That's what you do in Hong Kong, if you know the right people. He didn't do it in person, of course he didn't! Even I wouldn't do my own sister with my own hands! He paid some scum to do it for him.'

'But what would he pay them with? Flat broke, remember?'

'If there was an expectation of inheritance, they would've done it on credit, high interest rate. Or maybe he just sweet-talked them into it. Sales reps are good at this kind of shit ...'

Gillian has to smile. 'So how's that new car of yours?'

'Don't mention.'

'OK , I won't.'

'I'll get my fucking money back, if it kills me. I will! The gearbox is fucked.'

'Sorry to hear that.'

'Never mind. I'm cycling to work. Good for the heart.'

'Did you get to Nicola Eagles' mobile records?'

'Waiting. Should have something by tomorrow if they stop being obstructive and get on with it.'

'No worries. I'll look through her calls on the handset.'

'You've got it there? Did you lift the phone from the evidence box?' Jon is impressed. Thinking *outside the box* – he never would've suspected Gillian of that!

'The coppers here have no need for it. I doubt they even turned it on. Anyway, I'm hoping someone may call on it. There is a valid reason for hanging on to it. They may call on it to ask for a ransom.'

'If they haven't by now ...'

'I know – small chance.'

'Let me know if there's anything else.'

'There is, come to think about it,' Gillian remembers the scrap of paper with random foreign words and numbers on it, which she has also *lifted* from the box and forgotten all about. It is buried in her jeans pocket. She pulls it out, smooths out the paper. 'I can't make sense of this. I've got some handwritten notes. Foreign language, I can't read it. I'll send you a photo of it. See what you can make of it.'

Four courses later, Gillian is full. She is so full that she decides to stay at the table to help her overloaded stomach with its digestion. Having found no recent call history of any interest, she is paging through the phone's photos. Most of them she has already seen on Nicola Eagles' Facebook. There are also a few pictures of Fritz the cat – Jon hasn't reported any success in tracking the creature down, she will have to remind him tomorrow or speak to Miller about it. Then there is that one photo of 'Count Karenin': the only person featuring in Nicola's gallery of images. Gillian wonders if Nicola knew the man, whether he was a real presence in her life or just the fantasy of an old spinster with a penchant for Russian literature.

A group of diners takes a table behind her. She hears them comment loudly about the debatable quality of last night's venison – in English. She might as well strike up a friendly conversation, she tells herself, conveniently forgetting about Hassan's plea for *respect of his guests' privacy*. She turns around as soon as they order their drinks and before they wander off to the buffet.

'Good afternoon! I couldn't help overhearing you're from London!' She flashes her ID card. 'DS Marsh – Sexton's Canning CID. May I have a quick word?'

'Is something the matter, officer?' The man who addresses her looks positively shifty. He is slim-built, with wiry, grey hair and deep-set eyes that blink nervously. Gillian briefly contemplates the odds of his involvement with a dodgy scam, tax evasion or some other dubious practice that has paid for this holiday.

'George?' a woman on his arm asks him. She is bottle blonde and heavily made up.

The other man in the group, a chubby individual with a David Jason moustache, says, 'Sexton's Canning – where's that?'

'Somerset. Can I ask – how long have you been here?'

'What is this all about?' asks the woman on George's arm.

Gillian shows her Nicola Eagles' photograph that Jon printed from her Facebook page. 'I am looking for this woman. Do you recognise her? Have you seen her here?' They all examine the photograph.

George is visibly relieved, and already very keen to be of help. 'Yes, we did see her, didn't we, pet? Look at that,' he stabs his finger at the photo. 'She was older than in this photo, mind, but I remember her. She was one of them dykes, if you pardon my French.'

'George has a way of putting it,' his wife looks at Gillian, screwing her face in embarrassment, 'but yes, the lady in the photo was … well … friends … she was friends with the other ladies. In fact, we saw them dine together the other night. How long ago?'

'A good few days ago. A proper spectacle that was!'

'They were quite loud, weren't they, Paula?'

'Yes, I remember now. The woman in the photo was having a good chuckle with one of them. The younger one. They were all over each other!'

'She was well pickled if you ask me!' George comments.

'The woman in the photo?' Gillian finds it hard to follow.

'She was too, but the younger of the two dykes was –'

'George, we don't call them *dykes*!'

'So what *do* you call 'em? Merry-go-round?' George makes his companions snigger.

Gillian is beginning to lose her composure. 'I don't care what you call them. Can you get to the point, please? Who was pickled?'

'You tell her, Dawn. You're so much better at the … the … *vocabulary*,' George snorts.

Dawn draws Gillian closer and speaks into her ear, like they're conspirators: 'It was five days ago, maybe a week. We'd only been here three days at the most. So at first, the … *lesbian ladies*,' she glares pointedly at George, 'were dining alone –

128

together, I mean, with each other. Then the other joins them – the one in the photo. Lots of laughter. One of the *lesbian ladies* gets drunk as a skunk –'

'But not the one in the photo?'

'She's had a bit too much too, if you ask me!'

'No one's asking you, George. So the other – older – *lesbian lady* looks none too pleased 'cos the other two are falling over each other ...'

'Were they?' the other, so far silent, man asks.

'Oh, they were, Mick, they were! You was sat with your back to them. You didn't see their antics!'

'But we heard the argument, didn't we, Mick?' says Paula, stealing the limelight from Dawn.

'What argument?'

'The next day, or maybe two days later, there's this big row next chalet to ours.'

'That is the chalet where the *ladies* was staying,' George clarifies. 'And now there's only one of them left.'

'Hang on! Go back.' Gillian thinks she is, at last, onto something. 'Go slowly.'

'I'll say it, Mick, OK?' Paula says. 'It was, like Mick said, about two days after the restaurant antics. We didn't see the one in the photo after that, but the other two went on as if nothing had happened until about two days later. Huge row! There was shouting, things flying. Embarrassing for us to listen to.'

'Did you hear what was being said?'

'Well no. Not really. But something about *letting go.*'

'And *fucking up the other's life* ...'

'In so many words! The language, ouch!'

'Then one of them storms out –'

'The younger one!'

'The other one follows. They keep on arguing on the beach, but we can't hear what's being said. Then again, the young one breaks away and runs back inside their chalet. The old one sits alone for a while, till it gets dark. It gets dark very quickly here ...'

'What about the woman in the photo?'

'Haven't seen her since the scene in the restaurant,' Dawn says.

'That was two days earlier.' Mick seems to be the one who keeps the track of time in this place where time seems to stand still.

'So what happened after the argument?'

'Nothing,' Mick shrugs. 'Nothing happened. Or we've heard nothing more.'

'Except that now she's alone,' George gestures towards a lone woman at a table near the veranda.

'Is that the lady?'

'One of them. The older one,' Dawn says. 'Come to think about it, we haven't seen the younger one for days.'

'Not since that row. And the one from the photo is gone too. We reckon they did a runner together,' Mick looks pleased with his bit of deduction. 'Look at her! Sour as a lemon! Has been ever since the row. We've been wondering what she's still doing here. Sulking, more likely.'

'I feel sorry for her,' Paula says generously.

'Women should not meddle with women, if you ask me.'

'No one's asking you, George.'

Gillian approaches the woman – *the lesbian lady* as Dawn has put it – head on. Dressed in a pair of baggy jeans and a sensible white blouse, the woman doesn't belong in this heat-infused inferno. She looks like she is on her way out, back to the civilised world. Only a straw hat with a frayed rim sticking out of her backpack testifies to her being a holidaymaker. Gillian flashes her ID card. 'DS Marsh, Sexton's Canning CID,' she announces briskly. 'May I join you?'

The woman looks alarmed. 'What is this about?'

'It's about Nicola Eagles. Miss Eagles went missing from this island a few days ago. I'm investigating her disappearance.'

'Nicola Eagles?'

Uninvited, Gillian joins the woman at the table, and presents the photograph. The woman looks at it briefly, and nods. The expression in her face is inscrutable. She has a full face, soft

130

and chubby, but the eyebrows are thick and straight, which gives her an expression of stern disapproval. 'Yes, I believe I met her here. Nicola ... She disappeared, did you say? Mmm ...'

'She was meant to return to the UK four days ago. Failed to turn up. I'm trying to piece together her movements.'

The woman relaxes. She is obviously not particularly concerned about Miss Eagles. 'I see,' she says. 'I don't know what I can do to help you.'

'Like you said, you met her here. Perhaps you can tell me more about that meeting.'

'There isn't much to say. My ...' she bites her lip. 'We met Nicola here. She was alone. We asked her to join us for dinner. Once. Frankly, I can't remember seeing her after that.'

'We? That being yourself and ... ?'

'Me and my ... partner,' she shrugs, smiles, exhales, 'Me and my *wife* ...' The last word is spoken with bitterness. 'Amy befriended your missing person in the swimming pool, if my memory serves me correctly. We had dinner together. She didn't say much. Amy did most of the talking. And drinking. That's it. That's all I can tell you.'

'So the last you saw of Nicola Eagles was that evening when you had dinner?'

'Yes. A week ago now.'

'How did she seem to you?'

'Normal. Shy. A bit embarrassed by Amy's drunkenness. She excused herself as soon as she could, and left. We said goodbye, see you tomorrow, the usual.'

'She wasn't agitated, upset? Didn't say anything –'

'No! Just like I said – pretty normal. Not suicidal, if that's what you mean – though how can you tell if someone is suicidal, especially if you don't know them?'

'And you didn't see her after that? The following day?'

'No, I did not. But Amy did ...' the woman frowns. 'At least I think she did. She told me she saw Nicola with a man, swimming. *Frolicking*, Amy said. She said she was "frolicking with a man", which Amy found amusing. Whether it was true or

131

not, I can't tell. I was convinced Nicola was here alone and she wasn't the frolicking type. And Amy ... Amy will say anything to get me off the track ... No matter,' she gets up and reaches for her backpack. 'I must be going. Leaving today. I believe the boat is due to leave in half an hour.' She is striding ahead, a large woman with wide hips and an ample bosom. Gillian can hardly keep up with her. It is bloody annoying that she is leaving the island as they speak, but there is nothing Gillian can do to stop her. The woman hasn't done anything, nor is she under any suspicion. Her very passing connection to Nicola Eagles can hardly serve as an excuse to try to detain her.

'I couldn't help noticing your wife – Amy? She isn't with you?'

'Amy's already gone home.'

'That's a bit strange.'

'Happens.'

'To leave halfway through your holiday ...' *Honeymoon?* 'It's odd. It doesn't just happen. Did she have some prior commitments?'

'Not really. We split up. She left me.' The woman stops halfway through a stride. Her large face is flushed red. She is holding back tears and manages to turn her emotions to anger. 'Not that it is any business of yours!'

'It is my business if Nicola Eagles was implicated in any way –'

'Why would she be? She wasn't! For God's sake, I don't know the woman! I don't *want* to know her!'

'It is strange that you parted ways with your spouse soon after you met Nicola Eagles. If she wasn't the cause for you two arguing –'

'Arguing? Who said we were arguing?'

'You were overheard having a violent argument.'

'We were both upset.' Her tone is milder. There is something philosophical about it, something bordering on resignation. 'I was ... We've been together for seven years – I had the right to be upset, but it wasn't violent. And it had nothing to do with that woman. We've had it coming. I had it coming ...'

'What was the reason for you splitting up in the middle of your romantic getaway together, if you don't mind me asking?'

'Boredom. Age difference. Who knows?' She picks up pace again. 'Don't you people have better things to do than to pry –'

'A woman is missing. That is a great cause for concern. Frankly, I'm surprised you don't find it significant enough –'

'I do! I did! It did cross my mind that she was the reason for Amy's sudden U-turn.' She has stopped again and is facing Gillian. There is raw emotion etched in her face, something that cannot be disguised or faked. 'I put it to Amy. She denied it. That was when she told me about her and that man – frolicking in the ocean. She said Nicola wasn't into women. I hope to God that's true! But you will have to ask her. Ask Amy!'

'She isn't here to ask.'

'She went back home. I told you!'

'OK. We'll speak to her. I'll need your full names, your address in the UK, contact number. Before you leave, if you don't mind.'

'Why would I! You keep asking me if I do. Would it make any difference if I did?'

They are standing in front of the Reception hut. Just as the woman shouts out her name, Sarah Ludlow-Gray, Hassan floats into Gillian's peripheral vision.

'Is everything all right, madam?' he asks, an expression of grim concern in his bulging eyes.

'Perfectly all right. I just want to check out and go home.'

'I hope you enjoyed your stay with us.'

Sarah Ludlow-Gray bites her lip and does not care to answer his question, but asks her own, 'Can I borrow a pen and a piece of paper to give the detective here my *full details*?'

Having sent Gillian a furious glare, Hassan is quick to oblige. He sources a writing pad from the receptionist and presents his personal fountain pen from his palm-tree shirt pocket. Sarah scribbles something in capital letters and tears a page out of the pad. She passes the page to Gillian. 'Here! The address, telephone number, all you asked for. With any luck you may find them both there ... Am I free to go now?'

Gillian has her first solid suspect. She must speak to Amy, what's her name? She reads it from the piece of paper Sarah Ludlow-Gray gave her: *Amy Gray-Ludlow*. How quaint! She almost feels sorry for both of them. Did Nicola Eagles come between those two? And if she did, how does Count Karenin fit into it? Amy may have some answers. Is it possible that she and Nicola travelled to the UK together?

Gillian finds a stranded boulder by the side of the footpath. She perches on it – a scrawny bird with a tuft of feathery hair and lips puckered into a beak. She dials Amy's number. It rings and rings until an answer machine kicks in. A shiny female voice chimes with a twinkle and a chuckle: *You've reached Amy and Sarah. We're not at home. We are on our honeymoon! Leave a message if it can't wait. Back in business Monday week!*

Gillian doesn't leave a message. She is not sure what she wants to say. Or ask. She isn't sure she would get a straight answer. How do you ask for confirmation that a relationship – a marriage – is over? How do you ask who is to blame? How do you inquire if a third party was involved? This isn't a conversation for the telephone.

Gillian calls Jon.

On the fifth ring, a gravelly, disorientated voice answers. 'Gillian, this had better be a dirty call. It's two-bloody-a.m.!'

'I need you to get hold of someone.'

'And I need you to let me get on with my beauty sleep.'

'Amy Gray-Ludlow.' Gillian dictates the number.

'That's in London!'

'Yes, I'd have done it myself but London is much closer to you than me. Anyway, I just tried the number. No answer.'

'Are you surprised? It's two-bloody-a.m.!'

'Plus it isn't a telephone kind of conversation. Amy Gray-Ludlow may be romantically involved with Nicola Eagles.'

'Wow! It's getting spicy ...'

'I've just waved goodbye to a woman scorned – Amy's

134

dumped spouse. If Nicola is responsible for the break up, then we have ourselves our first strong suspect. Amy may hold the key to Nicola's disappearance.'

'Hang on, slow down. How is this Amy here in London holding any key to your disappeared person over there?' Patiently, Gillian begins to paint the picture of the love triangle she has formed in her mind, the violent fallout and the sudden departure of one of the newlyweds.

'You can see why I need you to talk to her face to face. Observe her reactions. She may still be protecting her former partner. Or she may be running scared. Or whatever it is, I have this feeling that getting Amy's version of events will lead us to Nicola. Just that one favour, Jon ...'

'I'm not going to London. I don't go to London, out of principle.'

Gillian is well aware of Jon's agoraphobia. The metropolis and Jon do not mix. Jon does not do people *en masse*. He struggles with the loud buzzing noise, the rubbing of bodies, the nudging and pushing, the collective eyeing of his person which he perceives as painfully invasive. 'Jon, I know. I just can't do it from here. Please! I'll make it a dirty call ...'

She can almost smell him squirm and sweat on the other side of the phone, but he doesn't weigh his options for long – he's too big a boy to believe in miracles. 'No. Webber's back tomorrow; I'll brief him. It's not my job, Gill, as much as I'd love a bit of naughty –'

'Ah! The cat!' Gillian decides not to fight a losing battle and, on a totally new note, remembers Fritz. 'Did you find the cat?'

'Miller went looking. No luck. It's probably run over and long dead.' Jon says without an ounce of feeling.

'Damn it! How will I explain this?'

'Let's hope you never find the owner alive then.'

'Are you really human?' Gillian gasps.

Jon chuckles. 'Where do you want me to start?' A stony silence answers his question, which he knows could only be rhetorical. He says, 'I have a nice juicy bit for you. Was going to call you at a more civilised hour, but,' he sighs, 'I've been pursuing my own lines of inquiry. Robert Eagles … Robbie, I call him.'

'Go on!'

'I was bored. Surfed a bit. You can follow a named passenger's travel history with this app. Choice!'

'And?'

'Out of interest, I checked Robbie's return journey itinerary. You know his way back to Ozzie from Hong Kong? He flew on a direct flight to Hong Kong, but funny thing, he went back via Colombo. Funny that, isn't it?'

It was odd, considering that the most obvious route would be a direct flight from Hong Kong to Australia with the same airline. 'Why stop in Colombo?' Gillian asks.

'You'll have to ask him that. He had a stop in Colombo on Tuesday, 3rd February. Six-hour stopover. Beats me … *unless* … You see, I've got my gut feeling about our friendly salesman. Call it woman's intuition … A man can have it too, you know?'

'Interesting.'

'I thought you'd like to know about it. It really brings it home. I'd forget about the gay love triangles and focus squarely on the brother, if I was you, which I'm not, but you know?'

'I do know, Jon. You may be onto something. I think it's time I had another chat with Mr Eagles. I may have to visit him in Melbourne.'

'Melbourne? Why Melbourne? He lives in Adelaide.'

'Sorry, Adelaide. My daughter's going to Melbourne. With some *chap* called Charlie she met in Thailand. I wish I was a fly on the wall –'

'In Melbourne?'

'Yes, in Melbourne. Never mind,' Gillian shakes off her anxieties. 'She'll be fine. She's a big girl.'

'Eighteen – the age of consent –'

'Don't! Don't go there, Jon. Keep your mind on the case.'

'It's your mind that's doing the wandering.'

'Have you got anything on those numbers and foreign

scribbles I sent you?'

'Yes. It's Finnish. An address and what looks like a telephone number, in Finland.'

'Hm. Did you try it?'

'What? Don't tell me you want me to go to Finland!'

'No, just calling the number would do – did you try it?'

'Why should I? You only asked me to find out what it was.'

Despite his numerous talents, Jon has the ability to exasperate Gillian. He makes a brilliant computer and forensic scientist, but he is a sad example of utter immunity to any human condition. He lacks compassion ... 'Give me that number again. I'll see where it takes me.'

'I left it at work. Do you realise I'm in bed. It's two-bloody-am!'

Gillian has been exploring the island for the past two hours, stopping every now and again for a glass of water at little thatched bars scattered along the sandy beach. She recognises a few places and objects photographed by Nicola Eagles and posted on her Facebook. She has spoken to a few more people, trying to jog their memories, trying to get them to place Miss Eagles, retrace her footsteps, favourite spots, habits. No patterns have emerged. A waiter, Ahmed, remembered that 'the lady drank Greyhound'. A couple of Russian kids nodded when Gillian showed them Nicola's photograph, but changed their minds when their father slapped one of them on the back of the head and told Gillian in broken English that they were making things up.

Gillian is exhausted with the heat and the effort of piecing together something that just won't fit. She is surrounded by people: on the beach, in bars and restaurants, lazing by the side of swimming pools, everywhere, yet hardly anyone recalls seeing Nicola Eagles and no one – no one at all – has witnessed anything that can explain her disappearance.

It is at a French restaurant at the top of the island that she finally comes across a small piece of the puzzle. A lean, swarthy Frenchman in charge of bookings informs her with an air of infallibility that he indeed recognises *madame* from the photograph and that she, indeed, dined at the restaurant a week ago *prècisèment,* that being Tuesday, 3rd February, in the company of a gentleman. 'They were very much in love, but that's nothing unusual on this island, *n'est-ce pas?*'

Gillian pulls out Nicola's mobile phone and skims through her photographs to the picture of the mysterious Count Karenin. She shows it to the waiter. 'Would you be able to identify that man? Is that him?'

He examines the picture carefully. 'It is *verrry* bad quality,' he muses, 'but he looked a *li-ttle* bit like zat, oui! Monsieur Lakso.'

Gillian pauses. 'Did you say his name was Lakso?'

'Oui, madame. Zat's ze name 'e made ze *rèservation.* Zat's ze name 'e used. A Russian gentleman.'

'Russian – are you sure?'

'Oui, madame, Russian. In ze last few years I am 'earing enough Russian speak to be sùre, madame.' The waiter gives her the superior look of someone who will not suffer gladly a *li-ttle madame* daring to doubt his say-so.

It is in quick succession that Count Karenin gets a name and George makes a vital disclosure. The four middle-aged Londoners happen to be at the French restaurant, sitting at an outdoor table, having an alfresco meal. They wave to Gillian from their vantage point on the veranda. It is Paula who waves; Dawn nudges George, he opens his arms, shrugs, refuses to look up. Dawn frowns. Mick is reading the menu. Gillian smiles, waves back. Dawn gets up, forcing George to follow suit. 'DS Marsh, can we have a word?'

Gillian walks over to their table.

'The drunken antics in the restaurant,' Dawn says excitedly, 'It wasn't the last time we saw that *lesbian lady* you're looking for. George saw her later. Go on, George, tell DS Marsh!'

George is reluctant, mumbles something under his breath, shakes his head, but gives in to his wife, 'Well, I saw them, sure enough. Wednesday it was. Anyhow, I saw them at the end of the pier. Hugging they was, kissing. The two of them: the younger of the two dykes and the disappeared one. They was right at it! Then the older one comes along, hands on hips – prises the lovebirds apart. They leave your disappeared one alone on the pier … She was sat there a long while. Crying, she was.'

Gillian stares towards the distant pier, the end of which is only a small wedge jutting into the ocean. 'You're sure you saw her there? On Wednesday?'

'Like I'm seeing you now!' Now that he got it off his chest, George is incensed at her lack of confidence in his talent for observation.

'It is a long way … You saw them hugging … you saw her crying? From the shore? Are you certain?'

'That's why he didn't tell you in the first place,' Dawn interjects. 'He's got them binoculars on him for bird-watching, he says. He didn't want you to think he been spying on people.'

'I was scanning the horizon, minding my own business …'

'Course you were, George! And the lesbian ladies just got into your line of vision.'

'That's why I didn't want to bring it up! You see – *that's* what I get for coming forward!' George seethes.

Gillian needs to do some damage control. 'You get a *thank you* for coming forward with this information. It's very important.'

'I told you so!' Dawn points her finger at her huffing husband.

'Did you see what happened later? Did she walk back? What did she do?'

'Don't know, do I?' George shrugs. 'All hell broke loose in the dykes' chalet, didn't it? We been watching them in action. They was at each other's throats, gloves off, claws out … Don't know what happened to your missing person one. Didn't see her after that. I wonder that myself – maybe she jumped and drowned. Wouldn't surprise me.'

The sultry evening air does little to help Gillian think. She is sitting on the deck of Chalet 42, feet on the railing, wearing her skimpy nightdress, hanging on to a misty bottle of water which she hopes will keep her mind cool. She has been inventorising the facts for the past two hours. In the distance people are laughing and cheering, their voices blending with the artificial glow of fairy lights.

The facts do not make sense; Gillian is at a loss. Probably the brother is the only one that fits the profile, though he could only be tracked down to Colombo airport, and no further. But yet, oddly, he was so close! So close he could smell her blood. Assuming that killing his sister was on his mind. After all, the only reason he would've had for killing her is the one fabricated in Jon's mind: a stab at a fat inheritance. It could be a compelling reason for some, especially those in dire straits, as Robert Eagles appeared to be – according to Jon. Gillian weighs the advantages of investigating Mr Eagles discreetly from a distance, without letting him know that he is a suspect. Once he knows, he may sever any links, destroy evidence. If there is any evidence ...

Nevertheless, it is a lead worth following. Gillian will need to convince Scarface to authorise inquiries with the Sri Lankan authorities. It would be interesting to find out what Mr Eagles was up to during his prolonged stopover in Colombo. Did he leave the airport? Did he meet with anyone? Gillian sucks in her upper lip. It does seem so far-fetched – the whole idea that a brother would order his sister's ... what? Murder? Kidnap? And yet, here, in this part of the world, far away from home, in an uncharted territory – it may be easier to buy into: some obscure Asian gang, pirates, abduction gone wrong. No one would blame the brother. Everyone would think the sister was silly travelling on her own, asking for trouble ... No, Gillian cannot eliminate the brother.

Then there are the two conflicting love scenarios. Now, that is where Gillian is really lost. There is the one Nicola: 'frolicking with a man' in the ocean, 'verrry much in love' with a gentleman in the French restaurant. And there is another Nicola: the hard-drinking, hard-living, gay marriage wrecker, canoodling with a newlywed Amy on the pier, under the very nose of the woman's hurting spouse. Both scenarios cannot be true, surely? And if Gillian is to trust her instincts at all, *neither* of those scenarios *is* true! Nicola Eagles is a shy, middle-aged spinster who cannot swim very well, is awkward with the opposite sex, attracts no attention from the same sex, is all alone in the great big world that sails by her, utterly oblivious to her existence. And that is why the brother cannot be eliminated. Because he fits. Because it would make sense if it were him.

Be that as it may, Gillian cannot disregard what she has heard from independent witnesses. She would have dismissed Sarah Ludlow-Gray's account of Nicola frolicking with a man had it not been for the Count Karenin photograph on Nicola's mobile and the French *garçon* attesting to the man's existence. *Monsieur Lakso* – someone to track down and talk to. Hassan will have to co-operate and share his guests' personal data. If it means getting a warrant, Nasheed will have to be rubbed the right way ...

And then there is Amy. She saw Nicola with the mystery man, or so Sarah would have Gillian believe. Because if Nicola did come between those two, then Sarah has to divert attention away from herself and Amy. She lied about not seeing Nicola after the drunken dinner. She saw her two days later. She saw her with Amy. *They were right at it*, George said. He saw Sarah approaching them, 'prising them apart'. She couldn't have forgotten that small episode. What happened to Nicola after she was left alone on the pier, crying? Crying ... She was crying. Upset. Depressed. Defeated. Could she have jumped? She wasn't a good swimmer. She had nearly drowned kayaking with Paul. Or was it Peter?

Gillian's telephone rings. It's the Sexton's Canning station, she knows the number. What time is it? She glances at her watch. It must be 10 a.m. back home. Good old Mark, she smiles, must've already tracked down Amy.

'Hi! An early bird, you! How was the hols?' she chirps.

'DS Marsh!' It's Scarface.

'Sir! I'm sorry. Thought it was DC Webber.'

141

'DC Webber is on the wild-goose chase mission you sent him on without discussing it with me first. In London, I believe. PC Miller is on another mission you sent him on without discussing it with me. He's looking for a cat, I understand!' Scarface's tone is getting dryer and chillier with every well-enunciated syllable he utters. He leaves no room for Gillian to explain herself. 'The Forensics are entirely at your disposal, DS Marsh, analysing blood samples and flight itineraries of various innocent individuals – innocent until proven guilty. But guilty of what, DS Marsh? We haven't got a crime yet. We have a missing person inquiry. A *discreet* missing person inquiry. Except that, hold on, not so! I've just received a second complaint about you harassing holidaymakers –'

'Sir, with all due respect, I'm only trying to interview potential witnesses before they all go back home. Somebody must have seen something, knows something. The problem is that the holidays come to an end, the holidaymakers go back home and take what they know with them. That's not a way to conduct an inquiry. I asked for a guest list. I was refused. I need your help to –'

'Quite rightly so! You had no right to ask. The consensus is Nicola Eagles has drowned. An accident. Her drowning has nothing to do with the guests at the resort.'

'We don't know that!'

'We don't know anything *otherwise*, DS Marsh!'

'I have clues to follow. If only I was given a chance –'

'No! You've done enough damage. You will be on the next flight back home. First thing tomorrow morning. You'll follow your clues from here. In your own time. And without engaging my entire manpower in your crusades! And that's final.'

Day Twelve

Gillian is lying in bed, wide awake. She is waiting for her 6 a.m. wake up call, which Hassan will no doubt execute personally. His ends have been achieved: he has got rid of Gillian and her snooping around. Without her, the resort will be back to its silky and luxurious self, without a care in the world and with well-looked after residents. Nicola Eagles and her unpalatable disappearance will be put out of mind, like a bad dream. Business as usual! Hassan must be gloating. He will make a point of seeing her off with a bottle of champagne. Gillian is fuming. How can she let it go? No one cares about Nicola Eagles and what happened to her. She is easy to forget, and that is just not on! Riotous thoughts wreak havoc on Gillian's mind. Does she have to obey orders, *stupid* orders? Her mortgage is paid off. Tara is about to fly the nest. Nothing to lose. Gillian could leave the force, something that she contemplates every now and again when things become too ridiculous to stomach. Stupid directives. Pointless, and unattainable, performance management targets. Convoluted priorities. Budget restrictions. Cotton wool wrapping, under-the-carpet sweeping, political correctness gone berserk! Gillian can't bear unfinished business, just because there is a new priority or the funds have been withdrawn. She thinks about Scarface's words: *In your own time* ... She could do it: in her own time, on her own terms. What does she have to lose? Her mortgage is paid off. Tara is about to fly the nest ...

Recycled ideas pass through her head, swirling, swelling. The telephone rings. Her wake up call.

'Yes! Thank you! I am up.'

'Gillian, Nasheed here. I told you you'd be the first one to know: we found her.'

It takes her a while to digest his words. She is leaning against the table, gathering her thoughts. 'You found her? Alive?'

'I'm afraid not.' Despite those words, Nasheed sounds triumphant. He was right: 'Local fishermen fished her out early hours of this morning, not far from Itsouru. Literally, pulled the body out of the ocean. Caucasian woman, apparently drowned. Just like we thought. We're bringing the body to Malè – I thought you may want to join us for the autopsy.'

'Thank you. I'll be on my way. We need to notify the next of kin. Her brother in Australia. He'll have to identify the body. No one else really knew her.'

'We've done that already. He's making travel arrangements.'

'So I wasn't the first one you contacted?' Gillian wishes she had been the one to break the news to Robert Eagles, just to hear his reaction, the extent of his grief, the exact words he would use. By the time he arrives in Malè, his reactions will be well-rehearsed.

Nasheed is astounded. 'You were the first one *after* the immediate family members! We thought it rather appropriate to contact the brother in the first instance.'

'How did he take the news?' she asks, for what it's worth.

'He was shocked. How else?'

The body is small and slim, naked. Whatever shreds of clothing they found on her, have been taken away and bagged. Gillian will examine them later. She wants to listen to every word the pathologist will utter. Unfortunately, the post-mortem will be conducted in Dhivehi; Nasheed will be translating. It will be a few days before Gillian will be able to read the full report in English.

Gillian's own assessment is inconclusive. The corpse is a mess. Empty eyeholes and a number of gaping cavities testify to a frenzy feeding by carnivorous fish. Hair is thin, bleached of colour. There are no signs of blood. The edges of all wounds look well-cleaned and disinfected by the salty water. She is frighteningly skinny, though bloated. Somehow Gillian has pictured her as voluptuous and fit. It is unbelievable how much life a few days in water can drain out of a body.

'How long has she been in water, did he say?' she asks Nasheed.

'His rough estimate is about four days.'

'Only?' Gillian is doing quick mental maths in her head. Nicola Eagles was last seen alive on the pier, Wednesday week, according to George. That is a whole week ago. That leaves the period between Wednesday evening and, say, Saturday unaccounted for.

'He wouldn't commit himself to anything more precise at this stage.'

'What is he saying so far?' Gillian wishes she could understand Dhivehi. Nasheed's version of what is being said may be tailored to what he thinks Gillian needs to know. She does not trust him.

'Going over the external wounds, all incurred post-mortem.'

'All?'

'Yes, the body has been in water for a few days. You'd expect it to be affected.'

Gillian watches as the pathologist makes an assured incision in the corpse, and begins the ritual of examining what is left of Nicola Eagles' internal organs. A photographer takes pictures, using a flash. The pathologist's speech is fast, but monotonous, matter-of-fact like a shipping forecast, and as indecipherable. Nasheed is passing on to Gillian scraps of irrelevant information. He stops, says something quickly to the pathologist. He sounds like he is annoyed. The pathologist replies with equal fire, and shrugs his shoulders. Nasheed frowns.

'What's happening?'

'He says there is no water in the lungs.'

'She didn't drown?'

'She was dead when the body entered water.' Nasheed carries out another rapid exchange with the pathologist.

'She was killed. How?'

He looks at Gillian as if it were all her doing. 'That's what we're trying to find out. If you just kept quiet. Let him do his job. I'll tell you as soon as he tells me!' His irritation is unabated and he isn't trying to hide it. Gillian doesn't mind. She has been vindicated. Nicola Eagles has been murdered.

The pathologist is conducting another, more thorough, external examination. His narrative has slowed down. He is attentive and detailed. More photographs are being taken: of Nicola's fingers, neck ... Nasheed translates.

'Broken nails indicate defensive wounds. Any tissue, any foreign DNA would've been destroyed by now. She's been in salt water for four days. The post-mortem injuries, especially segments of skin eaten by crabs and other scavengers, conceal most of the original wounds and discolorations. But there is the damaged windpipe and ... Hang on ...' He is listening to the pathologist who has cut across the base of the neck and buried his latex-gloved fingers in the corpse's throat. 'The spinal cord has been ... He's saying it looks like her neck has been snapped. No, hang on. She's been strangulated. Someone wrung her neck – that'd be more accurate, I think.'

'She couldn't have wrung her own neck and then dragged herself to the ocean and thrown herself in, could she, Ali?'

Nasheed realises it is a rhetorical question, and says nothing.

Within minutes Gillian is on the phone to DCI Scarfe. The circumstances have changed, Scarface accepts that. She can stay on, but the case belongs to the local police. She has to be respectful of their procedures. She must not tread on Detective Nasheed's toes. She is not to take charge. There must be no more complaints about her. 'Working together, Marsh,' Scarface preaches, 'is how you're going to go about it. Don't make enemies or they'll shut you out. Is that clear?'

'Yes, sir.'

'We want this case solved, not botched up.'

'Solving it is my priority, sir.'

'Assisting the Maldivian police in solving it – that is your

146

priority,' he corrects her.

'We have a common purpose, sir, but I do wish they shared *everything* with me. I have a feeling they're keeping vital information away from me. They don't want this case to reflect badly on their tourism industry. It's a big tax-earner here. An example: I've asked for a list of guests at Itsouru. It's been refused on the grounds of guest privacy –'

'The nature of your inquiries has changed. I'm sure the resort management will co-operate from now on. I'll see to it.'

Gillian doesn't doubt Scarfe's power of persuasion. He will make a case for her. Doors will start opening. 'Thank you, sir.'

'Incidentally, about that woman you're trying to track down in London – Amy Gray-Ludlow. No sign of her. Webber has been around the flat. It doesn't look like she's been back. The neighbours have not seen her, or the other one – her *partner* – in over two weeks. But they're due to be back in the early hours of the morning.'

'They *were* due, but they had a row. Amy left a few days earlier – that's according to Sarah Ludlow-Gray. The thing is, Amy left about the same time Nicola Eagles disappeared. That makes Amy a material witness. Possibly the last person to have seen Nicola Eagles alive ... Or, rather, one of the two people: her and Sarah. I think their bust-up was about Nicola Eagles. Pretty ugly, according to witnesses. I saw Sarah off yesterday. She's on her way home. She wasn't very co-operative when I spoke to her before she left. If nothing else, at least she must be interviewed again. Until we find Amy.'

'I see ... I'm assigning DC Webber to this case. He'll be reporting directly to me. Both of you will be reporting directly to me.'

A desk has been allocated to Gillian Marsh. The desk comes with its own, fully enclosed office, tiny as a walnut shell, but complete with all the mod cons a senior investigating officer may ask for. It is duly isolated from the rest of the open-plan area where the Mali detectives are working on the case. Obligingly, Gillian has been included in the briefing, which for her benefit, has been conducted in English by the officer in charge, Ali Nasheed. Gillian has shared her line-up of suspects and the few lines of inquiry she is working on. Going by the raised eyebrows and a number of unabashed yawns, she is not going to be taken seriously by this exclusively male investigating team. Nonetheless, to keep her occupied and out of the way, she has been given the desk and – to her pleasant surprise – the Itsouru Resort guest list she has been asking for.

And there, on that list, the name *Mikhail Lakso* strikes her. It is in fact, *Mikhail and Agaata Lakso*, Finnish nationals. They had been staying in Chalet 41, next door to Nicola's, but they left the island on Wednesday morning – Nicola was last seen alive that Wednesday evening. Oddly, they checked out three days before they were due to leave. Gillian cross-references their address and telephone number in Finland with the scribbles on the back of Nicola's itinerary – they match. It is time Gillian made an acquaintance of the man who possibly may answer to the name of Count Karenin.

The telephone hardly rings once before it is picked up and a deep male voice says curtly, 'Lakso.'

Gillian establishes quickly that the man can speak English. She introduces herself, gives her rank and gets straight to the point: 'You were staying on Itsouru Island, Chalet 41?'

'Yes, we were. What about it?' His voice is calm, almost disinterested. Perhaps the Finns are made that way: impassionate. Or perhaps he is making a deliberate effort to control his emotions.

'Miss Nicola Eagles was staying in the chalet next door to yours – Chalet 42. An English female, brown hair, average build, early forties … Might you have met her?'

'I'm sure … Why are you asking me about her?' The steel in his voice is hardening. He is beginning to answer questions with questions of his own – not a good sign.

'I've been investigating Miss Eagles' disappearance. She failed to arrive home from her holiday. She was due to be back five days ago. I'm contacting everyone who may have come in contact with her, anyone who may shed some light on her

148

disappearance.'

'I see. I don't know how I can help you.' Calm and collected. No exclamations of surprise or concern. And yet, Gillian is sure, he is Count Karenin.

'You could help me by telling me about the nature of your relationship with Miss Eagles.'

'Ha, *relationship*!' he laughs, but it is a forced merriment, fallacious. 'I wouldn't go that far. We knew each other –'

'You've been seen together.'

'We have? Well yes, I struck up an acquaintance with Nicola, if that's what you call it?' His English becomes more accented, heavier. Perhaps there is a hint of emotion in it. Gillian would swear it's a Russian accent. As little as she knows about accents, Russian is unmistakable. The waiter in that French restaurant on Itsouru was of the same opinion. What did he say? *In ze last few years I am 'earing enough Russian speak to be sure, madam.*

'Mr Lakso, if it is your wife you're worried about, let me assure you she doesn't need to be told. I'm merely investigating –'

'My wife is dead.' Steel returns to his tone. 'I'm not worried about her. My mother, on the other hand, doesn't mind. Yes, my mother. We both made good friends with Nicola.'

Mother! Oops! 'I'm sorry, sir. I didn't mean to imply anything untoward. I'm sorry about your wife.'

'My wife's been dead for years. She has nothing to do with this.'

'I'm sorry I'm intruding on you this way, but Miss Eagles has been seen in your company and now she's missing. I'm just trying to establish her moves on the island ...'

'Yes, I understand. I don't mean to be evasive. I just don't see how my ... *liaison* ... with Nicola can help you. But yes, we became very friendly. I took her out to dinner. She twisted her ankle, you see, and my mother and I took care of her. We became close, yes, but it came to an end and that's all I can tell you.'

'You left your address and telephone number with her? You

intended to stay in touch, I take it?'

'She asked for it. I didn't see why not.'

'Has she contacted you?'

'No.'

'One last question: why did you cut your stay short? It just so happens that you left within twenty-four hours of Miss Eagles going missing. Three days before you were due to depart.'

Another false chuckle. 'Ah! I would have stayed, but my mother – she isn't used to the heat. Her heart couldn't take it. She complained of chest tightness in the morning. She never complains. That got me worried. I thought about it, but I had no choice – we left that same day. The trip was her birthday treat and she wasn't enjoying herself, not being well ... I would have loved to stay. Nicola ...' his deep voice softens, 'We did have a good time and yes, we were planning to stay in touch. I ... She's a lovely lady.'

'Did she seem fine to you? Happy?'

'Yes,' he says slowly, 'very happy.'

'So you don't think she would've done anything –'

'Like suicide?' He laughs, and this time it is genuine. 'No, definitely not. We had a ... good time together. She was ... alive! I thought ... I like her a lot. She will be fine.'

'You were seen swimming together.'

'Snorkelling, yes.'

'Would you say she was a good swimmer?'

'Passable. She's all right. Anyway, the buoyancy in that ocean is amazing, and I was looking after her ...' he pauses. After a short silence, he adds, 'I hope you find her soon, alive and well. On my part, if I hear from her, I'll let you know.'

There is confidence in his tone and Gillian hates to break it to him, but ...

'I'm afraid you won't be hearing from her. We found her body this morning.'

'Nicola's dead?' It is not the same voice. It does not belong to the same man. It is ghostly, crumpled and weak. It is an old man's voice.

'I'm sorry.'

'She was killed.' This isn't a question – it's a statement of fact.

Nevertheless, Gillian answers, 'We believe she was strangled.'

'How long? How long has she been dead?'

'About four days. I need to find out what happened between the day she disappeared and the day she was killed. Where was she?'

'I can't tell you that. I don't know.'

He puts the phone down abruptly and without another word. Gillian knows it's the shock. He wasn't surprised to hear about Nicola Eagles' disappearance – he wasn't concerned, as if it was perfectly normal for a woman to go off the radar for a while – but he is shocked to hear she is dead. Gillian ponders that for a minute. If you're fond of someone – and he is fond of Nicola, that much is obvious from his fragmented admissions – you would be worried if they went missing. You would try to contact them. Does he have Nicola's number? He left his with her – did he ask for hers in return? If so, would he not try to call her? And yet Nicola's telephone has remained ominously silent throughout. No one ever called her. That, in itself, means little as far as Nicola Eagles is concerned. No one seems to be calling her whether or not she is available to take the call. Perhaps Mikhail Lakso simply follows the trend: Nicola was just a brief holiday encounter and he doesn't have the desire to keep in touch with her. It is not to say that her death didn't shock him, but it would have come as a shock to any half-decent human being who happens to have known her. So there may be nothing else to this line of enquiry. After all, Lakso and his mother had left the island days before Nicola was killed. And what motive would they have to kill her? And then, against all logic, leave their address and telephone number behind? Despite her misgivings, Gillian is reluctant to eliminate Lakso from her investigation. Something is not right. Something is niggling at the back of her mind: something she can't see yet.

Day Thirteen

Robert Eagles steps off the plane looking tired and dishevelled. His eyes are bloodshot and his breath smells of alcohol. He isn't the fit and lean man with a boyish grin and sun-tanned face that peers from his Facebook photos. He looks much older than that. It may be the merciless Australian sun that has drained away his youthful looks; it may be the hardships he has encountered in the New World. Gillian observes his demeanour with interest. He strikes her as a man on the edge.

He shakes hands with both Nasheed and Gillian. His grip is firm and business-like. In the car he asks if they have any clues about what happened to his sister. *My sister*, he says – he does not use her actual name. It sounds impersonal, makes one wonder whether he remembers *his sister's* name.

'We know she didn't drown,' Nasheed tells him what they know didn't happen to Nicola.

'So how did she die?' Mr Eagles demands impatiently.

'Strangulation. Her neck was broken. All we can say is that it wasn't an accident.'

'Who would've done that to her?'

'We wondered if you could help us with that,' Gillian interjects.

'Me?' he sounds defensive, as if an allegation has been made against him personally.

'Do you know if your sister had any enemies, anyone who would wish her ill?'

'No. I can't imagine my sister having enemies. She was always so ... harmless. But then I haven't seen her in seven years. I don't know what sort of people she mingles with. I don't remember her having any friends – never mind enemies –

153

back in the days when we went to school in Maidenhead. She … Nicola,' her name brings a wince to his face. 'My sister has always been plain shy – quiet as a mouse. She'd never stick her head out. In fact, I was surprised to learn she'd gone on a holiday abroad. When you told me on the phone,' he looks at Gillian, his forehead deeply furrowed. 'Such an extravagance! It's not Nicola's style.'

'It was on her Facebook.'

'I didn't know. I didn't even know she was on Facebook.'

'You are her Facebook friend! Surely you knew!' Nasheed sounds exasperated. Until now Gillian didn't realise he had gone as far as trudging through Nicola's Facebook. Maybe she has underestimated him. Maybe he's been carrying out his own background checks – on the quiet and without causing any backlash from Itsouru's management, unlike Gillian. Clever man, Ali Nasheed! It may pay to listen to what he has to say. It will certainly pay to share intelligence with him.

She says, 'And on top of that you were in Colombo the day before your sister went missing, that'd be Tuesday, 3rd February. What were you doing there?'

Robert stares hard at her, his bloodshot eyes bulging with indignation, 'Colombo is a long way from here … Are you trying to imply I had something to do with my sister's disappearance?'

'I only asked you a simple question. It was probably a pure coincidence – you in Colombo, your sister in the Maldives – but it is my job to ask questions.' She tries to sound non-confrontational, but she won't let him off the hook. 'So I'm asking: what brought you to Colombo last Tuesday?'

'Business. I travel for work. I was on business in Hong Kong, flying home via Colombo. It's cheaper that way. Does that answer your question?'

'It's just that when you travelled to Hong Kong, you took a direct flight there, so why, on your way back –'

'I told you – it was cheaper!' His face is flushed red. Is it guilt or indignation? 'I resent your insinuations! What are you implying?! I might not have been particularly close with my sister, but – for God's sake – I wouldn't have had anything to do with her death! Why the hell would I! She was *my sister!* And now she's dead, and I blame myself enough – without your bloody help – for not seeing it coming!'

'I'm sorry if I come across as insensitive –'

'You bloody well do!' His fists are closed, white-knuckled, and Gillian can almost smell his fury. If he could, he would hit her. She wonders what brought on all this anger. Are her questions too close to the truth? Did she hit a nerve? She won't let go. She is known to be the pitbull of interrogation – once she got her teeth into something, she just couldn't let go …

'Your sister was wealthy. I understand that as her next of kin you are her only heir. You'd be getting quite a handsome inheritance … Correct me if I'm wrong, but my sources tell me you're in a spot of financial bother at the moment?'

'I can't believe this!' Looking aloofly over Gillian's shoulder, Eagles is speaking to Nasheed. He has decided to disregard her, thus showing his righteous superiority. 'I didn't come here – all this way – to be insulted! You asked me to identify my sister's body, that's all. You didn't say I'd be bloody well interrogated! And anyway, who the hell is in charge here, you or her?'

Nasheed fixes Gillian with a firm stare. There is a muscle in his jaw that twitches as he clenches his teeth. 'I do apologise, Mr Eagles. It is a difficult time for you and your family, and we are grateful for your co-operation. I am the officer in charge. DS Marsh is working with my team.'

'So I don't have to answer her offensive questions, then?'

'You do, but I am sure DS Marsh will make an effort, from now on, to take the pressure off you and demonstrate a more sensitive approach – considering your loss.' Another meaningful glance at Gillian, who does not feel in the least contrite. She is suspicious of Robert Eagles: he had a motive, very likely an opportunity, and he doesn't appear much grief-stricken.

A grimace in his face could mean a lot of different things. He is led into the mortuary and waits for his sister's body to be rolled out of the freezer. When he sees the body is covered, he looks relieved.

'Are you ready?' Nasheed asks. 'Bear in mind the body has undergone some level of decomposition and there are deformities and tissue damage.'

'I'm ready.'

Gillian says nothing but watches his every reaction. He is standing stiff-upright, head tilted back, lips convoluted – bracing himself for what is to come. When the body bag is unzipped, he retches and, with his hand over his mouth, backs away. He is mortified, but who wouldn't be? The condition the body is in is awful. She passes him a paper tissue. 'Are you all right?'

'I didn't expect it to be ...' he starts but fails to finish the sentence.

'Is this your sister?'

Holding the tissue to his mouth, he returns to take a proper look. His nostrils are flaring, his breathing shallow and rapid. It is the shock of it. *He didn't expect it to be so gory* – Gillian finishes the sentence for him in her head. What did he expect? Did he order his sister's killing? Is this what he had in mind? His reactions seem to deny that, but this isn't a pretty sight. *Not what he expected* ...

'This isn't my sister.' He has now overcome the initial convulsion and is frowning with a strange, puzzled look in his eye.

'She doesn't look like she used to look –' Nasheed tries to tell him.

'No, it isn't Nicola.' Does Gillian detect a hint of disappointment in his voice? It most certainly isn't relief. 'No, it isn't her! Bloody hell! Can you turn her head? To the right?'

The pathologist does as he asks. With the tissue still firmly pressed against his mouth, Eagles bends over and examines an area just behind the ear. 'No. There should be a birthmark behind the left ear. You couldn't miss it. It's not her!'

Confused, Nasheed gapes at the pathologist, 'Could it be

bleached out by the salt water?'

The pathologist shakes his head, speaking in Dhivehi. Gillian does not understand a word, but the body language is clear: no, it couldn't be.

'Are you sure?' she demands from Eagles. 'Take a good look, please.'

His glance towards her is contemptuous. 'I am bloody sure. She should have a birthmark, just like this one,' he turns his head and displays a blood-brown patch, the size of a five-pence coin on his neck. 'Hers is higher, just behind the ear, but very similar to mine. We both have it. Runs in the family.'

Gillian and Nasheed exchange puzzled glances. The pathologist wheels the body back into the fridge as Eagles walks away, towards the exit door. He discards the tissue paper in the corridor outside with disgust as if it were contaminated with some deadly virus. It lands on the floor. He is back to his angry look.

'You've got the wrong woman! How did you get the wrong woman?'

It is a bizarre question to which neither Nasheed nor Gillian can offer an answer.

'You brought me all the way here – for nothing! I hope someone's going to reimburse me for the flight! What a bloody waste of time! And money!' he is raving, stomping down the corridor, his boots resonating on the stone-tiled floor.

'We had every reason to believe it was your sister,' Nasheed manages to say weakly. He himself looks bewildered – a rabbit in headlights.

'You put me through all this shit – for nothing!'

Gillian is not prepared to take this lying down. She says, 'It isn't *nothing*, Mr Eagles. Someone is dead, lying there. Your sister is still missing.'

'That someone is not my sister! Find her. Find her body, be sure it's her – then call me!'

Callous twat! Gillian is livid. He sounds like he is frustrated, like he was hoping to see his dead sister's body dispatched neatly and tidily out of this world, and all he got was someone else. Was there a mistake? 'We would still like to talk to you, Mr Eagles,' Gillian tells him. That stops him in his tracks. He glares at her, points a finger in her face. The finger is trembling; his face is flushed red just like it was when he first lost his temper.

'No! I'm not talking to you! I'm leaving on the next flight out. Unless you want to arrest me!' He turns to Nasheed. 'Am I under arrest?'

Nasheed shakes his head. 'You're free to go, Mr Eagles. Thank you for your co-operation. And I am truly sorry about the misunderstanding.'

They are sitting over a curry in a small takeaway outlet in the heart of Malè. It is a district full of miniature eateries and stalls lined up along the streets. Pungent spice aromas overwhelm the senses. Gillian's lips are puckered as she is musing over the latest development. She had to let Eagles go, which went against her every instinct.

She says, 'Did you notice how disappointed he was?'

Nasheed stares at her, baffled.

'Oh, come on, Nasheed! You must've seen it too! He looked disappointed – as if he was hoping to find his sister's dead body, as if he was *counting on it*.'

'No, not really. I thought he was distraught.'

Men simply cannot read men, Gillian is forced to conclude. Body language is lost on them. Only women can decipher the nuances of human behaviour. That is why women rear children, bring secrets to light and expose liars, who happen invariably to be men. Men like Robert Eagles. She insists on her diagnosis. 'He was furious, not distraught.'

'Who can tell? He was unnerved. I'd say you've done most of the unnerving.' He says that calmly, but not without a touch of sarcasm, and attacks his curry with chop sticks, displaying uncanny dexterity. Gillian prefers a fork.

'You see, I've got this theory.' Undeterred by the criticism, Gillian goes on, 'He was hoping to find his sister dead. He had ordered her killing when he was in Colombo. His handyman may have got the wrong woman. Remember what he said? He said: *How did you get the wrong woman?* Was he speaking to us, or ...' She raises her eyebrows, a cue for Nasheed to finish the sentence.

He does not. 'That is too far-fetched. We haven't got anything to back it up.'

'We have!' Gillian slams her small but perfectly lethal fist on the table. She points up one finger, 'One: motive. He's in financial trouble. He needs money. Nicola Eagles was rich and single, with him as the closest relative standing to inherit everything –'

'You did raise it with him, but that's just speculation.'

'But it got him on edge. What does that tell you?'

'He didn't appreciate us digging into his private affairs?' Nasheed raises his brows pointedly.

'And what on earth was he doing in Colombo! Why was he there? What was he up to? Why did he change his flight plans? Doesn't that puzzle you at all?'

'It was cheaper? He said that. It makes sense.'

'Does it really? If his employer pays for his flights, which I imagine they do, why would he care to take a cheaper flight – re-schedule his itinerary out of the blue? Why?'

Nasheed downs a cup of strong, syrupy coffee, and shrugs his shoulders. 'Don't know.'

'You shouldn't have let him go.'

'I had nothing on him to hold him. Subject closed.' He gets up. 'Now I have to find out whose body I have on my hands. I imagine *you* will be going back to the UK.'

Gillian is not finished here. She still has a missing person to find, a person who went missing here, in this country. Increasingly though, she is beginning to think that further clues will have to be found back home. Malè authorities seem to share that sentiment. She keeps stumbling on not-too-subtle clues to that effect left, right and centre. A message was given to her by a tight-lipped constable when she entered the building this afternoon: her little desk in her little executive office is to

159

be vacated. It has been re-assigned to Detective Nasheed. He has got an important job to do: a mission impossible to find out whose body he holds in the mortuary. Then a wild-goose chase for the killer. Stabbing in the dark! Gillian screams inwardly. This is *not* the way to go about it! Nasheed has got the wrong end of the stick! Gillian is convinced that all roads in this investigation lead back to Nicola Eagles' disappearance. That is the starting point. Once she has found out where the woman is and why she disappeared, she will know whose body is sitting on ice in the mortuary, and she might even know who the killer is. Her sixth sense tells her Nicola Eagles has all along been the intended victim. Gillian is rarely wrong – and she never admits it even if she is. She will have to prove them all wrong!

She sifts, once again, through the evidence. The Nicola Eagles evidence box is under her desk, with its contents strewn on the floor and the desk: the laptop open on Nicola's Facebook page boasting a kaleidoscope of photographs with lush exotic landscapes, and one with the foreign – Russian? – man Nicola nicknamed Count Karenin; her clothes – baggy, unassuming, spinster's garments with the allure of a retired church cleaner; books, mainly in Russian, including *Anna Karenina* from where, potentially, Count Karenin had sprung; passport showing no stamps other than the single one she received at the Malè Immigration desk; her crumpled itinerary with Lakso's details on the back; mobile phone that never rings … Somewhere amongst this inconsequential clutter sits an answer. Something happened to her, and it wasn't suicide. Earlier in the morning an old-fashioned fax has arrived, confirming that there was a DNA match with the traces of blood on the bed sheets found in Chalet 42. Nicola Eagles' blood. If she died in that chalet, where is her body now? And consequently – whose body is lying in the mortuary?

Webber's phone call brings Gillian back down to Earth. 'What have you got for me?' she asks unceremoniously.

'Oh! And hello to you too, ma'am. How was your holiday, Mark? Very good, thank you, ma'am. I enjoyed it, and so did my family … It saved my marriage. By the way, wife sends her regards. But let's get down to business, shall we?' Webber is a close friend. He knows Gillian's brusqueness, especially when she is head-on on a case, oblivious to the world around her, downright rude and socially inept. Webber is used to it. He doesn't mind, but that doesn't stop him from pointing it out to her. That's what friends are for, an idea Gillian finds difficult to embrace.

'Yes, let's get on with it. I'm busy. They're trying to get rid of me here,' she replies.

'Why am I not surprised?' Webber chuckles.

'What have you got, then? I need something, Mark!'

'Amy Gray-Ludlow is now officially a missing person.'

Gillian is hanging on every word. She has been vindicated. She is on the right track. This is exactly what she wants to hear. Could Amy be the dead body in the mortuary? 'You've no idea how vital this is!'

'The fact that you now have two missing women?'

'One missing, one found – dead. I bet you the dead one is Amy. But go on, tell me. Tell me everything!'

'Scarface sent me camping on their doorstep until Sarah Ludlow-Gray arrived. It was just after midnight. By the way, it's 2 a.m. now. Hope it's a convenient time for you?' he snorts, and continues as his complaint elicits no apology from Gillian. 'To cut a long story short, we looked around the flat – no sign Amy had been there. Bed not slept in. No notes. No clothes or personal items removed. Sarah intimated they had broken up and Amy should've come back for her things, but she didn't. That got the woman worried and she decided to report her missing. We also tried calling Amy on her mobile, but no answer. Gone without a trace!'

'We may have her here,' Gillian tells Webber matter-of-factly.

'Oh? How?'

'In the mortuary. I told you, didn't I? Weren't you listening?'

'You think that's Amy's body you've got there? Scarface said it was Nicola Eagles'!'

'Yes, that was the original idea, but her brother is adamant it isn't her.'

'But it can't be Amy. Riley checked with Heathrow. Amy Gray-Ludlow did travel back to the UK. She arrived five days ago, on Saturday, 7th, except that she has never made it to the flat. She vanished on her way between the airport and the flat.'

'Are we sure it was Amy who took that flight to the UK?'

'Her passport was used, pretty sure.'

'What if someone else used it? Another woman? Someone like ... Nicola Eagles?' Gillian pauses for effect, but Webber is too slow for her liking to pick up the cue. She has to guide him by the hand, 'My theory is Nicola Eagles is hiding. She knows someone's out to get her. She may have witnessed Amy's death and she knows it was meant for her. I'm almost positive we have a case of mistaken identity here. It's her brother –'

'Whose brother?'

'Nicola's. He wanted her dead; things went wrong. All I need is proof. Listen, Mark, get Jon Riley to check CCTV cameras at Heathrow. Let's see if the woman who arrived in London on Amy's passport was really Amy.'

Gillian is chuffed to bits. She can almost taste Robert Eagles' blood. He is her prime suspect. He had a hand in his sister's disappearance – that much she is sure of! Who else could be after her? She is a non-entity! By his own declaration, she has no enemies. No one but him could benefit from her death. And only a paid killer could have possibly got the wrong woman. *That's how, Mr Eagles, we got the wrong woman!* Gillian knows she has the right *man* though. All she needs is a scrap of evidence, something to hang on to, something to stop Eagles from fleeing back to Australia. His flight is leaving tonight, in less than eight hours.

Australia! That reminds her – she hasn't spoken to Tara in nearly two days. How easily that girl slips under the radar! Gillian must catch her before she wanders off again into the sunset. Tara must have already slept off the jetlag and be loitering in the dodgy alleyways of Melbourne. How much

Gillian wishes that whole globe-trotting adventure was over and she had Tara in one place under her watchful eye! It used to be such a luxury knowing Tara was somewhere between the school and home, fending for herself in the kitchen or at a friend's house, and not counting the days since she spoke to her last!

At least the child answers the phone on the first ring. 'Mum! Well remembered!' she shouts into the receiver, her voice untypically loud and excited, 'I thought I'd better tell you before you find out for yourself through other channels!'

Gillian's blood runs cold. 'Tell me what?'

'I am in a *relationship*, with Charlie. Remember Charlie?'

'You mean you're having unprotected sex with a total stranger?!'

'MUM!' The jolly spark vanishes from Tara's voice. She now sounds indignant, and soon, Gillian knows, the girl will turn petulant, like she usually does whenever Gillian hits the wrong note with her. 'We are in *love*. The s-e-x thing is only secondary. But ... it's great!'

Gillian groans.

'And it *is* protected!'

'You're only eighteen!'

'How old were you?'

'It's not about me!'

'Exactly! It's about me! I'm happy, Mum!' Twinkle returns to Tara's tone. 'Be happy for me!'

'But you hardly know him! What do you know about him? Do you even know his full name? I doubt it.'

'I know Charlie as much as I need to know him. He's perfect for me. We just ... we just click.'

'God, give me strength ... He's a total stranger, you silly girl!'

Another hollow dip to Tara's voice comes as a warning. 'Don't call me silly, Mother. Wasn't Dad a total stranger when you two met for the first time? People are always strangers when they first meet, and fall in love.'

Who can argue with that, Gillian ponders philosophically while her heart is bounding about her ribcage and her hands are sweating on the phone handset. 'Come home first. Get to know him better –'

'How much better than *this* can I get to know him? Don't be daft, Mum! Anyway, Charlie is coming with me to South Africa. I want him to meet Dad, then obviously you'll get your chance to meet him when we're back home.'

'Does your father know?' It is a sinking feeling, one that frequently piques Gillian, when she finds out that everyone else knows everything about her daughter ahead of her.

'Course he does. He's expecting us.'

'What can I say? You won't listen to whatever I have to say …' Gillian is slowly, but surely, descending into self-pity.

'You can say hi to Charlie! He's right here. Do you want to say hi?'

'Well …' It seems like a test – a test of Gillian's tolerance. She doesn't know what she is to say to pass the test. She takes the risk of saying, 'All right then. '

'Hello, Mrs Marsh,' says a youthful, almost boyish voice, hardly broken it seems to Gillian, fragile and quivering. The boy must be more petrified than she is.

'Hello, Charles,' she says in the lordly manner of someone who is in control. Instantly, her detective's persona kicks in. 'Do you have a surname?'

'Yeah, I do: Outhwaite.'

'And how old would you be, Mr Outhwaite?'

Before he has a chance to respond the phone appears to be wrestled out of his hand. There is a commotion, an outburst of laughter. Tara comes on: 'That'll do, Mum!'

'I don't even know what he looks like,' Gillian tries again.

'You need a mugshot, do you? OK, I feel generous today. I will put the phone down and send you our selfie. Ta-ra for now!' Click. Gone.

The selfie arrives within seconds. Next to the beaming Tara a young person is attempting a smile – unsuccessfully. He has a long blond fringe and a rather tousled feel to his hair. His face is long, slim. That's all. Gillian can't surmise anything else about him because he is wearing sunglasses that obscure his eyes. From his general scruffiness Gillian concludes that he couldn't look after himself, let along Tara. He can't be older than her either. At least he is not a middle-aged, slimy ogre with designs on unsuspecting young girls. And at least they're having protected sex. The thought of her daughter having sex physically chokes Gillian. She coughs and retches for a few minutes. It feels like it is her innocence that is being snapped in half.

It may be a blessing that she is prevented from dwelling on the matter any further and getting herself into a state – the phone rings. It is Jon. Gillian does a quick time conversion in her head. She has become quite proficient at that. It is the small hour of 6 a.m. in Sexton's Canning.

'Jon! That was quick! Thanks!' She is convinced he is calling with information about the identity of the person who travelled to Heathrow on Amy's passport. The only logical possibility, a possibility that fits Gillian's theory, is that it was Nicola. And it is a well-known fact that Gillian is rarely wrong: tenacity of a pitbull, intuition of a gypsy. She has to be right! 'It was Nicola Eagles, wasn't it?'

'No, it was Robert Eagles. I was right!' Jon sounds paralytic with triumph. Only this sort of personal triumph would get him out of bed this early. 'Robert bloody Eagles!'

Gillian is confused, 'Robert Eagles travelled to the UK on Amy Gray-Ludlow's passport? That's taking it a bit too far, even for you, Jon.'

'I don't know what's you're on about. Leave Amy Gray-Ludlow's passport out of it.'

'But I asked Webber! Didn't he ask you to go over the CCTV footage from Heathrow?'

'I haven't seen Mark.'

'I've only just spoken to him.'

'Well, I haven't – if that's OK with you! He's probably in bed with his wife while I'm working my arse off here for you!' Jon sounds slightly hurt. Gillian offers no consolation for his bleeding ego. Why is he so competitive against Webber? Didn't

165

she ask the two of them to work together? At least, Jon is working on something. He recovers and asks briskly, 'Can I get to the point now? I really want to hit the sack! I've spent the whole night watching paint dry at Colombo Airport.'

'Be my guest,' Gillian encourages him.

'Right … They sent the CCTV video files last night. I've been at it all night, but I found him! There he was – Bobby Eagles!'

Gillian is beginning to catch up. 'Great! So what was he up to?'

'Like I told you, Bobby is up to his eyeholes in shit! I'm emailing you the footage where he's caught on camera handing a suitcase full of money to a dodgy looking character. Big, nasty bloke! They shake hands. Bobby walks away with a smile, the nasty bloke walks away with a suitcase. It's all on camera. Gotcha!'

Robert Eagles had been dragged from the airport kicking and screaming, less than an hour before his plane was due to leave. He is quiet now, looking a bit shifty, but even more tired than when he arrived in the morning. It will be easy to break him. A duty solicitor, a smooth but young and, Gillian hopes, inexperienced buffoon, is sitting next to his client, with a reassuring black suitcase resting on the table in front of him. They are both watching the CCTV footage from Colombo, featuring the mysterious exchange between Eagles and the *nasty bloke*.

'Would you like to tell us, Mr Eagles, what exactly is going on there?' Gillian asks.

'No comment.'

'Can I put it to you that you travelled through Colombo in order to meet that man? It doesn't look like a chance encounter. Do you agree?'

'No comment.'

'What is in the suitcase, Mr Eagles?'

'No comment.'

'Who is that man?'

'No –'

'No comment, I know. We will find out his identity, Mr Eagles and will ask him the same questions. You see, it seems to me that you're paying that man for something. There is money – cash – in the suitcase. Am I right? Are you paying him to kill your sister?'

Eagles' eyes goggle out. He bangs his fist on the table. 'This is preposterous! I wouldn't hurt my sister. That,' he points to the laptop screen frozen on the act of exchange captured by the airport camera, 'that has nothing to do with my sister's disappearance!'

'Then you must tell us what that is to do with so that we can make up our own minds about it.'

The solicitor intervenes, 'The event at the airport is irrelevant to your investigation. You do not have evidence to the contrary.'

Gillian's eyes are fixed on Eagles. She hardly acknowledges the buffoon's comment. 'Mr Eagles, unless we know what's in that suitcase and why you handed it to that man, we won't be able to eliminate you from our inquiries. At face value, it appears that you are paying someone for something that you wish to keep secret. Something illegal? That's the most plausible explanation, don't you think? You have gone out of your way to carry out this exchange in secret. If, indeed, it is irrelevant to our inquiries, then please tell us what it pertains to.'

'No comment.'

'My theory is this: you changed your flight arrangements upon learning about your sister staying in the Maldives. You travelled to Colombo and met a man to whom you made a cash payment in return for him abducting and possibly killing your sister. Thus the secrecy. The motive was to secure inheritance which you desperately need, considering your current financial circumstances –'

'Where would I get the money from, then? If I'm broke, where would I get the money?'

'There are ways of securing a short-term loan, especially

when you have the expectation of an imminent windfall which your sister's death would generate.' Gillian is crossing her fingers. He is beginning to engage. He is beginning to fight back and that is only a step away from slipping on the first lie.

'You're wrong. It isn't even my sister you've got there. For God's sake, I wouldn't kill my own sister!' He clasps his hand on his mouth just as a sob escapes him. Belated contrition, Gillian thinks.

'Yes, we've got a different female in the mortuary. Your assassin got the wrong person. Your sister may still be alive. You still have a chance to put it right.'

'I didn't do anything to hurt my sister!'

'Then what is happening on that tape, Mr Eagles?'

'It's nothing to do with her!'

'That just won't do. You need to give us a full explanation. As it stands, with you remaining silent, we have grounds to remand you in custody while we're investigating further. You can help us, of course, and help yourself, but that is up to you.'

Eagles leans towards his lawyer. He is gazing at him, looking for reassurance or confirmation. The lawyer nods almost imperceptibly, then exhales heavily and says, 'My client will co-operate to help you eliminate him from your inquiries, but as the information he will offer may incriminate him we would like to ask for your assurance –'

Gillian does not do deals – out of principle. Deals tend to hold one to ransom. They tie one's hands. She has burned herself in the past. She won't go there. 'Just tell us, Mr Eagles. I am only interested in finding your sister! Don't waste my time!'

Eagles bites his inner cheek. His lips twist. He is clearly ashamed, but at the same time, he seems perversely relieved to be able to say it.

'Black market software, fake user licences – that's what's in the suitcase. I just wanted – had to – supplement my income. It's the first time I did it. The company I work for …' His voice breaks. He is beginning to realise the extent of troubles to come. 'I was put in touch with that bloke. He is a Sri Lankan. A businessman. Specialises in internet piracy. I made several illegal copies of the software, faked licences, all that ... They paid me by direct transfer to an account I set up in Hong Kong under an assumed identity. So there, you have it – nothing to do with my sister.'

Day Twenty-three

What woke her up the first time was the sound of footsteps above. Several heavy steps and male voices, talking. It was in broken English but friendly enough, and Nicola was able to pick up a few isolated words. They did not make sense, but there was something calming and reassuring about them. She surveyed the room. It was semi-dark, tiny and woody. It smelled of seaweed and something stale and alcoholic, perhaps beer. The bed, although narrow, was comfortable, with the white sheets beneath her feeling silky and smooth – good-quality sheets. She ran her hand over them. Again it was reassuring to know her creature comforts had been seen to. But her hand felt very heavy. She could just about slide it across the bed, but would be hard pushed to lift it. Her fingers felt numb and swollen. She was lying on her back. Her body was like a dead weight and she knew she wouldn't be able to get up or even roll over to one side. She was sprawled – a jellyfish on a bed of silk.

She turned her head. It felt infinitely huge and was throbbing viciously. Her eyes stung when she tried to peer out of the window. There was one solitary window in the room: a round one. Outside it was dusk. Or dawn. Nicola couldn't tell what time or even what day it was. Water was lapping lazily against the window and the wall. She could see the expanding ocean beyond the window: dark but not black. It was indistinct and bleary. She wasn't sure if it was her eyes or the dusk that made everything fuzzy and out of focus. But she was sure that she was on a boat or a ship. It didn't quite wobble like a small boat would, but it shifted ever so slightly from side to side, and creaked and the waves clapped against it, echoing hollowly.

She smiled to herself. Was it Mishka who had brought her

here? It had to be him. It was his big surprise for her. Strangely, she couldn't remember how they got here. Her head was spinning, a familiar reaction: she must have had too much to drink last night. Her fingertips massaged the silkiness beneath them. It was a very sensual sensation, almost erotic. Tiny electric currents travelled from her fingertips to her stomach. Butterflies. Yearning. This was still a new, uncharted territory for Nicola. She had been sexually awakened and now she was luxuriating in those thrilling new sensations. Better late than never, she kept smiling at her thoughts. Then she sobered up. She remembered the cruel joke Mishka played on her – made her believe it was over! It was as though the world had ended! Never again!

Her lips felt crusty. She ran her tongue over them. Water, she needed a drink. Where was Mishka?

'Water,' she tried to call out, but it came out as a groan. No one responded.

The voices outside receded. So did the steps. She heard a motor being started. Like a shot a speed boat swerved in a sharp arch past the round window. It had a blue strip across and Nicola recognised the word POLICE printed on the side. As the boat zoomed into the distance, a wave left in its wake rammed into Nicola's little window. It was at the same time that she heard a scream.

There was shouting. This time it was a woman's voice: agitated, high-pitched. Softer than before footsteps rang on the deck above, followed by heavier ones. It seemed like a chase. The woman was screaming. Her words were indecipherable. She sounded foreign, or perhaps her emotional state distorted her words. Perhaps there were no words, only that harrowing scream. Then a thud, and a silence.

Something was being dragged across the deck. Something was knocked over. Someone cursed. Finally a splash. It was very dark by then, but Nicola did register a heavy load plummeting into the water outside her window. Despite her exhaustion, she managed to stagger up to the window to look closely.

It was a person. At first, she – for it had to be a woman as she was wearing a stripy dress, ballooning with water – floated, but slowly she began sinking. No resistance was coming from her as she went under. She wasn't trying to swim. She most certainly was dead. Nicola screamed.

Crawling into the corner of her small cabin, she tried to stifle the scream and ended up whimpering like a baby. The door to her room, which she had not seen before as it was behind the narrow bed, swung open. At first, it was a square shadow of a person, but quickly he drew close to her. His face levelled with hers. He put his finger on his lips and told her to shush. Nicola stopped screaming. She recognised the man: his thickset frame, shaved head, heavy eyelids, Asiatic features. He was the man to whom she had opened her door, who had grabbed her by the arm, painfully bending it and holding it against her back, and stabbed her with a syringe. It had not been Mishka. It had been this man.

'Shh,' he hissed. 'You shouting and you go swimming with sharks. Like she,' he pointed to the blackness outside the round window. His voice was surprisingly soft and heavily accented. She had heard that accent before.

Nicola broke down in a cold sweat. The realisation hit her: she had been abducted. Probably for money. 'I've got money,' she mumbled, and nodded keenly. 'How much do you want? I can pay!' She could probably raise a million pounds. Was a million enough? She didn't have a clue. She regretted she wasn't in the habit of watching the news. Things like that were on the news: kidnaps, abductions, ransoms ... She would've known how much was enough. As it were, she didn't have a clue. She did hear somewhere, a while back, that no one paid kidnappers any more. It was a matter of policy. Except that this was her life, her life had just begun! It could not possibly end this senselessly! 'Please, don't kill me!' she implored him.

'Shh,' he said again, this time putting his finger across her lips. It smelled of tobacco. She swallowed the thick bile that had built up in her throat, and nodded silently. She did not want him to hurt her, and she could imagine many ways in which he could do that. His breath stank, rotten and alcoholic. He grinned unpleasantly. One of his front teeth was missing, or decayed. The space looked black. He was a vile man and the more vile he was, the more real was the threat he posed to Nicola. She prayed he wouldn't touch her anywhere else. His finger pressing against her lips slid down to her throat, pushing hard into her vortex. His hand gripped her neck, all his fingers digging into it, forcing her eyes out. She choked, fearing she was about to be throttled and thrown overboard, like the other woman. But he loosened his grip on her throat, letting her breathe. The flat of his palm pressed against her chest. Like a claw it clutched her left breast and fondled it, tightening and making it ache. Nicola held her breath as his hand moved to her other breast. Through her dressing gown he could feel her nipple. A glint of pleasure passed through his eyes. He circled her nipple with his finger, the same one he had held to her lips. His other hand reached for her pelvis. It rammed into it. His grin widened as he realised that under her dressing gown there was nothing. Nicola drew her thighs together. It was an involuntary reaction, but it made him angry. He prised her thighs open, lifting her left leg and thrusting his finger inside her. Nicola cried out and fought back. She punched him, her fist landing in his eye. That amused him. He laughed and released her. Standing over her for a few seconds, he made her watch as he licked his finger. Then he threw a bottle of water to her and once again, before leaving, told her to shush.

Nicola drank greedily. It was a two-litre bottle, but she managed to drink half of it in one go. She did not hear when the hum of the engine started, but she could feel and see the motion against the parting waves. It became a constant background noise, with time almost imperceptible. Over the days she got used to it.

She could not tell how many days exactly she was kept on the boat. It had to be roughly two or three weeks, but there were times when the vile man – he was the only person to deal with her through the entire sea voyage, though she could hear many voices from the deck above – would inject her with something which put her into a daze. It was a state of semi-consciousness interspersed with violent dreams and periods of wakefulness when she could hear and see things, but could not lift a finger or speak. She had gaps: hours of which she had no memory whatsoever. She did not allow herself to think what might have been happening to her in those blank hours.

No one had told her why she was there and when – if – she would be free to go. She could only imagine that a ransom demand had been made. She had money sitting in the bank, money she'd had no idea what to do with from the start. She would not miss it. She just wanted it to be over. Who would they approach for the money? she wondered. They never asked what her name was, how to contact her family ... What family? Would Robert be the person to address? He was the only sensible option. He was her brother. But he lived in Australia! Why didn't they ask her anything!

In her darkest hours, she doubted that anyone had noticed she was gone. Who would have? Robert in his Australian outback, busy living a family life with his wife and beautiful children, Robert who never bothered to as much as send her a birthday card? Friends ... What friends? Who was she kidding? She had no friends; she only imagined she had them. People at work? Yes, they would notice. And then what would they do? Find a replacement ... Her cottage would overgrow with weeds and dilapidate slowly. There was no bank with a mortgage over the house so no one would come to reclaim it. Fritz would be adopted by the tireless Devonshires, who would do anything for the memory of Great-aunt Eunice. They would probably condemn Nicola for abandoning the poor creature ... Maybe after seven years she would be declared dead and someone would go to the trouble of sorting out her estate – someone from the tax office. And that would be it.

Yet Nicola hung on. Not to any hope, by far! She just hung on. The instinct of survival is amazing! She diligently kept herself hydrated with the bottles of water the vile man brought her every morning, and she ate what he gave her, just to keep her alive. Obviously, he had a reason to keep her alive.

In the last few days she noticed the cold. From the overpowering heat at the start of the passage to the nippy cold ... She wondered about that. She wondered where she was.

And now she knows. This morning the vile man told her she smelled. He screwed up his ugly face, pinched his nose and waved his hand as if fending off Nicola's bodily odour. He then went on to unceremoniously tear off the sticky with sweat dressing gown she had been wrapped in for days. Her nakedness had no effect on him. He pushed her into a shower. Though he turned his back on her, he didn't leave the cabin. Instead, he sat on the bed and lit a cigarette. The smell of tobacco smoke made Nicola sick to the stomach. It was potent and suffocating, not the faint whiff that would sometimes brush by her nostrils at the entrance to an underground station. This was much stronger. Perhaps due to the nauseating stink, perhaps due to fear or hunger, she threw up. He turned and glanced at her with disgust. 'Wash!' he ordered her. Obediently, she turned the tap and let it run for a few seconds before she stepped into the stream.

She is now luxuriating in the warm water, washing off the filth of the man's hands and the glue of her own sweat and body fluids. Her hair is matted, but it dissolves into flowing streaks under the stream of water. She shampoos it thoroughly, hoping that the longer she takes, the further away she will push what is coming next. It's hard to believe she is looking down at her own body: she has lost lots of weight and gained an olive tinge to her skin. She appears alien to her own eyes.

The vile man turns off the shower and throws a towel at her. He does not ogle her, does not allow himself to glance at her. There is something reverent in his demeanour. Suddenly, she has acquired some value.

He points to black robes laid on the bed. 'Get dressed,' he orders her.

'Where are we? Where are you taking me? Can you tell me, please?' she asks, trepidation in her voice. She has not spoken to him in all those days. It feels like surrender that she has to

176

request anything from him, but she has got used to the relative safety – or rather familiarity – of this little cabin, and now she is being thrown into an unknown territory. It could be worse than what she has experienced so far. It could be the end of the line. But then would they ask her to wash and get dressed in order to put a bullet in her head?

'Get dressed,' he repeats.

'Turn around. Don't look. Please.'

He snorts. He is amused. His stupid grin makes a reappearance, but obligingly he turns to face the wall. Nicola dresses, pulling the garments on with trembling hands. They are odd garments: a long black robe and a headscarf with a gauze veil, also black: all in one, a burqa.

Two men escort her off the yacht. One glance behind her and she realises she has not been on some decrepit rusty old boat full of Somali pirates. The yacht is large and luxurious, streamlined, fresh – a beautiful white swan amongst other white swans moored alongside it. Whoever owns it does not need to kidnap Western women for ransom. Then why? And why is she now being released?

They step onto the pier and merge with the crowd. Now she understands why she is wearing a burqa – she is invisible. The vile man stays half a step behind her. The other man is walking arm in arm with her. He has shown her a pistol, which he is holding in his pocket. He told her he wouldn't hesitate to use it if she decided to run. He said he hoped she wouldn't do anything stupid; she was nearly free. His English is also heavily accented, but perfectly grammatical. She heard that accent somewhere before. She remembers. Of course, how could she forget! Mishka speaks with the same accent. They are Russian.

They have now entered the streets which are full of people shouting, laughing, arguing, trading. They speak foreign languages: Arabic and French. Lots of little outlets and run-down shops are scattered along narrow and windy alleyways, some of them shut down and boarded up, others full of life, exuding aromas of raw produce and cooked food. At one stall they are selling pigs' heads. The smell makes Nicola's stomach turn. She sees mainly men, dark-skinned, with keen eyes and wiry bodies. The few women out there are dressed in similar outfits to hers. That is why she is invisible.

She thinks she must be in some North African port, but as she has never travelled abroad, she cannot form any conclusive verdicts. Slowly, she and her bodyguards leave behind the loud market place and enter a quieter area, but still rather ramshackle and dirty. And it is there, at the far end of a busy street, she sees Mishka. Her heart jumps to her throat. Whether she is happy or shocked, her heart is pounding wildly. She doesn't know what to make of this encounter, whether she is betrayed or saved, whether this is supposed to be good or bad. All she knows is that it is not coincidental. He is looking around, and at last he sees her, too. His face is tense, but inscrutable. Not a hint of his old, boyish smile on it. He looks nervous.

The vile man behind her pulls her to a hold. 'Stay here,' he whispers into her ear. His grip on her arm tightens. The other bodyguard advances towards Mishka who steps forward to meet him halfway. They speak, briefly. The man is demanding something, his hand is outstretched, but Mishka pushes him aside. There is a scuffle. Mishka explains something and the man lets him through. Mishka is now face to face with Nicola. She is close to fainting. He pulls down her veil. Terror, shock, disbelief – all at once crowd his face.

'Nicola? You? I was told you were dead …'

'Mishka?' She has no strength to say anything else but his name. What can she say? How can she explain why she is *not* dead? Someone is dead, she remembers, the woman in a striped dress ballooning in the ocean; someone is dead but it isn't her.

Rapidly, angrily, Mishka turns to her bodyguard. They talk loudly, in Russian, gesticulating a lot. Her brain is too frazzled to even attempt understanding what is being said. The bodyguard has lifted his arms as if in a gesture of surrender. He is nodding to the one who is holding Nicola to take her away.

'No!' Nicola begs, but she does not have to. Mishka thrusts a thick envelope in the man's hand and his finger in the man's face. He is telling him something, laying down the law, it seems, for he is having the upper hand. On his orders, the man gestures to his accomplice to let Nicola go. She runs to Mishka, into his arms. He leads her away, his arm firmly on her back. They are walking fast, and faster. He looks back a few times.

'Keep walking,' he says, 'they're right behind us.'

It is a small café: only a few tiny tables tucked around a counter with a steaming espresso machine and a display cabinet brimming with creamy pastries. The menu on the table is written in French, and French is being spoken around them. A young waitress with a moody expression on her face brings their coffees, and gives Nicola an openly hostile look. She shakes her head in disapproval and strolls away to other customers, whom she greets with cordiality.

Nicola gives Mishka a questioning glance. He smiles. 'It's your veil. You're in the wrong part of town.'

They are holding hands across the table, his over hers, fingers curled under, squeezing. He still looks sombre, and his trademark carefree smirk is absent, but there is also tenderness in his eyes. Nicola feels safe and loved, and not at all forgotten. 'You paid the ransom?' she asks.

'You could say that – I paid the price. I gave them what they asked for.'

'I'll pay you back. I've got money.'

'No, it's not about money. Forget about it.'

'Mishka, thank you,' she whispers.

'Drink the coffee,' he says, evasively. She sips the hot black liquid slowly. She would've never bought espresso herself, she drinks milky coffee or, preferably, tea, but on this occasion, espresso is what she needs. It works its way down to her stomach and gives her a kick of energy.

He waits for her to finish the drink, then asks, 'Were you alone? Was there anyone else … there … with you?'

She tells him about the cabin, the silky sheets, the police boat, the woman in a stripy dress, and her gaoler. She leaves out what she doesn't wish to remember. It would only upset Mishka, and he cannot undo what is done. What would be the

179

point?

He listens attentively, his eyes hanging on her lips, but his face is frozen and inscrutable. He is holding back his smile. Why is he not smiling? Is he not happy to see her?

'Did they treat you with … respect?' he asks.

Nicola refuses to complain. She is happy to be free. Most of all, she is happy to be with him. She wants to make him smile. 'They were all right. They gave me water, food. I had a shower. One shower,' she chuckles, pushing bad memories – or suspicions – out of her mind. 'At the end of the day they didn't kill me. I am alive. I'm with you! That's a bonus. Let's forget about everything else.'

'Let's do. For now.' There is a pensive note in his tone, but he doesn't take it any further.

'Mishka, why did they contact you for a ransom? You of all people?'

He clears his throat, and tells her with obvious discomfort, 'I'll take you to your embassy. They'll get you home safely …'

She stares at him, round-eyed. This sounds final, again, like a farewell. She cannot bear it. She has been through too much to just submit to this renewed rejection without protest. She has toughened up. She wants to know: 'Why would you want to go to all this trouble just to send me away? All you've been trying to do so far is to get rid of me! Why bother? Why bother in the first place!' She is hurt, her ego is badly bruised, but it isn't about her ego. She does not want to be parted from him. The feeling of his closeness is too good and too precious to forsake. Apart from Mishka she has nothing else to hang on to – no one else.

'Look,' he points out of the window. Outside, on the other side of the road, the two kidnappers are standing on the pavement, shifty and vigilant, smoking their stinking cigarettes and casting furtive glances at the café. 'They'll be following us. They aren't finished with me. Not by far! I need to take you to safety. You're not safe with me. We must separate.'

'Mishka, I don't want to be safe, not without you!' she says hotly. 'And anyway, they aren't as bad as they seem. They could've killed me – I was totally at their mercy! But they didn't …'

He smiles at last. But it isn't the jovial, whole-hearted Mishka's smile. It is as if that smile has been wrenched out of his heart. 'Ah, you silly, silly girl! What a child you are! They would've killed you, given half a chance, but you were their only bargaining chip. Now that they've got what they wanted, very little will hold them back.'

'What did they want from you? What is it?'

'The less you know the better, trust me. I am not a good man to … to be friends with.'

She is cross. 'I thought we were more than *friends*. Don't I deserve to know what's going on?' Naively, in the typical fashion of a lifelong spinster, she has imagined that the few moments of carnal passion they shared give her insight into his mind and access to his secrets. Bizarrely, he thinks about it. His hands let go of hers, but his eyes arrest her in earnest. He weighs his options, considers whether he can trust her, thinks of the choices he has. He can send her back to England and forget about her. She has been nothing but trouble. But he won't do that, Nicola would not understand. He sighs, 'I'll tell you but you'll have to promise me you'll go home. You won't fight me on this.'

She nods. She wants to know what he knows. She wants to be part of his world, no matter how dangerous that world is. No such thing as cautious love.

'In Russia, in the Soviet Union days, just before it fell apart, I was an *apparatchik,* quite high up in the ranks – lots of power, little money. But money didn't matter in those days – what mattered was who you knew and what you could do. My job was something you would call Companies Registrar, modest station, you'd think, except I was a law unto myself. No one checked what I did. It was one big mess in those days. So there I was: the tsar of share trading. I recorded deals, issued certificates, verified buyers … I controlled stock in the vast post-Soviet industries, purely because I kept the central records. Power got into my head, like *shampanskoye*! So I made a mistake, a wrong sort of deal with very wrong sort of people. It was my mistake, but my wife paid the price. Too much was at stake for those bastards ... They had to show me who was in charge. She was a small fish to fry, is that what you would say?'

'I don't know,' Nicola is intimidated by the mention of his late wife. 'I don't yet understand.'

'Come to think about it, neither do I. Let's go to the beginning. We led the high life,' he smiles sadly to the memory, 'She was a prima ballerina of the very best, Kirov Ballet, me – a high ranking official ... Did I tell you Dariushka was a prima ballerina?'

Nicola nods.

'High life: state functions, drinking, extravagant dinners, gambling. I needed lots of money, we spent lots of money and my job didn't come with much. Money had to come from different sources. I got mixed up with the wrong crowd. Today they are the crème de la crème of society, but then they were just rough, unscrupulous climbers. Nothing was below them when it came to building their empires. They were busy tearing pieces from the falling Soviet industries, grabbing what they could ... Like hyenas ... the law of the jungle, it was ... We had this scheme going: *loans-for-shares*. People with their hands on money could lease big industrial plants, oil refineries and so on in exchange for loans to the government. The government needed cash, badly – it was going bankrupt. It was a free-for-all. If later the loans weren't repaid to the lenders – which they rarely were – the lenders would take over the ownership of the factories. Simple. The money lenders became industrialists. It happened all the time. It was easy, but you had to win the tender first. There was heavy competition – they were all at it: old KGB and the Communist Party barons.

'Sixteen years ago I helped Mrozkov win Irkutskiy Steel, worth billions. He had me under his spell, made me feel like I was invincible, like I too could get a piece of the cake. I was in debt, my gambling had got out of hand. Daria didn't know the extent of my troubles. I fiddled the books and Mrozkov won the bid. He paid me. Lots of money for me, believe me, I was set for life. It was an audacious scheme. No actual loan was advanced. On paper, yes, but not in reality. As Registrar, I issued share certificates in Mrozkov's name. No repayments of the loan were made, but then ... there had been no loan in the first place ... All was good, but then my conscience took the better of me. I couldn't hand over the certificates, I couldn't just let him steal the plan and get away with it. I still believed in Russia, the people – Mrozkov was stealing from them! Matushka would say of me: you can be stupid but you're always fair. It wasn't fair what Mrozkov was doing – it was daylight robbery. He was robbing Russia. I demanded that he paid – at least paid the amount of the loan! It wasn't much considering what he was getting out of it! He wouldn't. His money was tied up in other places. He threatened me. I didn't take him seriously, responded with my own threat: I was going to report him. There I was – a fool: a man with a conscience! Laughable!

'Mrozkov retaliated. In a big way ...' Mishka pauses, gazes blankly out the window where the two heavies are still on guard. 'Did I tell you my wife died in a car accident?' He does not wait for Nicola to confirm. He does not even look at her when she nods. 'It was Mrozkov, his men. Not him personally – he doesn't get his hands dirty. It was meant to be a warning. Her car veered off the road. They pushed her off, her car was driven off the road, into a river ... she drowned. I had nothing to lose, and I ran. I took the share certificates, the ledgers and the records of the deal. I took my mother. We went to Finland. My mother's Finnish, born Finnish ... Did she tell you? After the war, the Finns lost part of Karelia to Russia, my father fell in love with her – the usual ... She was very young. They were made for each other, despite the age difference. Finland was just a distant memory for her when suddenly I had to find a place to hide. It had to be Finland. Mrozkov knew nothing of my mother's background – it was something you didn't advertise in Soviet days. So we went to Finland. We took on Matushka's maiden name, Lakso. Mrozkov wouldn't find us and if he did, he wouldn't dare touch us as long as I had the share certificates safely stashed away.' He looks deeply into Nicola's eyes: 'I have just exchanged the certificates for you. Do you understand what that means?'

'That this whole nightmare is behind you?' she says hopefully.

Mishka laughs. The laughter resonates and it is deceptively carefree, his usual. 'I wish! There is nothing now to hold Mrozkov back. He'll track me down and he will ...' He does not finish the sentence, not wanting to upset her.

'Let's go to the police. Please, let's get protection!'

'I can't do that, Nicola. I'm too deep in it. The police can't know. I would be arrested, deported to Russia, thrown in jail ... Anyway, Mrozkov has them in his pocket. You may as well forget about it. No way out. They got me. I've had a good life: fifteen years of it! But they found me in the end. All good things come to an end ...' He takes her hand, kisses it with his typical chivalry. 'But don't worry about me. I still have the ledgers, enough evidence to keep them at bay. Though ... Ah, never mind! You – you must be safe! If you stay with me, you will be dead – like everyone else. You understand?'

'No, Mishka, please don't do this to me, to us ... Let's go to the police. Not all policemen are corrupt. This isn't Russia. We have laws –'

He laughs.

'Don't laugh. Please, don't,' she implores. 'If you don't do it, I've lost you. You'll have to hide for the rest of your life. You won't have any life! Going to the police is the only thing to do. That was your first instinct, remember? Doing the right thing?'

He stops laughing.

'I know you, Mishka, even though it's only been a moment.'

'You don't know me ...'

'But I do! You are a good man. You will do the right thing – I know. And I will stand by you no matter what! And I won't lose you. It's a win-win! We can have a life. Together. That's the only way ...' She doesn't know where the tears have come from. She is not a crier, and she believes – she is sure – he doesn't want to lose her either. So why is she crying?

'You promised.' His face is hard, expressionless. It is the face of an uncompromising man with a steely resolve and no room for sentiment. Almost a stereotype of what she would once have considered a hardcore Russian. He means what he says and Nicola knows she can't change his mind. That is why she is crying.

He tells her: 'We'll leave now. I'll take you to the British Consulate here, in Marseille. You'll go home. It will be easier for me to get away when I'm on my own. I'll lose them. I stand a chance. They don't know where I live. Let's go.'

She steals a few backward glances at the two kidnappers. Sometimes she sees them, sometimes they blend into the blob of pedestrian traffic, but each time they re-emerge, like two black ghosts. Mishka doesn't look back. His arm is wrapped protectively around her back. He is steering her amongst passers-by as if she were blind or made of glass.

Fifteen years, Nicola marvels, he has managed to evade them for fifteen years! How did they catch up with him now? Now that he has come into her life ... It's so unfair! She wants to lash out at them, run to them and scream in their faces, in front of all these people, to leave her alone, to get their hands off Mishka!

It is, in a strange, perverse way, flattering to think that they used her as a bargaining tool and he thought she was worth the sacrifice. He took a terrible risk. He came out here, to France, to face them, for Nicola! No one has ever done anything like that for her, and no one ever will ... He loves her – something warm and fuzzy envelopes her stomach. She doesn't regret meeting him and running into his arms. She stops looking back. Her mind wanders back to the sandy beach and the man – Count Karenin – pressing through the waves to the shore, towards her. The strong man who will make everything right ... She has that picture, that first picture she took of him and posted on her Facebook page. It wasn't a dream.

It hits her then: that is how they found him! Of course, it was all her fault! How stupid! She showed them where to find him. Her silly Facebook! Of course! How else! She is to blame for everything that happened. She – and no one else – put herself in danger. And it isn't just her own life – she put his life in danger too … Blood drains from her brain and she feels lightheaded. She has to tell him even though he may never forgive her. Then she will crawl back into the shell of her meaningless existence. Because everything will be lost.

'Mishka,' she says, breathless, as they wade through the crowd.

'Let's go, let's go!' He is not looking at her.

'No, I must tell you this.'

She stops. He stops. They are facing each other across the pavement, other pedestrians muttering abuse in French as they are forced to slow down and go around them.

'I put your picture on Facebook. That's how they found you. It's my –'

It is most bizarre to hear his laughter. In this precarious situation, with his life turned upside down, his defences down and he is laughing like only he can: a teenage boy with mischief on his mind. '*Tyi durak!* You humpty-dumpty! You're wrong. It's not so,' he says. 'Popov found me. I know it's him – Popov. A cunning rat! Don't fret over it. They found me without your help.'

'Popov?'

'The father of those two boys … His two boys led him to me!'

'Boys …'

'Remember that night when they were teasing you – playing cat and mouse with you? You fell?'

'You told them off …'

'I did. Popov must've heard me when I was talking to them in Russian; he must've followed me to make sure he had the right man. Popov works for Mrozkov. I wouldn't have recognised him. He was nothing to me but a pimple on the face of the earth, but he knew me. The day I was leaving Itsouru, I stood face to face with him, and I knew it was over for me. It

186

was too late to run – they would get to me one way or another … I made my mother board the boat and decided I'd lie low on the island overnight. We had to separate, you see? They knew me, Popov recognised me, but they didn't know my mother. She was safer without me, I thought … I travelled out of Itsouru the next day, sneaked out unnoticed. I was sure I outsmarted them. *Durak!* But it wasn't you – it was him, Popov.'

'Are you sure? It wasn't my silly photograph?' She is relieved but still needy for his reassurance like a little girl who stopped believing in ghosts but still needs the lights on at night.

'Sure, sure, sure!' He kisses her. He takes her into his arms, like that big powerful Russian bear, and kisses her full on, on the lips. It feels wonderful. Everything is going to be fine because of that kiss.

She wishes –

He urges her on. 'We must go. The consulate is only a few metres from here. You're almost safe.'

Mishka pushes her through the door with some force. She is trying to hang on to him, but stands no chance against his strong arm. He vanishes quickly, without a backward glance. In her black robes, like a disorientated raven, Nicola flies across the marble floor and lands on her knees. She is sobbing. She cries out, 'Help me! Help!'

A small crowd of people around her, visa applicants and compatriots who've lost their passports and have to queue at a small window, gawp apprehensively at a shrilling woman wearing a burqa and looking like she has got nothing to lose. Some run away, hunched down, and hide wherever they can; some fall to the ground and lie still. Alarm is raised. Two armed security guards approach her with great caution. They are shouting at her, telling her to stay calm and move her hands away from her body, to put them above her head where they can be seen.

Day Twenty-five

Amy is a pin-up girl. She has a tiny but perfectly formed Ally McBeal body and light, almost weightless, disposition. She is reclining on a sofa, her head resting on Sarah's shoulder, her eyes focused on DC Webber. They are twinkling with a mixture of intrigue and flirtation. She is playing with a wisp of her hair, curling it round her forefinger. Her big, blue eyes, her childish gestures and a small woman's vulnerability render her dangerously seductive. Perhaps she is trying to seduce poor Mark; perhaps there is very little *trying* in it – the pose comes naturally to her. It is little wonder that Sarah struggles with bouts of jealousy. Amy is the type that could seduce any man, or any woman for that matter, and both would have every confidence that she was theirs for life. Amy puts people in touch with their inner sensualities, and Mark has just got in touch with his. She has mesmerised him into submission.

Sarah's arm is placed firmly around Amy's shoulder – where it belongs. Amy needs it, Gillian thinks, Amy needs looking after and she knows it. She has returned into the bosom of her marriage for that reason alone.

'I am so sorry, officer, if I caused any trouble.' She addresses DC Webber to the exclusion of DS Marsh. That sends a clear message: she has no interest in other women. Perhaps that is what puts Sarah's mind at ease. 'I needed time to think. I never thought, not in a million years, you'd be looking for me. It's insane!' She chuckles. 'We've had a little misunderstanding,' she tears her eyes away from Webber and gazes lovingly at her partner, 'an identity crisis, I guess. *My* identity crisis. Sarah is my mainstay. We're inseparable. You knew I'd be back, didn't you, darling?'

Sarah exhales through her mouth. It looks like she's blowing on something hot. 'I wasn't sure this time,' she says.

'I am so, so sorry! I just wanted to disappear for a while, get my thoughts in order. I stayed with old friends of mine, in the Lakes. It was my time out. All I did was curl up in front of the fire, and think. And I realised how much I missed you. I felt like such an idiot – I really did! I didn't know what had possessed me. Maybe that's why it took me a while to come back home.' She enounces the world *home* with great conviction. 'But I couldn't do without you. It was a mistake. I think it was the heat. In fact, I'm sure of that. It fried my brain!'

'Mrs Gray-Ludlow,' Gillian ventures an interruption, 'Nicola Eagles is still missing. I know you made ... an acquaintance with her,' – Sarah winces, of which fact Gillian is acutely conscious. It is likely that she blames Nicola for Amy's meltdown on Itsouru – 'and I hope you can shed some light on her disappearance. Our hopes are pinned on you.'

'I really don't know what I can say ... Nicola was a ... quiet sort of person, shy, I'd say. I felt sorry for her: on her own, kind of lost ... I chatted to her. She was easy to talk to. I don't know what else there is ...'

'You were seen with her on the pier on the day she disappeared.'

'That's where I left her.'

'What did she seem like to you?'

'Well ...' Amy spares Gillian a glance, and pauses to think. 'Tired, I think. I don't know. Now that I think about it, she looked tired like she hadn't slept well. Or maybe like she'd been crying ... Red, puffy eyes, quiet – quieter than usual, sort of resigned. I don't think she said much. Well,' Amy shrugs, 'I did most of the talking. I was upset. I was on and on about Sarah and me ... I didn't pay that much attention to Nicola, to be honest. It's terrible, isn't it?' She gazes apologetically at DC Webber.

'I wouldn't blame myself if I were you,' he says, rather pointlessly, Gillian believes, since he is not her, and never will be.

'So she said absolutely nothing to give you a clue why she was looking downbeat and tired?'

'No, not that I recall. But it was odd,' Amy perks up, 'considering how she was the day before when I saw her with that man … She was playful, threw all caution up in the air. You should've seen her, Sarah!' She is addressing her long-suffering partner as if she wants her to know – her in particular – how happy Nicola was with *that man*. 'Until then I was sure she was gay – just didn't know it yet. But then I saw them. They were kissing, canoodling, God knows what else, right there in everyone's sight.'

Gillian shows her the picture of 'Count Karenin'. 'Is that the man?'

Amy examines the image and nods. 'Yes, that's the man. Tall, much taller than Nicola. I must give it to her – she took me by surprise. I didn't realise she had it in her. She saw me too, waved to me. She wasn't at all embarrassed, which I thought she would've been – she was the type, all prim and proper … But not then, not when I saw her that day. She was happy and she was flaunting it!' Amy clasps her hands together and peers at Sarah with childlike exhilaration. 'Just like we were seven years ago … I felt a tinge of envy. I wanted that spark back … Maybe that was *it* – that was what made me doubt us, silly me.' She gazes at Sarah and her gaze is returned, a guilty plea in Amy's eyes, tender forgiveness in Sarah's.

Gillian is fed up. Do these two really need to exorcise their demons right this minute? She makes a discreet noise. 'Nicola? Can we go back to Nicola?'

'Yes, Nicola. It's about Nicola.' Reluctantly Amy tears her eyes away from her lover. 'What can I say? She looked – alive! And then … such a transformation! That Monday morning she was spent. Flat, like she didn't care to breathe.'

'Suicidal?' Webber suggests.

'Maybe.'

On the train, Gillian tells Mark, 'She couldn't have killed herself and then hid her own body so well that no one would bloody well find it!'

'You still don't accept the drowning?' He yawns. A big and heavy man, only thirty-four but already looking middle-aged and on the flabby side, Webber exudes the air of a man in authority. Gillian certainly lacks his gravitas. She looks like his older prodigal sister who had never grown up, while he'd had to take care of the whole ailing family since he was twelve. She is glad to have Webber back from holiday and on the case: hands on. He is good at putting his family on the back burner: all four of them – the wife, Kate and the three girls, whose names Gillian forever forgets. Sometimes she watches him, efficient and dedicated, and wonders: is his work an escape from the mounting challenges of his family life? She never bothers to pause long enough to answer the question. More pressing matters are usually at hand.

'No, I don't accept suicide. For one, we have Nicola's blood in the chalet. Two, we have no suicide note. Three, we have a body.'

'Somebody else's body,' Webber points out. 'Maybe that body is unrelated? Nicola Eagles disappeared on Wednesday, 4th February. That person was killed at least two days later. Maybe one has nothing to do with the other?'

'There's a link, I'm sure of it. We just have to find it.'

'You were sure it was Amy's body. Now that we have Amy back alive and kicking –'

'We'll have to look elsewhere,' Gillian finishes his sentence. 'Could it be Nicola after all? Maybe Robert Eagles lied. Maybe he was mistaken. Maybe it is her …'

Webber shakes his head. 'The postmortem translation came when you were on your course last week. He wasn't mistaken. No DNA match between the body and Nicola Eagles. It's someone else.'

'It ties in with Nicola. Somehow it does …' Gillian insists. She has to think about it. Now that the wretched DI's course is behind her, useless as it was but dutifully attended at Scarface's insistence, she can refocus her energies on the case. He has tried to keep her away from it – *damage control* he calls it – after

Robert Eagles made an official harassment complaint, but the dust has settled, nothing came of the complaint and Gillian is back in the saddle. The pit bull has her teeth into it once again. 'I want to see that postmortem first thing tomorrow morning,' she tells Webber, but he can't hear her. His chin is bouncing on his chest and a wheezy snore escapes his gaping mouth. He is asleep.

Fritz greets her at the door. He is caressing her legs with affection. She has to play hopscotch to avoid being tripped over by him. As soon as she enters the kitchen the game is over and Fritz sits to attention by the fridge, demanding food with the insistent yodel he had once exuded at the police station. 'All right, I'll feed you first, shall I?' She takes an opened can of cat food out of the fridge to Fritz's visible delight. 'Then I'll have my tea.'

Fritz had never gone missing. He'd run off and hidden somewhere in the house, silent and invisible, playing dead. He waited for Gillian to leave before he took matters into his own paws, surviving the five days of her absence by drinking from toilets and feeding on the large indoor population of spiders. He made a mess but only in one corner of the downstairs closet, where he used a floor mat as a litter box. When Gillian returned from the Maldives she found Fritz alive and well, asleep on her bed. At first, there was something of a Mexican standoff, Fritz refusing to accept Gillian was the rightful owner of her house, but soon they kissed and made up. A cat flap was installed in the kitchen door. Fritz became a household name.

Gillian makes her tea while he is crunching cat biscuits. It is a comforting feeling to have a living creature in the house, making noises, breathing and generating enough fuss to take Gillian's mind off the eerie emptiness that fills every nook and cranny. She misses Tara and her constant dramas, her untidiness and her moods. The house has flatlined since she went away. Even though there were many days when they would pass each other like two ships in the fog, without a word, just knowing that Tara was up there, in her messy room, with headphones on her ears, painting her toenails livid red and ignoring her mother blatantly and unashamedly, was all Gillian needed to be happy. She simply had to know she was not alone.

She puts her mug on the floor – the tea is too hot and there is no milk in the house to cool it down with – and decides to have a little talk with her child. Tara is staying at her father's, in South Africa. Another three weeks and she will be back. But Gillian can't wait that long. She knows only too well what Africa is like: rife with danger, callous and unforgiving. When she was young and – let's face it – stupid, Gillian brushed by dark characters and narrowly escaped the many lethal encounters that Africa threw at her with an abundant hand. She was stupid enough to hardly notice them then, but today a cold shiver runs down her spine when she thinks back to those days.

There is no answer on Tara's mobile. It rings, in vain, and takes her to the all too familiar message on the answer phone. Gillian won't give up: she dials Deon's home number.

'Sorry, did I wake you?'

'Nothing new,' he says, almost indulgently. 'I wasn't sleeping. They aren't home anyway.'

Gillian's heart jumps to her throat. 'What time is it? Shouldn't you put a curfew on them? You know how dangerous the streets are at night.'

'It's only ten. They went to a nightclub. It's safe. It's a safe part of town. As safe as they come. Relax.'

She tries to do just that. This may be a good time to discuss Charlie. 'I'll have to trust you,' she says, 'but can you trust that boy? Charlie … What do you make of him?'

'He's all right.'

'But … ?'

'No buts. He's all right.'

A groan escapes her. Deon's economy with words is frustrating. Not to mention his lack of observational powers. 'Did you find out what his second name is?'

'No. Why should I?'

Gillian is at a loss. 'You invite a stranger into your house. The least you can do is ask his name.'

'It's Charlie, isn't it?'

'It's Charles Outhwaite. That's what he says his full name is. I think you should know.'

Deon tut-tuts into the receiver. 'Good grief, Gillian, you never used to be like that!'

'Like *what* precisely?'

'Neurotic. Unreasonable.'

'For God's sake, Deon! We're talking about a total stranger whom our daughter picked up, like a bloody stray, halfway round the globe! We know nothing about him. For all we know he could be a serial killer or a psychopath! Tara, on the other hand, is a fresh-faced, gullible young girl. Not a clue! And she's totally irresponsible. God knows what they're getting up to –' The rest of the sentence won't pass her lips, perhaps because she is too embarrassed to voice her reservations, perhaps because she doesn't quite know how to phrase them or perhaps because deep down she realises how ludicrous they are.

'Not under my roof – they're not. I put them in separate bedrooms.' He murmurs something else under his breath, but all Gillian can make out is: 'pretty randy in the night ... it's either them or the rats ...'

The knock on the door saves her from further torture.

Her late-night visitor is a woman. She is in her late thirties, average height, average build, her face drawn and showing signs of tiredness or lack of sleep. Her eyes are underlined with dark circles. She has the appearance of someone who has recently lost lots of weight – her clothes are too baggy, her skin sagging around the jaw. Something weak and vulnerable shifts in her eyes, something immature. By looking at her, Gillian ventures a guess that the woman is both unmarried and childless.

'I'm sorry to trouble you this late, but I believe you have my cat, Fritz. I found this note,' she passes a scrap of paper to Gillian. 'My name is Nicola Eagles.'

Of course! Gillian was right: the woman *is* unmarried and childless. She recognises the face from the photo she still has somewhere in her unpacked bags. The bouncy curls are missing and so is the strawberries-and-cream complexion, but the childlike expression in the eyes is unmistakable.

'Miss Eagles, come in! I've been looking for you all over the ... world!'

Fritz recognises his mistress without the need for an identity check. He watches her at first from a safe distance under the coffee table, then produces a couple of his trademark yodels and trots towards her merrily with his tail up. 'Oh Fritz, my boy!' she lifts him from the floor and cuddles the creature lovingly. 'I hope he wasn't too much trouble?'

'No, none at all!' Gillian thanks God that Fritz won't be able to verbalise his concerns, especially the ones about being left home alone for several days without food or water. 'He was as good as gold! I'll miss him when he's gone,' she lies.

'Thank you for looking after him.' Nicola is heading for the exit with the gratified feline in her arms.

Gillian is alarmed. Surely, the woman intends to explain herself to her? Surely, there is an explanation! All she had got so far was a few pleasantries and an expression of gratitude for cat-sitting. 'Would you like a cup of tea?' she asks briskly.

'I don't want to trouble you any more.'

'Oh no! It's no trouble. Except that I've no milk. Is that all right?'

Miss Eagles is trapped in the armchair with Fritz in her lap as she struggles through her story. She is a very bad liar: her lips are dry and she keeps moistening them with her tongue; she is pulling at her cardigan's buttons, doing them up and undoing them continually. She points out that she has already explained everything in the consulate, to the Head of Security, the very kind Mr Jones, who insisted on being referred to by his first name, Ross (presumably to put the poor creature at ease). She told him everything she could remember and he took down notes which, he said, would be passed on to the police. Could Gillian – perhaps – obtain those notes and let her go home now?

Considering that she is rather exhausted? She only got home this morning ...

She positively shrinks when Gillian insists on hearing it all over again. She is flushed, and flustered and clearly very, very anxious to get her story right the second time round. Gillian is sure the only uncensored part of Miss Eagles' account is the bit about the very kind Mr Jones – Ross.

'So, please, help me get my facts in order,' she presses her, 'I'll have to investigate this matter in full, write a report ... Plenty of paperwork, believe me! It simply won't go away by itself. A crime has been committed. It's a clear case of abduction. It cannot go unresolved.'

'I don't wish to press charges,' Miss Eagles ventures gingerly, a glint of hope in her eyes.

'It's not that easy. We're talking about a serious crime. It's in the public interest to bring the perpetrators to justice. Those people, if they go unpunished, will do it again, to another innocent person. Next time round it could end in a tragedy. We can't let it happen.'

'Of course not.' She is quick to surrender. 'It's just that I know so little. They kept me locked up in a tiny cabin. I saw nothing, heard nothing ... I slept – I slept a lot. I was drugged, I think. There's nothing I can tell you.'

'Are you sure they released you without any ransom being paid?' Gillian is relentless. 'It's not a crime to pay a ransom to kidnappers ...'

'No ... I mean, yes! I am sure. They just let me go. In Marseille. Perhaps they realised I had no way of paying them anything.'

'You are worth quite a bit. We checked.'

'Well, I don't know ... I really don't. Maybe it wasn't enough for them? I wasn't worth the trouble?'

'So they just let you go?'

She nods, wordless. She probably knows Gillian doesn't believe her so she has given up on trying to convince her.

Gillian sighs. She is frustrated. She stands up, looks out of the window into the obscure night outside. She hasn't drawn the curtains. The rain is pounding on the glass as if it's trying to get inside. She gazes back at Nicola Eagles – an enigma. Here, in her lounge, sits a woman whose death she thought she was investigating. The woman, for whom Gillian has been looking high and low, has come into her house of her own accord to tell her a pack of lies. What sort of bloody game is she playing! She seems to be protecting her kidnappers – why?

'I am amazed they let you go. It's amazing!' Gillian repeats herself, rather pointlessly.

'Yes. I don't understand any of it myself. Perhaps I was lucky?'

Despair makes Gillian clench her fists. She wants to claw the woman and shake the truth out of her. She drills her with her eyes, forcing her to look back at her. She says, 'Look here, Miss Eagles. You might've been lucky. Damn lucky, if you ask me! But we have a body on our hands. A woman. She is cold dead. No identity. She wasn't as lucky. Can you help me here? Anything? Anything at all?'

There is a tangible change in Nicola Eagles' face: the discomfort of an unseasoned liar is replaced with guilt. Her fingers abandon the buttons of her cardigan and clutch her chest. She speaks in a small, frightened voice.

'I saw a woman. She was wearing a striped dress. *They* threw her overboard. I think she was dead. I watched her dress fill with water. She went down and she wasn't … I mean, she wasn't doing anything, didn't try to swim or … She was dead.'

'When was that?'

'Right at the start … When I woke up for the first time. The thing that woke me was the police boat. It was loud. I saw it leave. I heard a woman scream after them, *"Pamagitze! Viernis."* She was screaming for help, calling for them to turn back – she must've been Russian … Then I heard shouting – an argument, or something to that effect. Agitated voices … I couldn't make out what it was about – it was in Russian –' She halts halfway through the sentence, draws in air sharply and falls into a despondent silence.

'Russian? Are you sure?' Gillian clings onto the vital piece of information. There were Russians on the island, Russians travelling by yachts and cruisers. They could come and go unnoticed, carrying whatever cargo on-board. In fact, Nasheed did mention his men searched the boats moored on Itsouru, but what sort of *search* was that! They wouldn't dare to upset or cause any inconvenience to their Russian patrons. It was more of an afternoon tea from a samovar than a search.

'No, I'm not!' Nicola exclaims, and looks at Gillian round-eyed and petrified as if she has just been caught red-handed. She starts stammering, clearly in an attempt to muddy the waters again. 'I can't be sure they were Russian. I was drowsy, confused ... They couldn't have been Russian. I don't know where that idea came from. There were a few Russians on the plane, speaking loudly, when I was flying home from France. I guess that's where I got it from. Sorry, I'm tired.'

Gillian swallows yet another lie without protest. She is excited. There is no doubt in her mind that Nicola Eagles, despite herself, has just given her something real to hang onto. 'I understand. Why don't you take Fritz home – I've got his cage somewhere ... It must be in the garage. Let me take you there.' She gets up and leads the trembling Nicola Eagles, and her cat, towards the front door. She tries to sound encouraging and considerate – a friendly little Miss Marple, which she can be when she puts her mind to it. Her hand is on Nicola's back as she chats softly, 'Why don't you have a good night's rest. Tomorrow I'll need you at the station to sign your statement. Just a formality, mind, but it has to be done,' she smiles and immediately adds firmly, 'We will also need a description of your kidnappers – I'll organise a sketch artist to work with you.'

'I am a bit fuzzy on –'

'And you'll be able to collect your belongings,' Gillian won't be interrupted. 'All those items you left on Itsouru – we have them at the station.'

Gillian watches Nicola Eagles as, hunched and with her head between her shoulders, she braves the rain and limps off home.

She cuts a pitiful figure. The cage with Fritz rattling inside bounces off her leg. Soon the night swallows her whole.

Gillian shuts the door. She marvels at the hapless, vulnerable creature she has just dispatched away. It is astounding that the woman has somehow survived abduction as well as a journey across the seven seas on a bottle of water a day. Strangely, Gillian feels reassured by this miracle. After all, if someone as hapless as Nicola Eagles had made it through all that and come out on the other side, her innocence unscathed, then there was hope for Tara.

Day Twenty-six

DCI Scarfe has made himself perfectly clear. The investigation is at an end. The missing person has been found, not in the least through Gillian's efforts. A sufficient number of police officers around the globe have been antagonised, entirely through Gillian's efforts. A complaint about police harassment has been made – again thanks to Gillian. Operational funds have been substantially depleted – Gillian. Public relations have been severely strained, especially in the sensitive area of respecting gay rights to privacy – Gillian. Scarfe is foaming at the mouth, the dip in his upper lip livid red. He is sitting upright and tense while Gillian stands before him, pale and desperate to look reverent. A dead goldfish, belly up, in his Feng Shui fish tank, which caught Gillian's eye and made her feel queasy, doesn't help with concentration. In the window behind his back Gillian observes Nicola Eagles scuttle away with the treasure box of her belongings. Scarfe hollers, 'You've done enough damage, DS Marsh. More than you bargained for! Now, you're off the case! No, hang on – there IS no case! Whosever body they've got in Madagascar –'

'The Maldives, sir.'

'Don't interrupt, DS Marsh! Whatever body they've down there, it has got nothing to do with us. With you in particular! So you have no case.'

'Sir ...'

'No!' He lifts a foreboding finger. 'No, no discussion. Let me tell you this, DS Marsh, so that you're clear about it: I looked into it myself. The description of the kidnappers will be circulated – it's being sent to Interpol as we speak. That's all we can do on this count. As for the murder: one – it has been committed outside our jurisdiction; two – the victim is not

British. If you bothered to read the postmortem, which I did while you were gallivanting in London, harassing that gay couple … anyhow, where was I?'

'The postmortem, sir.'

'Right! Yes! If you bothered to read it, you'd find the bit about the victim's fillings. Almost definitely Russian. So the victim is Russian. And that means that you will keep your nose out of it. Am I making myself clear?'

'Perfectly, sir.'

Another goldfish – a big fat orangey one with a tail like a frill – swims up to its dead friend and nudges it with its nose. That generates a small ripple in the tank, but the orangey fish loses interest and glides away.

Webber pings her a semi-sympathetic smile when she slumps at her desk. Everyone on the floor has heard Scarface bellowing at her from a dizzy height, telling her in no uncertain terms to lay off the Maldivian case.

Gillian is unfazed. 'Have you got that postmortem report for me?' she asks Webber.

'On your desk.' There is a glint of admiration in his eyes. He has to give it to her: the woman is unyielding, the pit bull just won't let go!

Gillian digs in. She reads the whole thing, cover to cover. Something is staring at her from those pages, something she can't see. She finds the section about the Russian fillings. She doesn't have to be told twice. The abductors are Russians. The victim is Russian. And yet right in the middle of this whole mess sits Nicola Eagles, a hapless spinster from Sexton's Canning. How does she fit into it? She has to. Somehow she is part of it. What is her Russian connection? She speaks Russian. She reads in Russian. Gillian recalls her collection of books in Russian, including *Anna Karenina*.

Anna Karenina … Count Karenin. He is the missing link! Mikhail Lakso, Nicola Eagles' very own Count Karenin! Her mystery man, her lover … Finnish, but with a Russian accent. He has to be the Russian connection! She's infatuated with him.

She names him her royalty, her count – *Count Karenin*! How much more outlandish can it get? Love, the untamed beast! By Amy's account, Nicola is in love with him. *She was so happy and she was flaunting it,* Amy's very words. And if she is in love with him, she will protect him against all reason. That explains why Nicola is covering for her kidnappers. Because they are linked to the man she loves – Mikhail Lakso!

'Yes! Yes! Yes!'

Gillian is having her *When-Harry-Met-Sally* orgasmic moment. Webber stares at her. 'You're all right?'

'Better than all right!' she grins. She picks up the phone and punches in Jon Riley's extension. 'Hurry up, man!' she urges him. 'Get off your fat arse!'

Webber keeps staring.

Riley answers, 'Gillian! Thought you'd never phone!'

'I need a favour, Jon. I need fast-track background checks on Mikhail –'

'If that's to do with the missing woman case then I can't. Scarface's strict orders.'

'It's personal, Jon.'

'It's always personal with you.'

'Thanks, I knew you'd understand.'

'Who said I did?'

'So the background checks – I want to know his place of birth, nationality. Actually,' Gillian pauses for thought, 'it's two people I'm after: Mikhail Lakso and his – *allegedly* his – mother, Agaata ...'

This is the point where she finally recognises that *something* that was staring her in the face from the pages of the postmortem report. She slams the phone down and picks up the papers. It's right there in front of her, page one: *The body is that of an elderly woman, of approximately mid to late seventies.*

Agaata Lakso!

Nicola is sitting on the floor, contemplating a cardboard box with the word *ARCHIVE* written on it and Nicola's name accompanied by a case number. Her memories of Mishka are buried in that box. It feels like a funeral.

She reaches into the box and takes out her spanking new laptop. Plugs it into the wall. It becomes alive with images from the Maldives. It displays her Facebook page as she left it weeks ago – it just went to sleep. It is overdue for an update. But Nicola can't bring herself to pick it up from where she has left it. The continuum of her pallid, uneventful life has been broken.

She zooms in on the photograph of Mishka and smiles at the caption: *Count Karenin*. He is no Karenin, she knows that now. He isn't a sensible old man; he isn't as upright, hardly a mainstay of society, nobody's role model ... He is a daredevil, a man with a past! So enchanting: pure glitz and glitter! And that boyish grin of his – full of mischief, and full of promise of amazing things to come ... And he made promises, did he not? He said he would not let her go. They would not be separated. He would not let that happen. He said he would take her to St Petersburg and show her the high life. He said she would be dazzled!

And then he told her she would be better off without him ...

She finds her summer dress, rolled up in a bundle with other items. She wore that dress to the French restaurant. She presses it to her face – she can just about detect the scent of his aftershave. She still doesn't know the brand but she would recognise it any time.

She wore that same dress the first time they met when she was slumped to the ground, disorientated and frightened, crying her eyes out, desperate to go home to Fritz and the strawberry fields behind the cottage. Today, she cares little for the fields and the cat can look after himself better than she ever could. Everything paled into insignificance the moment *that man* picked her up from the ground and took her home, and offered her a drink of water ...

He loves water. He told her so. He told her about the Black Sea. He gave her an underwater kiss of life, pressed a starfish into the palm of her hand and showed her miracles. He promised to show her more. He promised ...

Nicola puts the dress on the floor and throws more clothes

on top: pairs of sensible knickers, a one-piece swimsuit, shapeless tops and a Laura Ashley skirt – her old, orderly life without a reason or purpose. Fritz sniffs around the pile and plonks himself on top of it. He looks content in his nest. It is cosy and the smells are familiar.

Anna Karenina, in Russian, is at the bottom of the box. Nicola takes the book out. She never used to like the heroine. That was before, however. Now she knows how Anna felt: she was plainly and simply in love. There is no escaping it. There is no going round it. There is no biding time. She was condemned to follow her heart and be damned for it, but at least she had the courage to live, and to love. It was worth it. Given a second chance, Nicola knows now, she would have done it all over again. Those few precious moments justified everything. Excused everything.

Mishka is Nicola's Alosha Vronsky. He is no Karenin! He's Vronsky! He is her sin. Probably he will be her doom, but before it comes to it he will take her to St Petersburg and show her the high life. He will laugh with her. He will make love to her. He will be her knight in shining armour. Even if it is only for another five minutes, it will be well worth it.

Between the pages of *Anna Karenina*, in Russian, she finds a scrap of her itinerary with Mishka's address and telephone number scribbled on it. It is meant to be!

She shows the paper to Fritz. 'Sorry, Fritz, I'll have to love you and leave you. It won't be for ever. I'll send for you as soon as I can.'

Fritz presents her with a disdainful glance and whips his tail once – a cue for her to go away and leave him alone.

Day Twenty-eight

Things have been moving slowly. Infuriatingly so! It was the boss's decision that took the time. Scarface took an age to make up his mind despite the facts that Gillian put in front of him. Undeniable facts! Her instincts have been vindicated again. Riley was able to verify that Mikhail and Agaata Lakso left Russia for Finland fifteen years ago and as soon as physically possible changed their surname to Agaata's maiden name. Riley further confirmed that Agaata never returned to Finland after their holiday in the Maldives. Mikhail travelled on his own. What's more, he failed to report Agaata missing. Gillian briefed Nasheed on the latest developments. It wasn't hard to convince him that the unidentified body in the Malè mortuary was that of Agaata Lakso. From then on she had to leave it in Nasheed's hands. It was his murder – his investigation. It would no doubt lead him to Finland. She wondered how he would take the change of air. At this time of year Finland was in the cold grip of winter.

As much as it wasn't difficult to convince Nasheed, it was near impossible to do so with DCI Scarfe. He took his time to thrust his chest forward and puff up his feathers before getting down to business. After he reprimanded Gillian for disobeying his orders and pursuing the matter behind his back, he sat down in his chair, pursed his cleft lip and sulked while Gillian presented the facts of the case. He wouldn't budge when she suggested that Nicola Eagles was implicated in Agaata's death and that she was covering for someone, in all probability for Mikhail with whom she'd had an affair.

'And you have Amy Gray-Ludlow's word for it, plus your powers of deduction to substantiate it?' he retorted. 'That won't stand up in court!'

'He didn't report his own mother missing, sir.'

'So that's your rock-solid proof that he – and Miss Eagles – killed her. What would be the motive?'

Gillian didn't know.

He wouldn't budge when she proposed an alternative possibility. 'According to Miss Eagles she was abducted and then released without a ransom. Without a ransom! If we believe she was abducted, we can't possibly accept that there was no ransom. There had to be! Who paid it and why? Did Lakso pay it? If he paid for Nicola, why didn't he pay for his mother?'

'We may never find out. Be it as it may, Miss Eagles is alive and well.'

'And that's what doesn't make sense, sir. Why is she alive and well while the other woman is dead? If we take Miss Eagles' word for it, Agaata was on the same boat, presumably kidnapped by the same people. Why did they let one of them go? Why did they kill the other? It doesn't make sense. Nicola Eagles has to do better than that. She knows more than she lets on. She is up to her ears in it!'

'You are throwing idle accusations at a woman who has been through quite a lot. We are not bringing her in, and that's final.'

He only relented when Gillian offered a compromise. 'Sir, could I at least interview her as a witness? I'll visit her at home. I won't put her out in any way and won't bring her to the station. An informal interview, how about that? New facts have come to light. We may have the identity of the victim. We need to put this to the witnesses – to Miss Eagles, our only witness.'

At last, Gillian is knocking on Nicola Eagles' front door, about to knock the truth out of her. It has taken a day of to-and-fro, but now she has Scarface's blessing to get to the bottom of it. She won't be taking prisoners. The damned woman is protecting Lakso and Gillian wants to know why. She also wants to know exactly what happened and what led to Nicola's release and Agaata's death. In her bag, Gillian carries the unsightly photographs of Agaata's corpse, fished out of the ocean. She has every intention of showing them to Nicola. Maybe that will refresh her memory!

There is no answer to her persistent knocking. Only Fritz appears on the footpath from behind the cottage, followed by none other than Mr and Mrs Devonshire. Fritz rubs himself on Gillian's legs and purrs, which is a welcome departure from his habitual yodelling. Mrs Devonshire speaks, 'Fancy finding you here, DS Marsh! What brings you back?' She doesn't wait for an answer and hurries to inform Mr Devonshire of her discovery even though he is only a step behind her and can see it all for himself. 'Look, Vincent, dear! Look, who we have here: DS Marsh!'

'I need to speak to Miss Eagles.'

'You're not in luck, I'm afraid. She's gone, isn't she, Vincent?'

'Gone where?'

'To Finland! Where else?'

Mr Devonshire nods affirmation.

'Would you believe that she left us in charge of Fritz? We're only doing it for poor Eunice if you must know. Nicola has proven herself very unreliable in the past, you may remember? Oh yes, she said it'd be only a few days, but that's what she said the last time, didn't she, Vincent? And look what happened then!'

Day Twenty-nine

The taxi driver drops her at the end of the hard-beaten track. He won't go any further. It is a country road: windy and unpredictable. Flat, snow-covered fields lie on both sides of it, the monotony of them occasionally broken by a gnarly white birch or some other specimen of sub-arctic fauna.

He points to a distant dwelling and in broken English tells her to head in that direction. The house she wants is there. He can't venture to drive her to the doorstep. His small-tyres weren't designed for the deep ruts of country paths.

Nicola pays him, and he drives off.

She sets off in the direction of the house. All she can see is a high-pitched roof and dark, wooden decking. This is a cold, desolate place, like Siberia. It is moody and unrestrained. It feels like the very soul of Russia.

Even though she is dressed for winter, the dry, cold air penetrates through her coat, to the bare bone. She wraps her arms around her and trudges on through snow that reaches up to her calves. The snow cracks and crumbles under her feet like a meringue.

The light is already thinning though it is only three in the afternoon. Nicola detects tyre tracks. Mishka has been driving in and out, getting supplies for the house: fresh bread, milk, fruit ... Agaata has started on the dinner. They will be so surprised to see Nicola! Mishka may even be angry at first. He told her to stay away, but that was in Marseille. He had to get away from those nasty characters, couldn't afford to have his hands tied up with Nicola lagging behind him. She accepted that. That was then. This is now.

Today will be different.

Today he will sweep her off her feet and carry her inside the

211

house just like he carried her into the ocean when her ankle was sore and swollen. He will shout to Agaata, 'Look, Matushka! Look who has come to visit!' He will kiss her all over: her hair and her eyes, her hands and her lips, and later on, when they are alone, he will kiss her neck, her breasts, her stomach and the inside of her thighs. His cheeks will be covered with day-old stubble and it will feel rough against the delicate skin of her inner thighs, but she will welcome the discomfort. Blood will rush to her head. She will gasp with pure pleasure. She will kiss him back and dig her nails into his back. They will be safe and happy in each other's arms. He will forgive her for not listening. More than that – he will thank her for not listening because he has missed her unbearably and he simply cannot live another day without her.

On the weekend they will drive across the border, to St Petersburg. He will show her the glitz and glitter of the city. They will drink champagne that flows like rivers, and eat caviar canapés. They will gamble and play cards, go to see *Uncle Vanya* in a theatre with crystal chandeliers and gold-plated picture frames. And next week – perhaps next month – they will go to the police. It will have to be done. For peace for mind. For that woman in the striped dress that ballooned in water but could not keep her afloat, because she was a dead weight. Nicola has been dreaming about her. She won't go away. Just like Mishka's wife – *Dariushka* – won't go away until her killers are brought to justice. Then Mishka will be free of his past. Free to love Nicola.

She has waited for him to come to her all her life. It was worth the wait. Every minute of awkwardness with other men, her spinsterhood and her acute loneliness – all of that was worth the wait. The terrible man smelling of booze and stale cigarette smoke, and whatever he did or didn't do to her on that boat – it was worth the wait.

She is nearly at the door, drawn to her darling Mishka like a moth to a candle flame, like Anna was to Alosha Vronsky. Beyond this moment nothing matters. Beyond this, to hell with the rest of the world!

She can't wait to see his face – the expression of shock, immediately replaced with joy. She knocks on the door. Silence. She closes her hand in a fist and bangs on the door. She hears steps. The door opens.

It is the man from the boat, the one smelling of booze and stale cigarette smoke.

Day Thirty

Gillian has only herself to blame. She should have never let that woman go. She should've detained her – she should have kept her safe. Nicola Eagles was the most vulnerable, helpless creature Gillian has ever come across in her career. She had the word VICTIM printed on her forehead in bold capital letters. She had to be looked after and the problem was that there was no one out there to do the job. It was down to Gillian.

Right from the beginning Gillian has had this irrational feeling that she was investigating Nicola Eagles' death. Not just her disappearance, but her death. Now it has come to it. By the time Gillian had got Scarfe's permission to travel to Finland, by the time she had met up with the Finnish police, by the time they got their act together and made it to Lakso's house, Nicola was dead, her throat slit – one surgical cut. Her death must have been instant.

Mikhail Lakso was found bound to a chair in the middle of his kitchen. He had been tortured and left for dead. They'd probably thought he was already dead: the stab wound between the third and fourth rib was deep, narrowly missing the heart. But he clearly has the constitution of an ox – for he survived.

Gillian has been sitting in a brightly lit hospital corridor for what seems like days. Her back aches. The chair is hard and uncomfortable. Her eyes can't get used to the light. She has been sustaining herself on caffeine, a collection of polystyrene cups by her side testifying to that. Her eyelids feel heavy, her mouth dry and her head is reeling. Her telephone is switched off. She won't be distracted and she won't leave until she has spoken to Mikhail Lakso, whenever that's going to be.

A Finnish policeman is sitting in another uncomfortable chair on the other side of the door, guarding the patient. Gillian is grateful. She can't afford to lose her only witness. She no longer believes Lakso a murderer and kidnapper – he wouldn't be where he is now, and in the state he's in now, if he were. But he knows answers to all of Gillian's questions. She won't leave until they are answered. Not that any answers will bring Nicola back. Her preventable death is something Gillian will have to live with.

The doctor whom she saw enter Lakso's room a few minutes ago comes out. She is a tall, slim woman with no time for appearances: her hair is in a knot so tight that her eyes slant; there is no trace of make up on her perfectly pale face with its high cheekbones. She reminds Gillian of an alien.

'He'll speak with you now,' she tells Gillian. 'You have five minutes. Then he will need his rest.'

It is the man from the pages of Nicola's Facebook. Even in a hospital bed he looks strong and invincible in a large, square way. His arms are long, lean and covered in fair, reddish hairs. The fingers of both hands are bandaged together – apparently his assailants broke all ten of them. They also used him as a punchbag, crushing most of his ribs, and finished it off with the stab that had just missed the heart. The final blow to his head with a blunt instrument left him bleeding profusely and concussed. His head is now bandaged, his bloodied left eye peering from under the dressing unblinkingly. A far cry from *Count Karenin.*

'Nicola?' he asks. The apprehension and urgency of that question are harrowing.

Gillian shakes her head. 'I'm sorry,' she says. 'It was instant.'

'It is my fault.'

Gillian could argue with that, but she leaves it. 'I need to ask you a few questions.'

'The body you found. Tell me.' He has his own questions.

'An elderly woman, in her mid to late seventies. Russian, very likely.'

'My mother?'

216

'I think so. I wanted to ask you –'

'Yes, my mother. I thought – I hoped – they kept her alive … They took her from the boat just as she was leaving the island. I stayed behind so they would not make a connection between us. I hoped they would not know who she was, or maybe I hoped – *durak*! – that they would just let her go. It was nothing to do with her … I thought she had made it; I thought she was safely on her way home. I was wrong. When you called, told me you found Nicola's body, I never –' His voice falters, but he recovers it quickly. 'Then when I saw Nicola in France, I knew it was Matushka. My mother was dead.'

'Sorry, we made a mistake.'

'What does it matter? They are both dead now.'

'Why?'

'Some papers, that is why. *They* wanted the papers – shares, records. Important documents. My mother and Nicola – collateral damage … *They* took them both to exchange for the papers. But why did they kill them?' he looks at her, puzzled and hurt.

'I don't know. I was hoping you could tell me. I don't even know who *they* are.'

'Ah, I could have taken the secret to my grave. Mrozkov was sure I would.'

'Mrozkov?'

'Except, you see,' Lakso sucks in his lips and makes a hollow popping noise, 'I have already sent the papers to Nicola: the ledgers and the records, copies of all shares. I made copies in case … I told her to do with them as she liked. In a letter. I knew – I thought – she would take them to you, to the police. I just didn't – I did not count with the possibility of her coming here! *Durak!* Silly, silly girl! But how was she to know what sort of people we were dealing with …'

'Who is Mrozkov?'

'I wrote it all down, in a statement, and sent it to Nicola. With the papers. It is all there. She would have taken it to the police. That is what she wanted to do. I thought she would. If only she had waited …' His bloodied eye drifts out of focus.

217

He's gazing at the bland wall opposite his bed when he says, 'She made me think there was a way for us to go on. A chance! I wanted to believe it. I am a gambler, you see? Gamblers are eternal optimists, ha! I thought I could give it a go – we could start again. The two of us, hot sand, middle of nowhere. I wanted Nicola there with me!' He refocuses on Gillian. 'You think I'm lying ... In five years' time I will think I was lying. I was naïve, so naïve! I was going to get Nicola when it was safe, when I was sure ... I found a place, in Thailand. It would remind us of how we met. I was so close! *Durak!*' He punches the bed with his bandaged fist, and winces in pain. 'When I saw her in the doorway ... *Durak!* I said to myself, *Durak, tyi ubiw Nicola! Ubiw!*'

'Sorry, I don't speak Russian. Can you –'

'They found me. They were bound to find me! What was I thinking! But still ... They wanted the papers and I laughed in their faces! I did! I laughed! Because I had sent them all to Nicola. They would not find those damned papers! So I won, I thought, I paid Mrozkov back for everything – for Daria, for *Matushka*! And then I saw Nicola at the door. My blood ran cold. I knew it was no good. I knew they would kill her. I knew I could never win with Mrozkov. *Durak!* It's my fault she is dead. I killed her. Like I killed Daria. Like I killed my mother. They are all dead.' He is crying. It is a pitiful sight – an adult man crying. Gillian wishes she had it in her to offer him comfort, hold his hand, do something!

The alien doctor spares her the trouble. 'Your five minutes is up. The patient needs to rest.'

Day Forty

The sense of failure persists. Gillian derived little satisfaction from the arrest of the two henchmen: Vladimir Hanik and Sasha Raskalin. The moment they were picked out by Lakso in the police line-up, the moment Igor Mrozkov severed all his links with them. After all, what those two had been getting up to while on holiday in the Maldives and soon thereafter in Finland was none of his concern. They were loose associates – sort of ... *freelance contractors*. In their turn, Hanik and Raskalin had never heard of Igor Mrozkov. It was a dead end.

Only this morning, Mrozkov's smug, £150-an-hour solicitor wearing a hyphenated name and an Armani suit, got his client released without the faintest possibility for Mrozkov ever returning to as much as *assist the Police with their inquiries*. There was no evidence to link Mrozkov to the murders of either Agaata Lakso or Nicola Eagles. Even though the leisure cruiser upon which Nicola was smuggled across the seven seas did belong to Mrozkov. Again, according to the smug solicitor, the two *freelance contractors* had taken the liberty of helping themselves to the vessel without the owner's knowledge or permission. Mr Mrozkov was most displeased when he heard about it ...

Gillian was not allowed to tread into the murky waters of fraudulent share trading in Irkutskiy Steel. For Igor Mrozkov is a law-abiding resident on an investor's visa with high stakes in the British economy. As such he is presumed innocent until proved guilty – and beyond. Scarfe got his instructions from above and passed them on to Gillian in no uncertain terms: keep your hands off Mrozkov. Lakso's papers, together with his willingness to testify against Mrozkov, have been dispatched to

Foreign Affairs to be passed onto the Russian authorities. Apparently. Gillian will never know whether they will ever see the light of day. In all likelihood they will be buried alongside Dariushka, Agaata and one rather insignificant other in the greater scheme of things: Nicola Eagles, a 42-year-old spinster from Sexton's Canning.

Thus the sense of failure.

The traffic is slow-moving. It's the rush hour. In London every minute of day and night blends into one endless rush hour, though *rush* has nothing to do with it. She is going to be late! Another failure – this time as a mother. Once again, invariably, Gillian will find herself on the wrong side of the word *reliable* when it comes to her parenting style.

Now it is a definite standstill. She takes her frustration out on the steering wheel. Inadvertently, she hits the horn and within seconds other vehicles respond with equal force. It is a motionless cacophony. Road rage. But it won't change the fact that she is late.

In the Arrivals Hall she instantly spots a tiny, lone figure sitting on top of a bulging backpack. Gillian dashes towards the little person, her heart racing ahead of her.

'Tara, I'm so sorry! The traffic was awful!' Gillian throws her arms over her daughter like a fishing net of motherly love. In her embrace, Tara is a shivering bird with a broken wing. She has lost plenty of weight. Is that what puppy love does to youngsters?

'Let me look at you!' Gillian pulls her child away and clutches her by the arms, scrutinising her drawn face, swollen eyelids and red patches of raw emotion on her skin.

'What's the matter?'

'Nothing.'

'Where did you lose Charlie?' Suddenly, she has remembered to mention the significant other half. The plan was to meet them both at the airport – Charlie was coming home with them for a few days. Gillian has a Chinese takeaway in the oven on 150 degrees, keeping warm. She has made the bed in the spare room. Everything, short of a WELCOME HOME banner, is ready and waiting. She has already reconciled with the young man's presence in Tara's – and her – life. She did some background checks – who wouldn't? At least Charlie Outhwaite has no criminal record.

Tara motions towards the escalator. 'There,' she says. 'His girlfriend is taking him home. I think her name is Phoebe.'

A young couple are strolling nonchalantly, holding hands, their backs to her. The man with gangly limbs and messy blond hair carries a camouflage-green backpack. The woman keeps turning her face towards him, talking animatedly. She kisses him on the cheek and it is then that he turns briefly and looks back. It is a fleeting glance. Furtive. Bastardly. It is at this point that Gillian makes a few steps towards them, white fury engulfing her mind, fists clenched. She cannot think, but even without thinking, she knows what she wants – she wants to punch the bastard in the face. Break his nose.

She stops in her tracks, and turns back. Tara doesn't need to see her irrational mother's fury. Tara just needs her mother. She is only a little girl – as little as Gillian once was, when life dealt her a blow or two of her own – and all she needs is holding tight. Gillian holds her tight. Despite the initial protest, the shrugging of the shoulders, the twisting of the face to stop tears.

'I'm sorry, darling.'

It feels good to have her little girl buckled up in the car, next to her mother who will never let her down. Because mothers don't, even if they're habitually late.

They brave the raging traffic together. Thelma and Louise. All men are bastards, a thought that gives Gillian a strange sense of accomplishment. Mainly because she is not a man.

She does not dare ask Tara any questions. Answers would not heal any wounds anyway. Charlie Outhwaite is gone. On some level Gillian could consider sending him a thank you card. He has returned her daughter to her bosom. It isn't a very charitable sentiment, not to Tara, but Gillian finds comfort in it: it isn't yet Tara's time to flee the nest. She has stuck her hand out and got burned. Retreated. Gillian has her baby back.

At the end of the day, Gillian ponders further, it isn't that bad. Tara is young, so young! She has many rejections ahead of her, and plenty of time to get over them.

Unlike Nicola Eagles.

As if reading her thoughts, Tara asks, 'How is your case? The missing person case?'

Gillian glances across at her daughter before responding.

'That case is closed.'

THE END

222

ANNA LEGAT
NOTHING TO LOSE

The second DI Gillian Marsh mystery by Anna Legat

When a head-on collision involving four cars occurs on a stretch of peaceful country road, resulting in four deaths and a fifth person fighting for his life, DI Gillian Marsh is sent to investigate. There are no simple explanations as to why the accident happened: there were no hazards on the road, and it was a quiet, sunny morning with clear visibility and little traffic. There was no obvious cause, so why did four sensible and capable drivers end up dead in a pile-up?

As Gillian delves into the victims' lives and unpicks their stories one by one, she uncovers secrets that lead her to discover the cause of this tragedy. And tragedy is brewing in Gillian's own life ... can she help her daughter before it's too late?

ANNA LEGAT
THICKER THAN BLOOD

The third DI Gillian Marsh mystery by Anna Legat

Liam Cox is at his wits' end: he owes lots of money to a South African crime lord who has forced him into a world of shady deals. The police are on his back and he needs to buy his way out of trouble, so Liam looks to his mother Mildred to bail him out – but, despite sitting on a goldmine in the shape of her farm, she refuses to sell up. With his back to the wall, Liam is desperate – and he's not the only one. Someone is bound to snap … it's only a matter of time.

When the situation blows up and someone is murdered, DI Gillian Marsh steps in to investigate. As she uncovers deceptions and heinous acts, Gillian stumbles upon a man who could well be the love of her life … but will the circumstances allow her any happiness?

Anna Legat
life without me

Georgie Ibsen is a successful, cynical hotshot lawyer. She runs her life, professional and personal, with precision and clear purpose. She's just made a breakthrough in a crucial case, her family is growing more independent … things couldn't be better. Until it all comes to a screeching halt when she's hit by a car and ends up in a coma …

Somehow, in her comatose state, Georgie is given unique glimpses into the lives of her nearest and dearest, their most intimate secrets: her boring husband's involvement with a colleague; her son's lovelorn yearning for his mother's nurse; her fifteen-year-old daughter's bad boy boyfriend, who *just might* be linked to the criminal mastermind involved in her last big case …

Throw in a neurotic actress sister, a senile mother with a traumatic past, and a smug subordinate barrister who's out to ruin her case … oh, and a sex-god lawyer extraordinaire who's a deeply troubled soul with a penchant for some unsavoury practices … although Georgie is out of action, life certainly isn't boring without her!

Crime Fiction from
Accent Press

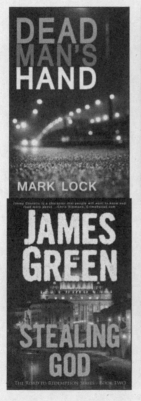

For more information about **Anna Legat**
and other **Accent Press** titles
please visit

www.accentpress.co.uk